HOT SEAL BRIDE

HOT SEAL Team - Book 4

LYNN RAYE HARRIS

This is a work of fiction. Names, characters, places, and incidents either are the products of the author's imagination or are used fictitiously. Any resemblance to actual persons, living or dead, businesses, companies, events, or locales is entirely coincidental.

The Hostile Operations Team® and Lynn Raye Harris® are trademarks of H.O.T. Publishing, LLC.

Printed in the United States of America

First Printing, 2018

For rights inquires, visit www.LynnRayeHarris.com

HOT SEAL Bride
Copyright © 2018 by Lynn Raye Harris
Cover Design Copyright © 2018 Croco Designs

ISBN: 978-1-941002-30-8

Chapter One

SHE FEARED she couldn't go through with it.

Antonella Rossi gazed at herself in the mirror, her wedding veil pinned to the glittering crown on her head. Her eyes glistened with sudden tears. She did not recognize herself. Who was this girl with the ruby-red lips, the smoky eyes, and the winking jewels at her throat?

For fourteen years, she'd lived in the shadows—not because she'd wanted to, but because she'd had to. When her cousins were wearing the latest fashions and getting their hair and makeup done at salons that cost a fortune, she'd been left behind. What was acceptable for her cousins was deemed too extravagant for her.

So she'd holed up in her room, reading books and dreaming of the day when she would be old enough to make her own decisions.

She hadn't realized that day would never come to pass.

In twenty minutes, she was marrying a complete stranger and jetting off to a foreign land so that her aunt and uncle and cousins could continue to enjoy themselves here in Virginia with their fifty-acre estate, their wine cellars, their racehorses, and their busy social calendar.

Apparently, being the exiled royal family of Capriolo was an expensive job—and they were running out of money.

Ella was the expendable one. For sale to the highest bidder. The sheikh with a penchant for virgins had won out against the other men they'd tried to sell her to. She didn't know what he'd promised them, but she knew it had to be something akin to the moon.

If only she weren't a virgin, he wouldn't have wanted her. He'd have moved on to someone else, and maybe Ella could have had a life of her own choosing someday.

A hard rap at the door made her jump.

"Ella!" her cousin Luciana snapped. "It's nearly time. Get out here and stop being so spineless."

"I'll be out in a minute," she called. "Fixing my veil."

"Hurry up then. Sheikh Fahd is getting impatient."

The name made her shiver. She'd tried not to think of the sheikh too much, but she was soon going to have to face him at the altar. He was more than twice her age—fifties or so—and while he'd been pleasant enough, there was something about him that unnerved her. Perhaps it was the gleam in his eyes when he'd talked about how he would be gentle with her when he bedded her the first time. Or perhaps it was the hooded hawk that a servant carried around behind the sheikh. She felt sorry for the bird and afraid of it at the same time. What kind of man demanded that he be accompanied by a hooded raptor in polite company?

Her stomach twisted. No, she couldn't do it. She *wouldn't* do it. If she did, she'd be like that hawk. Hooded, controlled, a possession to be paraded.

Before she could change her mind, she ripped the

crown and veil from her head and set them on the counter. Then she unclasped the jewels and left them too. There was no time to change from the white satin gown with the seed pearls and Swarovski crystals sewn into the bodice. She lifted the heavy skirts adorned with acres of lace and swished toward the exit.

She pressed her ear to the door to listen. Then she opened it carefully and peeked out. The hall was clear. Her cousin had gone back outside to the garden where the ceremony was to take place.

Ella hurried down the hall, her skirts sliding silkily together. There wasn't a lot of time. She reached the front entrance without running into a soul, thank God. Her heart pounded in her throat as she considered her next move.

Outside lay a long stretch of lawn and tall wrought iron gates that closed off the estate from the road. There would be security guards.

And she was in a wedding gown. Ella frowned. She shot a glance over her shoulder. The house remained empty, but it would not for long. Everyone was in the back garden, beneath the tent set up for the occasion. If she didn't show up soon, they would come looking for her. She had to go. *Now*.

She yanked the door open. Rain fell lightly onto the steps. She gathered her skirts and stepped outside. Two valets stood off to the side, intent upon the cars and whatever animated conversation they were having.

She thought of her uncle—of what he would do today with a wedding on the estate. There would be guards at the main gate, checking IDs. She couldn't go that way.

Unless she drove out. She stood, thinking. Yes, driving was the way to go. If the guards gave her any trouble, she could just keep driving until they got out of the way.

She knew from experience of previous gatherings on the estate that the keys were in each car. All she had to do was choose one on the farthest edge of the parking area and steal it.

Heart in her throat, Ella made her way down the stairs as the rain picked up. The valets still hadn't stopped talking as she ducked between a row of cars and crept toward the end. She had to get the last car. A car that faced out. And she had to pray it was not a standard transmission.

When she reached the last car in line, she opened the door and slipped inside. Her skirts were heavy with rain and awkward, but she piled them inside, balling them up beneath her, and locked the doors. The car was a Mercedes.

And there was no key. Simply a button. Her stomach flipped. Now what?

She'd only ever driven golf carts around the estate. But a car couldn't be much different. Except for this push-button thing.

She pressed it—and nothing happened. She glanced up in a panic as the rain began to beat down on the car. The valets were nowhere to be seen. Ella ripped open the glove compartment and found the car manual. After a few moments, she found what she wanted.

She put her foot on the brake, pressed the pedal, and the car purred to life. Another quick check of the manual and she had the car in gear, easing it out of the line. She spun the wheel toward the gates and pressed the gas.

The car lurched, but she didn't give up. She found the sweet spot and it rolled smoothly—if slowly—down the drive. The windshield wipers came on automatically, shoving the rain away. She was glad for that.

There were two guards at the gate, but neither of them tried to stop her. The rain was hard enough now that all they must have seen was a car with a woman inside. She eased through the wrought iron gates, her skin clammy with sweat, and came to a stop at the road. She didn't know which way to go.

A glance in the rearview revealed one of the guards sprinting toward her. Ella panicked and spun the wheel left while pressing the gas. The tires spun and the wheel jerked.

"Please," she begged. "Please don't make me go back."

The tires stopped spinning and the car shot forward. She held on for dear life and prayed she didn't go into the ditch.

Because if she got caught—if they dragged her back to marry Sheikh Fahd—her life was over.

Chapter Two

"Pussy whipped," Cash "Money" McQuaid said as he drove down a country road. Rain pounded the windshield of his Mustang GT. The trees swayed in the wind. He hoped the sudden storm passed as quickly as it had arrived.

On the other end of the line, Cody "Cowboy" McCormick snorted. "Dude, call it what you want, but no way in hell am I giving up three days of my life to fish with you when I could be in bed with my lady. No offense."

"Not offended. I'll catch all the fish on my own. Don't need you or Cage to help me."

The three of them used to take this trip together, but now it was just him. Remy "Cage" Marchand was married and Cowboy was on his way to the altar. Cash shook his head. Dumb fuckers. Not that he didn't think Christina and Miranda were worthy of his boys—he totally did—but shit happened and people changed. One day it could all go to hell. And then what?

"Thought you were asking Camel on this one."

Alex "Camel" Kamarov was the team sniper. "Fucker hates fish. Can you believe it?"

Cowboy laughed. "Sorry, man. Next time, okay? Miranda wasn't supposed to be in town but her assignment was canceled. Can't refuse a gift like that."

"Pussy whipped."

"You can't piss me off, Money. Have fun. Don't do anything stupid."

"Like what? It's fishing, not fucking."

"They've got bars in the Shenandoahs. And waitresses."

"Since when do I go barhopping on a fishing trip?"

"You might get bored out there all alone."

Cash rolled his eyes. "I'm fine, mom. Now go hold Miranda's purse and ask her if you can have your balls back."

"One of these days I'm going to enjoy watching you fall for a woman. Then we'll see who's pussy whipped."

"Not happening."

"Never say never."

"Yeah, I'm saying it."

Up ahead, a car sat haphazardly on the side of the road. Another car partially blocked the road in front of it. It was the woman in a wedding gown who drew his eye first. Her wet hair clung to her face as she spun on her heel and started to run. A man sprinted after her, catching her by the waist and throwing her against the car.

Every one of Cash's hackles leaped to attention. There was something very wrong about the situation. It was more than a bride and groom having an argument on their wedding day. He'd bet his left nut on that.

"Gotta go. Talk to you later."

He didn't wait for a reply before punching the button on his steering wheel to end the call. He skidded to a stop and flung the door open as the man advanced on the woman again.

"You guys need help?" he called, reaching for the Glock he'd left on the seat as he unfolded himself from the driver's side. He tucked it into the Kydex holster wedged against his body as he started toward the couple.

The man spun around. The woman's gaze jerked to Cash as he advanced. She looked terrified. His protective instincts flared. He'd spent his life removing that hunted look from people's faces, and he couldn't ignore it now. Cool rain dripped into his face, soaked through his clothes as he sized up the situation.

"No, we don't need help," the man said harshly. "This is none of your business."

"Aw, man," Cash drawled as adrenaline pumped into his veins. "Those are just the words to make me think it *is* my business." He fixed his gaze on the woman. She looked cold and scared. "Are you okay, ma'am?"

She had dark hair and dark eyes. Her cherry lips parted. The lower one trembled. "No."

Before Cash could say anything, the man drew a .45. Cash stopped moving. He had the Glock within reach, but he didn't draw. Not yet.

"I'm not hurting her. I'm taking her back to her wedding."

Fury boiled inside him. "Looks like she doesn't want to get married, boss. Maybe you should accept her decision."

The asshole made a show of the pistol. Cash shook his head. "You don't want to do that. Not to me."

"Yeah, I think I do. Get back in your car and keep driving."

Cash stood for a moment. All he'd wanted was a quiet fishing trip. Not this bullshit. "All right. Think I'll do just that."

He climbed inside the Mustang and slammed the door. Then he revved the engine, released the brake, and shot toward the asshole. The man hadn't been expecting it, so his aim was off. He fired, but the bullet ricocheted off the top of the quarter panel on the passenger side. Cash might've eased up a bit if not for that. Dude fucking shot his car, so Cash didn't stop and the man had to dive out of the way or get flattened.

The Mustang slid to a halt and Cash jumped out. He was on the dude in half a second, disarming him and knocking him out with an uppercut to the jaw. "That's for ruining my paint, asshole."

Cash got to his feet with the .45, ejecting the magazine and clearing the chamber before tossing the full mag into the muddy water flowing through the ditch beside the road. He dropped the weapon next to the guy's head and held out his hand to the woman. She hadn't moved from where she'd plastered herself against the Mercedes.

"I suggest you come with me. Before this guy wakes up."

She hesitated for a long moment. And then she seemed to make up her mind. "Yes," she said, putting her hand in his. Her voice had the barest hint of an accent, but he couldn't place it.

He escorted her over to the Mustang and opened the door for her. He piled her mud-splattered skirts into the car, surprised at how heavy they were. It was only when he was shifting them around so they'd fit that he realized she was barefooted.

Her eyes met his and something jolted inside him. "Where are your shoes?"

"In the ditch, I think. They're not important."

He glanced over. There was no sign of any shoes in the swirling water. He shut the door, then went around and got into the driver's side. Within moments, he'd maneuvered them around the car that blocked the road. He wiped the water from his face and flipped on the heat. Not for him, but for her. Her teeth were chattering and her body shook, vibrating the seat beneath her.

"Where do you want me to take you?"

He could feel her eyes on him and he glanced at her. She was wide-eyed. "I… I don't know."

"Family? Friends?" Though maybe they were all at the wedding. Still, they'd have to know it wasn't going down by now.

She shook her head. "There's no one."

"You're dressed like that and there's no one?" It was possible, he supposed.

"No."

"I can take you to the sheriff's department. They'll help you get this sorted out. Get you back home."

"No!" The panic in her voice made him gape at her. She swallowed. "No police. Please."

Okay, going to have to take this one slow. He pulled in a breath and hit the mental reset button. *Nice and easy, Cash. Don't spook her.*

"My name's Cash. What's yours?"

She hesitated. "Ella."

"Okay, Ella. Look, nobody's going to force you to go back to him. But the police can make sure you get home safely. You can file a restraining order against him. And then you can get back to your life and move on, right?"

"I…" She dropped her chin and shook her head. "I have nowhere to go. And I wasn't marrying *that* man. I was marrying someone else, but I ran away. That was one of my uncle's security people. He caught up to me—it wasn't hard since I'm not much of a driver—and ran me off the road. If you take me to the sheriff's department, they'll take me back to my uncle. And I'll be forced to marry Sheikh Fahd before the day is over."

A prickle of unease slid down Cash's spine. "Sheikh Fahd?"

He knew that name. The man was a Qu'rimi oil magnate and a cousin to the king of Qu'rim. He was also rumored to support the Freedom Force, the terrorist group that backed the rebels in the Qu'rimi civil war. There was no proof of that connection, but there'd been some chatter in intelligence circles.

"It's not important. What's important is that I don't want to go back. I can't pay you, but if you'll help me hide for a few days, I'm sure the sheikh will leave."

He was still struggling to understand how this wisp of a girl was supposed to be marrying Sheikh Fahd. She couldn't be more than twenty. Maybe twenty-one. Clearly she came from money. Fahd wouldn't marry a waitress he met in a bar. This woman was someone. But who?

"This is America. Nobody can force you to get married. Just tell them you've changed your mind."

She shook her head. "You don't know my uncle. Or the sheikh. If I go back, I'll be married before nightfall." She sucked in a breath. "I-I can't give you money to help me. But I can give you something else. If you want it."

He frowned. He didn't want money. Or anything. But he was curious what she was offering. "What's that?"

She bit her cherry-red lower lip, her lashes dropping over her dark eyes. "My virginity."

Cash nearly choked on his own tongue. He shot her a glance. She still wasn't looking at him. "Are you fucking serious?"

She lifted her lashes. The look in her eyes made him want to kick himself. He didn't even know her and he hated that he'd hurt her.

"You aren't interested?"

He gripped the wheel. Hard. What the hell was he supposed to say now? Whatever it was, he got the impression he needed to tread carefully.

"It's not that you aren't attractive, Ella. But I don't expect payment. I helped you out because it was the right thing to do."

She twisted the bejeweled fabric of her skirt in one small hand. "And now? Will you still help me, or do you plan to drop me at the sheriff's department and wash your hands of me?"

Shit. It's what he wanted to do. No doubt about it. But what if she was right and turning her over resulted in her marriage to Sheikh Fahd taking place anyway? Cash knew he wasn't going to take that chance. She might be crazy or exaggerating—but if there was any chance she really could be forced to marry against her will, then he wasn't putting her in that position.

"Jesus," he bit out, staring straight ahead at the rain coming down. He still had two hours to drive before he reached the fishing cabin. It was isolated, sitting on a mountain and surrounded by woods and streams. Nobody would think to look for her there. And he'd have a couple of days to figure out alternatives.

"Yeah, fine," he said. "I'll help."

"Thank you."

She slumped in the seat and a shot of anger ricocheted through him. Not at her, but at the situation that would make this woman trust a stranger with her life rather than return to her family. It wasn't right. Or normal.

What the fuck was he supposed to do with her in three days when the fishing trip was through? Hell, what was he supposed to do with her *now?*

Not take her virginity, that's for damned sure. He had a

policy about virgins: hell to the *NO*. Because virgins hadn't yet figured out how relationships worked—i.e., they wanted one. He did not. Relationships were superficial at best, and he wasn't about to pretend there could ever be more.

No matter what his teammates thought about it, love wasn't real. At least not for him. Cowboy could cuddle up with Miranda all day long and convince himself he needed her more than he needed to breathe, but Cash knew the truth—if she left him tomorrow, he'd eventually get over her and find someone else.

Love was a con. And Cash wasn't playing.

Chapter Three

ELLA WAS IN SHOCK. Sort of. Yes, it was her own choices that had gotten her here, but when she'd run away from the estate, she hadn't expected to find herself in a car with a stranger, begging him not to take her to the authorities.

What did *you expect, Ella?*

Yes, what had she expected? That she'd drive away from the estate and... do what? She had no money, no ID, and no cell phone. Where would she have gone? Who would let her stay in a hotel when she had no ID or means to support herself? The scheme had been doomed from the moment she'd hatched it in the bathroom. She was woefully unprepared—and would even now be on her way back to the estate if not for this man.

Ella chewed her bottom lip, then stopped when she heard her aunt's voice in her head. *Stop that right this instant. You're a princess, not a commoner. You must learn poise and grace.*

Poise. Grace.

Ella wanted to snort. What did she need those for if she was only ever going to be locked away from the world? Her cousins were permitted more freedom than she'd ever had. Her life was almost a cliché—the mean aunt and uncle, the evil cousins, nobody who loved her or looked out for her. If they'd forced her to sleep in a closet under the stairs, she could have at least dreamed of getting a letter from a magic school and being freed her from her humdrum existence. For part of the year anyway.

But they hadn't gone that far. They'd given her a big room of her own, exquisitely furnished, and then reminded her every day for the past fourteen years what a burden and a drain on their finances she was.

Ella sucked in a calming breath and clasped her hands on her wet lap as she took stock of the situation. The dress was soaked. Ruined. It was a gorgeous creation, but not to her taste. It was ostentatious and heavy and she wanted out of it.

But she hated that she'd ruined it. Someone—or several someones—had worked hard to make this dress beautiful. And it was arguably the most expensive thing her aunt and uncle had ever bought her.

She reached for the vent and turned it toward her. Cash—she was still processing his name, testing it out in her mind—had turned the heat on. She didn't know why he'd done it, but she was thankful he had. He didn't look cold at all. As if to emphasize that fact, he flipped the middle vent, which was still pointing at him, toward her.

"Thank you," she said.

"Sure."

She slanted a look at his face, and her stomach did a slow tumble thing that she was trying to get used to. She knew he was tall from the confrontation with her uncle's security man. He was also lean, his body packed with muscle that popped and flexed as he moved. She'd watched him back there, and she'd been mesmerized by the grace and beauty of him.

But it was his face that made it hard to breathe.

It was a perfect face, symmetrical, with a sculpted jaw and high cheekbones. His eyes were green, rimmed in black. It made them stand out against that perfectly beautiful face. His hair was a deep, rich chocolate color, wavy and full. His mouth invited all sorts of thoughts that made her skin prickle with heat.

Ella's belly clenched. She might be a sheltered virgin, but she'd read books and she'd viewed a few porn videos. Her aunt had considered that the best way to educate her about sex. Ella's belly had clenched in much the same way the first time she'd watched a man and woman have sex on-screen.

She shook herself and turned to look out the window as the rain fell and obscured the fields in the distance.

"We need to get you out of that dress," he said, his voice all growly and deep, and she nearly jumped a mile out of her skin.

Was he interested after all? She'd been taught that men prized virginity. Perhaps he'd changed his mind. Which made her heart start to hammer.

"I, uh, yes," she said helplessly. Because she'd offered. And because if she wasn't a virgin anymore, then Sheikh Fahd would not want her. She could do this. She *could*. It was the best idea.

"We'll need to find a place to stop and get you some clothes and shoes," he continued, and her heartbeat slowed a fraction.

So he wasn't planning seduction after all. And why had she expected it? She must look like the proverbial drowned rat. Her hair had been coiffed and piled on her head with exquisite care, the crown set just so and pinned into place. She'd jerked the crown from her head and mussed her hair then. But that was nothing like the moment she'd been tugged into the rain by her uncle's security man.

Her hair was plastered to her head. Ropes of it dripped down her face, sticking to her cheeks. She pushed it back carefully and started feeling for pins. At least she could remove them and finger-comb her hair. It would dry faster that way.

"That would be good," she replied.

"There's a Walmart in the next town. We'll stop there."

"Thank you." She'd never been inside a Walmart. How exciting! But her excitement was short-lived as she thought about buying anything. Ella balled her hand into a fist. "I'm afraid I don't have any money."

Cash shot her a glance. "Didn't think you did. Not many women tuck credit cards into their cleavage on their wedding day."

"Maybe more should," she grumbled. Not that she had a credit card to tuck anywhere. Or any cash, come to think of it. Hell, she didn't even possess her own ID card—no driver's license or government ID—or passport. She *had* a passport, but her uncle kept it in his safe.

"It's okay. I've got it."

"I'll pay you back." Somehow.

"I'm sure you will."

"I really will. Honest."

"It's not designer shit, okay?" There was a hint of amusement in his voice. It made her feel better. "You'll pay me when you can. I'm not worried."

She finished pulling pins from her hair. There was a nice pile on her lap. She combed her fingers through her hair and shook it out. Cash reached behind her seat before shoving a cloth in her hands.

"It's clean," he said. "I keep it in here for drying the car after a wash, but I haven't used it yet. Go ahead."

She wrapped the soft cloth around her hair and squeezed. It soaked up a surprising amount of water. She dried her face and arms with it too, then squeezed her hair again.

The heater was doing a nice job and she was starting to finally feel warm.

"Well, shit." Cash was looking in the rearview mirror, his jaw set in a hard line. Ella spun to see what the trouble was.

A black SUV bore down on them, lights flashing. Her heart dropped to her toes and her belly turned to ice.

"Don't let them take me," she blurted out, grabbing his arm. It was a solid arm. Hard.

He seemed to be considering something. Maybe he was thinking about turning her over anyway. Letting her uncle drag her back to Sheikh Fahd. Ella's life flashed before her eyes as she considered what the next few hours might look like.

In the next instant, the car accelerated so hard she was pressed against the seat back. If he'd been thinking about turning her over, he'd clearly decided against it. Cash gripped the wheel with both hands, looking angry and determined at the same time. She prayed he didn't change his mind anytime soon.

The road was wet, the rain pelting against the windshield. She didn't know how he could see. Ella closed her eyes and gritted her teeth, praying that she made it out of this alive. She was too young to die. There was too much she hadn't experienced.

Love. Freedom. *Sex.*

"Hang on," Cash said a second before time stood still.

The car swung hard, the back end spinning beneath them as the front end gripped the blacktop. Ella couldn't open her mouth to scream even if she wanted to. Her eyes stayed screwed tight.

The car jerked hard and then shot forward again as if someone had lit a fuse and it'd been propelled from a cannon. Ella finally managed to open her eyes. The rain was no better, but the man beside her drove as if he knew exactly where he was going. As if he had X-ray vision. The engine roared as if possessed, screaming at high speed along country roads that should have refused to let it pass.

She didn't know how long they drove like that or how many turns they made, but eventually Cash whipped onto a road that seemed to appear out of nowhere. It was well hidden by the woods lining either side of the road for miles. It was obviously a driveway, but you'd have to be looking for it to find it. Otherwise you'd drive right by and never know you'd done it.

Ella gripped the center console and the door for support as they rocked over bumps in the track. Eventually they reached a clearing where a small house sat. Beyond the house, a river swelled with rain. It rushed angrily along the banks, the white water swirling and bubbling.

Ella's belly twisted as she considered the situation. She was alone in this remote place with a stranger. A man who might not be any better than those she'd run from. She'd already told him she was a virgin. What if he had sex with her and then killed her? He could dump her in that river and nobody would know.

Stop.

As if he'd sensed the word in her head, Cash brought the car to a halt. He swung around to look at her, his brows drawn low over those incredible eyes. Eyes that sparked with anger.

"All right, Ella—out with it. Who the hell are you?"

Chapter Four

Her dark eyes widened. She swallowed, blinking rapidly.

"I... uh... I..." She closed her eyes and clasped her hands in her lap. It was a calming gesture, and Cash felt a rush of guilt that he'd scared her. But holy hell, that had not been a fun escape. Whoever'd been in that SUV had been determined.

He'd figured she had to be somebody, marrying the sheikh, but hell, that could mean anything. The fact someone was after her within moments of his rescuing her from the first guy meant they wanted her back pretty badly.

Which meant she was probably more than a lovely, connected woman marrying a wealthy foreign national.

"Spit it out, Ella."

"My full name is Antonella Maria Rossi. My family is, uh, Italian by heritage. I was born in Italy though my family is from the sovereign island of Capriolo. We are all Capriolan. I came to live with my aunt and uncle fourteen years ago when my parents were killed in a car accident.

They—my aunt and uncle—arranged the marriage with Sheikh Fahd."

"Without your consent."

"Consent is not necessary in my home country."

"We aren't in your home country."

She nodded. "No, we aren't. My mother was American, by the way. I'm fairly certain she married my father out of love."

Love. Cash didn't scoff, though he wanted to. Judging by Ella's gown and the fact she was marrying Sheikh Fahd, money was involved. A lot of money. Which meant her mother'd had incentive to marry her father too.

"You want to marry for love."

She dropped her gaze, her fingers fiddling with the lace on her gown. "I do."

Cash resisted the urge to roll his eyes, but only barely.

Ella's dark eyes blazed as she lifted her lashes. Her expression hardened. "But not yet. I want to make my own choices, live my own life. When I'm ready, I'll choose my own husband. I don't think he should be chosen for me."

Cash tapped his fingers on the steering wheel. This whole fucking trip had gone sideways, and all because he'd had to pick up a bride. A runaway bride. It would have been funny if not for the fact some asshole had shot a hole in his Mustang—a car he was *still* paying for, dammit—and another group of assholes had then tried to run him off the road.

"Look, I'm not a miracle worker. I can give you a place to stay for a couple of days. I'll help you figure out a plan if you want. But I'm not risking my life for you, got it? If someone comes looking for you here, I'm not standing in the way."

Guilt slashed through him, but dammit, he wasn't here to risk his life for this woman. She didn't want to go through with an arranged marriage. He got that. He didn't blame her, but it wasn't his job to get between her and her family. They'd been a little heavy-handed in their pursuit of her, but he wasn't sure she was in any real danger.

Color flared in her cheeks. "I understand."

He tipped his chin toward the house. "There's a key under the seat of that rocker on the porch. Let yourself in while I hide the car."

The color drained from her face. "Don't leave me out here. Please. I don't have a phone—I don't even know where we are. If you leave, I'll—"

"I'm not leaving, Ella. But I can't leave the car sitting in the open either. They obviously know to look for a black Mustang GT."

Hell, by now they had his plate number too. The original guard wouldn't have gotten it because Cash only had a plate in the rear, but the people in the SUV would have gotten a good look. *Shit.*

She opened the car door and gave him a long look. "I'm counting on you."

Then she hefted herself and her monstrosity of a dress out of the car. He'd gotten her as close to the porch as he could. She climbed the steps and he focused on her slim ankles and her bare, muddy feet. When she reached the top, she went over to the rocker. A moment later she had the key. She held it up and he nodded. Then he squeezed the gas and eased the car over to the shed built a little distance away. If he was lucky, he'd find a tarp or something inside. Then he could cover the car and hope nobody came looking for her.

Because he *would* turn her over if they did. He'd risked enough already. He wasn't risking more.

Ella watched him drive away, her heart pounding. But he didn't go far. There was a shed a few yards distant and he parked beside it. Then he got out of the car and went into the structure. She stood undecided for a second and then turned and went over to insert the key into the lock.

If he'd intended to leave her here, he wouldn't be cautious about it. He'd simply drive away. Besides, she was tired and cold and she wanted out of all these acres of wet satin and lace.

She opened the door and stopped just inside. The house was rustic but pretty. Wood paneling covered every last inch of the interior, and the ceiling soared into a point over the living area. Windows covered the entire wall from floor to ceiling, and a deck jutted out from the house.

The view, commanded by the river, was gorgeous. The trees were a beautiful second. They were lush and full, their leaves that bright shade of new green that heralded spring. There was a dock that squatted over the river, and a lift with a boat on it. For a moment, her heart was full as she stared at the scenery.

Free.

That was the word that came to mind, and yet it wasn't quite right. She wasn't free. Not yet. She was, in fact, in a worse position than she'd first imagined when she'd ripped off that crown and escaped the house.

No money, no clothes, no identification—and nowhere to go. Only the kindness of a stranger had gotten her this far—and his kindness had a hard limit, which he'd told her only moments ago.

If her uncle's security men showed up here, it was all over. She didn't really blame him. He'd gotten shot at and chased, and now he had to put up with her. She was still a burden, but for Cash instead of her aunt and uncle.

Dammit, why couldn't she do anything right?

Ella walked into the room, rubbing her hands over her arms. She was cold and wet and very disheartened. There was a fireplace, a huge stone thing that perched against one wall. She looked at the wood piled in the box next to the hearth. She didn't even know how to start a fire.

Useless, Ella. You are useless.

The door swung open and she whirled. Cash stalked inside, carrying a duffel bag and a handful of plastic grocery bags. He kicked the door closed and went over to put everything except the duffel on the kitchen island.

He started taking stuff from the bags and putting it into the refrigerator. "I was supposed to make this trip with two buddies," he said, dropping a bag of potato chips on the island. "Grocery shopping is always my task." He shot her a wry look. "Seems I'm incapable of buying for only one person."

"I see that," she said as he kept putting things away.

He shrugged. "I like to cook. And whatever I don't use, I take home again. No big deal."

"You like to cook?" She didn't know how to cook. She'd never been allowed to learn. That's what servants were for, according to her aunt.

"Well, I like to eat. Cooking seemed like the next step if I didn't want to eat takeout my whole life."

"Is this your house?"

"It belongs to a friend."

He frowned as she drifted closer. She realized he was looking at her hands. Specifically at the way she kept rubbing her arms.

"You're cold."

"A little."

"You should take a hot shower. Or a bath. This place has a Jacuzzi tub. You can soak for a while if you like."

"I would like that a lot."

He nodded toward a hallway. "You can take the master. That's where the tub is. I'll bunk in one of the other rooms."

Ella hesitated. "I need, uh, I need help…" She couldn't stop her gaze from dropping away. "There are a lot of buttons."

His movements stilled. He didn't say anything for a long moment. When his gaze finally met hers, she wasn't certain if it was frustration or something else coloring his expression.

"I guess you can't very well reach behind your back, can you?"

Ella glanced over her shoulder. "I could get a few in the middle maybe. But not the top. Maybe if you just start it, I can finish?"

He sighed and wadded the grocery bags into a ball before stuffing them away in a drawer. "No, that's all right. I can unbutton you. Unless you want me to slice them away—be quicker."

Ella shook her head. "No. I mean I know the dress is very likely ruined already, but I can't willfully cut into it."

He frowned and then laughed. "So you can stomp through mud and get soaked in a rainstorm, but you can't harm the dress on purpose? Sounds a little crazy, don't you think?"

"Probably so." She gazed at the wet lace. "But it took a lot of work, you know? Someone spent time sewing the beads on, and the buttons. It needs a good cleaning, but it'll be all right."

"I can't believe you care about that dress. Seems like you'd think of it as the memory of your near-marriage to the sheikh."

She blinked. "It's not the dress's fault. Someone else may get joy out of it. You never know."

25

It was his turn to blink. "That dress probably cost a fortune, and you want to drop it at a thrift shop or something?"

She hadn't quite thought of that—but why not? "That sounds like a good idea. They'll clean it up. Someone will enjoy it."

He shook his head. "Turn around, Ella."

She did as he commanded. And then she held her breath, waiting for the feel of his fingers against her skin. But he didn't touch her. Not for a long moment.

She shot him a look over her shoulder. "Is there something wrong?"

He was staring at her back, at the junction of her shoulder blades beneath the silk. He cleared his throat and lifted his hands. "No, nothing."

His fingers were warm as they made quick work of her buttons. Her skin tingled beneath the onslaught in a way that surprised her. The porn leaped to her mind and she thought of the way the man had caressed the woman's back before sliding his erect penis into her wet folds.

So erotic, that memory. The woman had been shaven clean, and the sight of all that male flesh disappearing inside her had both amazed and aroused Ella. How had she taken it all? How had she stood it?

But the male flesh disappeared again and again, and the woman moaned and thrashed her body against the man. Then she stiffened and cried out, and the man pumped harder. All Ella could see was his thickness sliding in and out, in and out. Rasping tender flesh. Dragging feelings from deep within. She hadn't thought of any of that with Sheikh Fahd, but now she couldn't quite stop herself.

She bit her lip, and Cash's fingers stopped moving against her back. She didn't say a word, didn't move. He didn't speak either. Then he took a step closer, and for a moment she could feel his hard body ghosting against the back of hers, so light as to not even be a touch at all.

But it was most definitely a touch. She started to lean back out of instinct, but two broad hands fixed on her shoulders and stopped her. They were strong hands. Insistent hands.

"That should be good enough," he said, his voice huskier than it had been. "Go shower, Ella. Take your time, and I'll cook something to eat."

She nodded as heat crept into her cheeks. It wasn't the heat of arousal though. It was the heat of embarrassment. Had he known what she'd been thinking?

Oh God.

She clutched the dress to her chest as she followed his directions to the master bedroom. Once she found the bathroom, she ran hot water and discarded the gown in a heap on the floor. Then she stepped inside the steamy tub and sank down in it until she could sink no more without drowning.

Though maybe drowning was a good idea after all. At least she wouldn't have to face Cash again.

Chapter Five

HOLY SHIT. Cash watched Ella walk away, then turned and went back into the kitchen with his heart thudding in his chest in a way he wasn't quite accustomed to. He liked— no, _loved_—women. Loved sex. And he was pretty good at it too.

But what he wasn't good at was the emotional component. He could rock a woman's world with his tongue, fuck her into oblivion with his cock, but he didn't do the emotional stuff.

Ella Rossi needed the emotional component. He'd been unbuttoning her dress, revealing creamy skin and reminding himself that she was a virgin. But he'd noticed something as he'd kept going.

Arousal. _Hers._

Because he wasn't an idiot, and he could tell when a woman was getting excited. The shivers and shudders. The soft inhalation of her breath. And that moan there at the end, the barely uttered sound that had made all the hackles on his neck rise as if he were a predator scenting prey.

If he'd turned her around in his arms, she'd have gone limp. He could have kissed her. Could have peeled that dress right off her body and explored every inch of her.

Which he was *not* going to do. No way. No how. She was a virgin, and he was allergic to virgins. He'd learned that lesson a long time ago. No initiating a woman into sex for the first time. It gave them ideas.

He adjusted his cock—yeah, it was hard—and walked over to the kitchen to start something for dinner. It was still early, not quite five, but it'd been a while since he'd eaten and he figured Ella was hungry too.

He took out some chicken, pasta, and mushrooms. He'd make chicken marsala for dinner. It was a good seduction dinner. One that had served him well in the past.

No. He stopped in midgrab of the chicken and shoved it back into the refrigerator. He was not cooking a seduction dinner for this strange—and strangely appealing—woman. Instead, he grabbed the pasta and some butter, cream, and parmesan. He'd make an Alfredo sauce. Plain enough and delicious. He'd picked up some shrimp, so he'd put those in there too—

And, shit, that was also a good seduction dinner. Shrimp Alfredo, bread, butter and good olive oil.

Fuck me.

Cash hesitated for a long moment but finally grabbed the ingredients anyway. He wasn't planning a seduction, and they needed to eat. He'd have cooked this for the guys, though he'd also have cooked hamburgers and steaks. But he liked the grill for those, and it was still raining outside.

So pasta it was. *Not* seduction.

He got busy putting water in a pot for the pasta, getting out a skillet for the sauce, and heating the oven for the bread. It took all of twenty minutes. He hesitated, fists on hips, wondering if he should start cooking or wait for her to emerge again.

He would have turned on the television, but he knew there was no signal right now. This cabin belonged to the second-in-command of HOT, Lieutenant Colonel Alex "Ghost" Bishop, and Ghost had told him that the satellite wouldn't work if it was raining hard. This was Cash's second trip up here, and he knew that was true.

He and Cowboy and Cage had stayed here once before, a few months ago. Before that, they'd stayed in a dive of a cabin a bit farther along the river. When Ghost offered this place, they'd jumped on it. It was much nicer than they'd expected. Ghost said it was a family property and refused to take any rent for it. Free was better than cheap, at least in this instance, so Cash and his buds planned to come here often.

Except here he was. Alone. Or not alone but with a surprisingly sensual virgin who'd managed to give him a hard-on by doing nothing at all.

Geez. He wasn't desperate. He'd spent the past few nights with a cute dental hygienist he'd met at the grocery store. He'd have thought for sure he wasn't ready for sex for a few days yet. Not that he would turn down a good lay if it came his way, but it wasn't precisely front of mind at the moment. Or at least it hadn't been.

He shoved a hand through his hair and turned back to the stove. The stick of butter sat waiting for him to put it in the pan. But once he did that, the sauce would cook quick. Butter, cream, parmesan. Toss with the pasta and, boom, dinner.

He flipped on the burner for the pasta water. Then he went to set the table. He didn't light the candle sitting in the middle of it, nor did he pull out the cloth napkins from the drawer he knew they rested in. Nope, this chick was getting a paper towel. Hell, if this place had plastic cutlery, he'd have given her that too. And a paper plate.

Instead, he had to make do with stainless steel and porcelain.

The pot soon started to boil. He went over and turned it down, unwilling to start cooking when he didn't know when she was coming back. He glanced at his watch—she'd been gone for forty-five minutes. Surely that was time enough to bathe.

He hesitated a moment before heading down the hallway to the master. The door was closed and he knocked. When there was no answer, he pushed it inward. The wedding gown lay in a heap on the floor. The door to the bathroom was open. But she hadn't answered his knock.

"Ella," he called out.

There was a small shriek, a splash, and then a tentative "Yes?"

His heartbeat slowed at her reply. Did he really think anything had happened to her in here?

"Just checking on you. It's been a while."

"Oh, I'm fine. Thank you."

"Hungry?"

"I... Yes, I think I could eat something."

"Can you be done in twenty minutes?"

"Yes."

"Good. I'll have dinner ready then."

"Um, Cash...?" she called as he was headed toward the door.

"Yeah?"

"I don't have any clothes."

He closed his eyes. "No, I guess you don't. Give me a sec."

He strode into the nearest guest room where he'd

LYNN RAYE HARRIS

stowed his duffel and yanked it open. He hadn't brought a lot with him, but he had a few things. He picked up a pair of sweats and a flannel shirt. It wasn't precisely cold out, but it could get cool at night. He went back to the master and tossed them on the bed.

"I've left sweats and a shirt out here on the bed. It's the best I can do."

"That will work. Thank you."

He left the room, pulling the door shut behind him, and went back to the kitchen. He turned the water back to a boil, tossed in the pasta, and got to work on the sauce. By the time he had it all finished—pasta drained and tossed in the sauce, bread heated and cut into thick rounds, butter and oil set on the table—Ella appeared.

Cash did a bit of a double take at the sight of her. She'd scrubbed off the makeup and her hair was long, dark, and thick. She'd managed to dry it, but she had nothing to contain it with. It hung heavy and full and wavy over her shoulders. Her eyes were dark and sparkling, and her body in his clothes was practically dwarfed. The shirt hung to her knees. She'd rolled the sweats up, but they were baggy and she kept pulling them up.

Her feet were bare. Small feet that must surely be cold. He should have given her some socks.

She smiled at him, and his heart did a little leap-skip thing that was odd.

"Smells wonderful," she told him. "I'm starved."

"Are your feet cold?"

She glanced down. "Not yet. I'm still hot from the bath."

"Let me know when you need socks. I'll get you a pair."

"Okay."

He pulled out a chair and sat down. "It's all ready," he said. "Help yourself."

She looked a little strange. But then she sat down and primly took the paper towel and laid it in her lap. She hesitated a moment, then picked up the two long pasta forks he'd set in the Alfredo and helped herself to a pile of food.

She didn't touch the bread until he did, and then she eagerly dipped a piece into the oil and pepper before eating it. When she closed her eyes and moaned, he felt that sound all the way to his cock.

"It's just bread," he said.

She opened her eyes. "I know. But it's so good. I didn't think I'd be eating simple bread with oil ever again. Silly, maybe, but I don't know what desert sheikhs eat."

"Oh, I imagine Sheikh Fahd eats quite well. You would not be denied with him."

She chewed the bread thoughtfully. "Maybe not. But I don't want to find out."

He rolled pasta onto his fork. "You don't think this could have been solved in a different manner? That you could have just said no?"

She stopped the motion of rolling pasta onto her own fork and stared at him. "That was not possible."

"Because your uncle wants you to marry the sheikh."

She nodded. "Yes. My aunt and uncle both. They are…" She looked thoughtful. "They need the money that he will pay them for me."

Something about how matter-of-factly she said it pissed him off. "You realize he won't be paying them anything now?"

And they deserved it. People who sought to sell their own flesh and blood into a situation she did not want were no better than human slavers. And he'd seen enough of them in his line of work to last him a lifetime.

"Yes, I suppose that's true," she said softly. "But there was no other way. If I'd married him, I would have gone insane."

He hated to hear her say that. Hated that anyone had to think of such things. But he did not doubt she believed it. Or that she would have lost whatever spark she currently had.

"Then I guess you had to run away."

She smiled, just the corners of her mouth tilting up in a shy little smile, and he had to harden his heart not to feel anything. "It was my only choice. But without you, I wouldn't have succeeded at all. So thank you. Thank you from the bottom of my heart, Cash."

Heat crept through him. He was used to saving people, but somehow he didn't feel like he'd done enough to save her. Not yet anyway. He'd picked her up off the side of the road, but he'd done nothing significant to get her out of her situation.

"Have you thought about what comes next?" he asked, certain that she hadn't.

She stuffed a forkful of pasta in her mouth. When she moaned, his senses went on alert. How many times could this woman moan about simple things like food and touch? Worse, why was it affecting him so much?

"Oh my God, this is delicious. Simply delicious."

Cash frowned a bit. "It's good, but it's not that good."

She lifted her gaze to his. "I haven't had pasta in so long I can't remember—trust me, this is delicious."

"Why haven't you had pasta? I thought you said your heritage was Italian." Not that Italians had to eat pasta all the time, but all the Italians he'd ever known ate it with some regularity.

"My aunt thought I would get fat."

He was really starting to hate this aunt of hers. Ella

34

didn't have any meat whatsoever on her bones. She was thin and small and looked like she'd blow away in a stiff breeze.

"Eat as much as you like," Cash told her. "But don't make yourself sick."

She grinned as she reached for more bread. "I'm going to stuff myself silly."

He wanted to laugh but he didn't. "Okay, so what's next, Ella? After today? Where do you want to go?"

The flicker of delight died in her eyes and he kicked himself for making it happen.

"I don't know. I honestly don't. Could we maybe not talk about this tonight? Please?"

"The problem isn't going away just because you don't address it."

She twirled the fork on her plate, eyes downcast. "I know. But I'll think about it tonight. I'll have a better idea by morning."

He could see the exhaustion and stress lining her face. He wasn't going to be an asshole to her, not when she'd been through so much. Besides, he was here for three days. If it took her that long to figure it out, then fine.

There was still the matter of his car—the hole that'd been shot into it and the fact that her uncle's people knew to look for it. He couldn't very well drive away from here as if nothing had happened, no matter what.

"They're going to be looking for you, Ella. I can't guarantee they won't find you here."

She bit her lip. "I can't go back. If I do…" She shrugged, but it was a sad gesture.

"We'll figure something out. I won't let them take you."

Though earlier he'd told her he wouldn't interfere. *Way to go, Cash.*

She studied him for a long moment, tilting her head to the side. "Are all American men like you?"

He frowned. It was an odd question, and yet he thought she was sincere. In truth, he didn't know what she meant by it. "You live in America. What do you think?"

"I don't leave the estate much," she said softly. "I don't encounter many people."

His dislike of her aunt and uncle was growing exponentially. "How long have you lived there?"

"Since I was eight and my aunt and uncle took me in after my parents died."

Fourteen years ago, or so she'd said earlier. So she was twenty-two. Young.

"You didn't go to school?"

"I had tutors. My cousins and I did, I mean."

"But you've traveled, right?"

She shook her head. "I've been on supervised trips to the mall with my cousins a few times. But not in a couple of years now."

What she was telling him was mind-boggling. "You haven't left their estate in two years?"

She looked small again. As if she were folding in on herself. "No."

"Jesus," he muttered. She'd been a prisoner. There was no other word for it. He'd spent the past few years freeing people from hostage situations—and Ella had been enduring a gilded prison so near the nation's capital that it was shocking to think nobody had known about it.

But why would they?

He needed to know more about her. "You have no idea what to do now that you've left there, have you? You had no plan. Hell, you've already said you have no money. What do you expect you'll do? Get a job at a grocery store or something?"

Her face was red. "I told you I'll think about it overnight. I'll figure something out."

He could only shake his head. "I don't think you will, Ella. I don't think you have the first idea what happens next."

Chapter Six

_____

ELLA'S HEART thudded in her chest. He was right, of
course. She didn't know. She was very conscious of the
knowledge she had no identification, no history, and no
money. She was Princess Antonella Maria Rossi, and she
had never been prepared for living her life on her own.

Oh, she'd watched television and movies. She'd
combed the internet for information, though carefully
because her aunt and uncle watched her and knew which
sites she visited. She'd learned that lesson the hard way.
They'd taken away her access for a month when she'd
dared to visit the US government site on citizenship and
becoming naturalized.

After that, she was careful what she searched for. She
watched mindless shows on Netflix, but they weren't totally
mindless because they showed her what it was like to work
for a living. How to go about renting an apartment, paying
bills, getting a license and driving.

She knew they weren't entirely accurate, but it gave her
a picture. And then there were the home shows on HGTV.
Oh, how she loved to watch those couples buy homes and

renovate them together. It was a hopeful thing to shop for a home with a man, to buy it and turn it into a place where you were happy together. She loved those shows like she loved this pasta.

She took another bite and tried not to moan her happiness. She wasn't quite successful. Cash's eyes narrowed, but he didn't say anything.

She'd asked him if all American men were like him. He hadn't given her an answer, but she was pretty certain the answer was no. He was big and muscular, but he didn't frighten her. Not like her uncle's security forces did. That man earlier today—he'd run her off the road and then yanked her from the car as if she were nothing.

He'd fully intended to throw her over his shoulder and shove her in his car so he could return her to the estate, but Cash had driven up and ruined his plans. She could still see the angry look on Cash's face, the way he'd sized up the man and her, and the odd way she'd been drawn to him.

He could have been a serial killer, but she'd known in her gut that he wasn't. That leaving with him wasn't a fatal choice. She'd taken the risk and now here she was, wrapped in clothes that smelled like him and eating pasta that tasted as delicious as anything she could remember.

She was happier than she'd been in a very long time. And that was pitiful in a way. But she *was*. Pasta and small talk during a heavy rainstorm was heaven compared to the past few days of preparing for the sheikh's arrival.

Cash was still watching her and she realized he was waiting for an answer. But she didn't have one to give him. So she made something up, because she had to.

"I have a friend in California. I'm going to stay with her."

His gaze narrowed. "California. How do you know this person?"

She'd said California because it was the first place that popped into her mind. *The Real Housewives of Orange County*, of course. Ella swallowed her bite of pasta.

"We met online. She's married and has a big house where I can stay until I figure out what I'm doing."

"I thought you said you had to think about it overnight."

Ella resisted the urge to lick her lips. "I *am* thinking about it. But you said you didn't think I had a plan. I do, but it's not fully formed yet."

He didn't look convinced. "Okay. Let me know when you have it together."

He stood and took his empty plate to the sink. Ella finished the pasta, no matter that she was already full, and ate another slice of bread for good measure. Cash did the dishes while she ate. She watched his backside, the strong lines of his body, the flex and give of muscles that had been honed to perfection.

When he finished washing dishes, he turned to her. "Are you done?"

She looked down at the empty plate and the bowl of pasta still in front of her. But she *was* full. Eating another whole plate of pasta wasn't happening.

"Yes. Thank you," she said as he took the plate and went to wash it.

She buttered another slice of bread and ate it slowly, savoring the flavors. She managed not to moan, however.

He put the dishes on the drying rack, hung the towel, and turned back to her. His face made her heart skip. So handsome. Like a movie star.

"What do you do, Cash?" Because she didn't know,

and she could suddenly see him swaggering across a movie screen.

"I rescue people," he said without a touch of irony. And then he continued. "I'm a Navy SEAL. Special Ops," he added when she felt as if she'd frowned for too long.

"What does that mean?"

"It means I rescue people."

This time he smiled, and she couldn't help but smile too. "You drive around looking for people to rescue?"

"Not precisely," he said. "More like I get sent to war zones to get people out."

She frowned. "And today?"

"Today I was on my way here. To fish. You were a bit of a surprise."

"I'm sorry." But she wasn't. She was glad he'd found her. Glad it had been him who'd happened upon the scene. If not for Cash, she'd be in Sheikh Fahd's arms right now. Perhaps they'd only be dancing, still playing the part for the guests, but she would have dreaded what was coming.

Sheikh Fahd wasn't unattractive. Not really. He was a bit older than she was, but that was nothing. It was just that he didn't do anything for *her*. There was something about the way he leered at her. The clammy feel of his palms against her skin. The word *defiled* sprang to mind.

And then there was the fact she hadn't *chosen* him.

"I couldn't leave you there. It's not who I am."

Her insides warmed. As if he'd poured hot honey over her. "I'm glad for that. You saved my life."

He glanced at his watch as if embarrassed. Or maybe he just didn't know how to respond. "It's still early, but I'm afraid television is out of the question with this storm. Satellite won't work."

"That's okay," she said, nodding toward the book-shelves. "I like to read."

"So do I."

"Favorite author?"

"Tolkien."

She nodded. "The Lord of the Rings. I loved that."

"Who's your favorite?"

A blush crept over her. "I like romance novels."

"Those aren't real," he said automatically.

"And Lord of the Rings is?"

He had the grace to look perplexed. "No, of course not. But nobody's in danger of thinking it is, are they?"

"Meaning that women are more likely to think romance novels are real, right? That we can't distinguish between real life and fantasy?" She shook her head vigorously. "I assure you I know the difference. Romance novels are how we wish the world worked—how we wish men really were—but I'm pretty sure the reality I've endured is closer to the truth. The men my uncle hired are interested in rewards and keeping their jobs. Sheikh Fahd is interested in having a virginal wife. My uncle—well, who knows what he wants, but it's not heroic, believe me. And you?" she added. "You saved me, but not because you were violently attracted to me and knew I was the *one*. You did it because it's what you do. You have said as much."

———

Cash had to admit she shocked the shit out of him. But she wasn't wrong. For a woman who seemed to have so little experience of the world, she was surprisingly wise at times. In spite of her words, he wasn't so sure that she really meant them though. In his experience, there were definitely women who thought romance novels were templates for real life. He'd encountered a few of them, women who'd swooned when they learned he was a SEAL. They had *ideas* about SEALs, which wasn't necessarily a bad thing for him. Got him laid.

But then reality set in when they started wanting more than sex. He'd ruined the marital fantasies of more than a few. Then there were the ones who claimed he'd gotten them pregnant. That had only happened twice, but he'd shut them down quick. It hadn't been true anyway. They weren't pregnant at all, and certainly not with his baby. He was careful. Super careful because he knew what happened when parents didn't love each other. It wasn't fair to the kid to be brought into that kind of dynamic, and he wasn't about to be a party to that.

Now he was more cautious about getting involved at all. In fact, he never had sex with the same woman more than five times. It was a personal rule, and one that served him well.

"I doubt there are any romance novels here."

"I'm sure I'll find something. Maybe the words won't be too big."

He glanced at her sharply. She arched an eyebrow and then dropped her gaze. It took him a minute to process her lightning reaction. When he did, he wanted to laugh.

Ella Rossi wasn't just a virgin on the run from her arranged marriage, she was also a smart-ass. How had that happened? She was sheltered and clearly out of her depth in some ways, but she didn't let it define her.

"You need anything else? Dessert?"

She cocked her head toward him, her lips splitting in a sudden grin. Damn, he liked the way she looked in his shirt. Without all the makeup and the wet hair, she was stunning. Pretty in a way that made his balls tighten.

Whoa, boy. Virgin. Red alert.

"Dessert?" she repeated. "What do you have?"

43

What did he have? Hell, he didn't know. He couldn't remember. Cash opened the freezer. Oh yeah.

"Ice cream," he said. "Vanilla or chocolate."

"Mmm, vanilla with chocolate sauce?"

He imagined squeezing chocolate sauce over her nipples. *Shit.* "Yeah, I've got chocolate sauce."

"Then I'd love some ice cream." She stood. "I can get it. You don't have to wait on me."

He waved a hand at her. "Sit. It's no big deal."

He scooped ice cream into a bowl, poured on a generous squeeze of chocolate, and pushed the bowl toward her. She took it, curling her fingers around it and holding it against her breasts as she stood across from him.

She was small. About five-four, maybe a hundred and ten. Not tiny, but small. She dipped the spoon into the ice cream and lifted it to her lips. He didn't expect the shot of arousal to his groin when she closed her eyes and moaned.

Damn, did this woman ever do anything else? All she'd done since he'd started feeding her was moan. The sound dug into his brain, made him imagine her moaning under other circumstances.

"It's just ice cream," he said a bit gruffly.

Her eyes popped open. "To you, maybe. I haven't had ice cream in months."

Her aunt. Of course. Now that was a woman he'd like to horsewhip. Ella could have afforded a few pounds on her slight frame.

"You can have as much as you want," he told her.

"Thanks. But I think this will do. I haven't eaten this much in forever." She frowned slightly. "In fact, I'll probably be sick. But oh well."

"Don't do that," he said. "You can eat it tomorrow. For breakfast if you like."

She spooned in another mouthful. "Nope, has to be now. My uncle could arrive in the middle of the night."

Not on his watch. "It'll take longer than a night."

She grinned. "Then I'll just eat more ice cream in the morning."

He shook his head. "Yeah, you're definitely going to be sick. Don't expect me to clean up after you."

She blinked. "Oh wow, I never thought of that."

"You should since you'll be cleaning it up."

She ate another spoonful. "That's okay. I'll get a towel from the bathroom. It'll be fine."

He snorted. She shocked him and made him laugh at the same time. "You're kinda crazy, Ella. Nobody purposely eats until they puke." He frowned as a thought occurred to him. "Unless that's your thing. Are you a binge eater?"

Her eyes widened. "Are you kidding me? I've never been allowed to binge on anything in my life."

He was relieved. Binge eating was a serious disorder and could be life-threatening. Last thing he needed was for her to have a crisis out here. The closest hospital was over an hour away. And it was dark, wet, and there were people looking for his car. Not the best way to get help if she needed it.

"Maybe you shouldn't start now," he said. "Pace yourself."

She pressed a hand to her belly after another bite of ice cream disappeared. "Whew, I am feeling rather full." She set the bowl on the island. "Guess I'd better stop."

"Wise decision."

She sighed and tipped her head to the side once more. Then she smiled at him. He didn't think she had any idea how sexy a gesture it was on her, but then again he didn't really know her and she might know precisely how pretty and appealing she appeared. Her rich dark hair hung in a long silky curtain to where she propped her elbows on the island. Her eyes sparkled.

"Thanks for dinner. It was amazing."

"You're welcome."

A wrinkle formed on her forehead. "I should be scared of you, but I'm not. I don't know why I feel safe, but thanks for that too."

"You'll be safe so long as you're with me. I swear it."

Her voice was soft. "I know I will."

Chapter Seven

CASH CHECKED THE SATELLITE PERIODICALLY, but it hadn't yet come back. The rain was starting to let up outside though, so he figured it was only a matter of time. After dinner, Ella did indeed find a book to read. She curled up in a chair by the window and hummed from time to time as she turned pages.

She fascinated him for some reason, and he found himself looking at her again and again. For one thing, she didn't have a cell phone that she kept dragging out and fussing with. Everyone did that these days, so it was unusual to see someone who didn't. Almost as if she'd landed here from twenty years in the past.

More likely she'd left it behind when she'd fled her wedding. Or maybe she didn't have one, which he found hard to imagine.

But she sat in the chair with her legs beneath her, reading and humming and looking for all the world like she couldn't care less about checking an electronic device.

Cash couldn't say the same for himself, however. The signal out here was spotty, especially while it was raining, but he had at least a bar at all times. He tried to check the news, but nothing would load, so he gave up after a while.

He went into the bedroom he'd chosen and inspected the ammunition he'd brought. He had a Sig and a Glock with him. There was a gun safe with a couple of other rifles in one of the rooms. He knew the combo because Ghost had given it to them all the first time they'd stayed. Just in case they decided to go hunting.

It was starting to get dark when the rain finally eased. Cash threw on a rain slicker and Ella looked up from her book. The panic in her eyes was automatic, but he held out a hand, palm up, to reassure her.

"I'm just going to check the car and the perimeter. I'll be back in a few minutes."

She sat up straight, pulling her knees underneath her, and he had a crazy urge to go over and drag her into his arms for reassurance. The book hung from one hand. The other rose in what he thought was an unconscious gesture to touch the base of her throat.

"I could go with you."

"No, stay here. It'll be fine, Ella."

"You promise to come back?"

"I told you I won't abandon you."

He left her staring after him and stepped outside. The evening was cooler than the day had been. There was still a bite in the air this time of year, and his breath frosted. The rain trickled from the roof and the trees, but it didn't fall from the sky anymore. He squelched across the yard to the shed, his eyes scanning the surrounding area even as he made plans for how to react should anyone come at him from the shadows.

Nothing happened, however, and he reached the shed soon after. Everything was good. The car was untouched, nothing was disturbed, and everything looked as it should.

The men who'd chased him in the SUV weren't up to his skill level. He'd bet his career on that. Didn't mean they couldn't send someone else, but so far he and Ella were out here in the woods alone.

They had his plate number, but he'd lost them and spent a good amount of time driving around to confuse the trail before he'd turned down the driveway.

After a check of the perimeter, he made his way back to the house. His phone rang as he stepped up onto the porch. It was Dane "Viking" Erikson, the CO of his SEAL team.

Fuck, if he was being called back for a mission, what the hell was he going to do with Ella?

"Money, what the fuck is going on out there?" Viking said as soon as Cash answered.

Shit, he'd known this was going to come back to haunt him once his plates were run.

"I picked up a woman," he said, and Viking snorted. "Not that kind of pickup, I swear. She needed my help. Some dude was trying to force her into a car and make her get married."

Cash knew, since his plate number was out there and Viking was calling him, that the official story differed somehow. Especially if Ella's aunt and uncle were marrying her to Sheikh Fahd. Dammit, he hated rich people. Except for Gina Hunter, aka Gina Domenico, the pop star who'd married HOT sniper Jack "Hawk" Hunter. She was cool. So cool she'd let them use her plane when they'd needed to help Colonel Mendez out of a tight spot recently.

But Ella's aunt and uncle weren't Gina. They were people who'd kept Ella hostage for fourteen years and then tried to marry her to a sheikh against her will. Sold her to him, in fact.

"You need to tell me everything that happened."

"Don't leave anything out, sailor," a commanding voice added, and Cash's insides turned to jelly for a second.

Fuck, if Colonel Mendez—soon to be General Mendez —was listening in, it was serious. Cash pulled in a breath and turned to stare at the woods. He tucked one hand beneath his arm and watched the steady drip of water from the roof as he recited everything that had happened from the moment he'd seen Ella standing on the side of the road until he'd walked outside just now to check the perimeter.

Well, maybe he left out the details of the dinner, but he told them he fixed her something to eat and she was inside, safe and well.

"Have you seen the news?" Viking asked.

"No. It's been raining and the satellite hasn't been working." He gazed up at the sky. "It'll probably work now though."

"You'll want to, but I'll save you some time. There's an APB out for you, Money. You've kidnapped a member of the royal family of Capriolo. She's a *princess*, dude. Like a royal princess with a crown and everything, and her family is distraught. They're waiting for a ransom demand."

Cash's insides turned to liquid. And then a bolt of anger fired up in his stomach. Ella was a *princess?* She'd failed to mention that detail. But she'd still been in danger. He hadn't done wrong in stopping to help.

And he wasn't going to let the knowledge she was a princess derail him. Not yet.

"They don't care about her," he said, repeating what she'd told him. He was certain she hadn't lied. She wasn't sophisticated enough. "They've held her hostage at that estate for years. She's being forced to marry Sheikh Fahd—

and we all know what kind of upstanding citizen he is, right?"

"Doesn't matter," the colonel said. "The Rossi family is tearfully begging for her return on all the networks. And *you're* the one who stole their precious girl, Money."

"If you're asking me to take her back—"

"I'm not," he cut in, and Cash's tongue got stuck tumbling over itself. "You're a HOT operator. I believe you. But this is a serious situation, son. I can't let you or the girl fall into the hands of the police. The media doesn't know who you are, not really, but it won't take long at this point. We have to control the situation."

"Yes, sir," Cash said. Because what else did you say to the big boss?

Viking cut in. "I'm sending backup. Everything about this mission is off the books—but you aren't alone. We have to contain and control, as the colonel said. Stand by for incoming."

Cash was seriously reeling by now. "ETA?"

"Morning," Viking replied. "You got the Mustang hidden?"

"It's covered. And we're clear. I just checked the perimeter."

"Then batten down the hatches and hold tight until morning. If you're attacked, take evasive action."

Cash sucked in a breath. He wasn't scared. He was never fucking scared. Even when he should be. "It's just me out here, Viking. The girl is useless when it comes to defense."

"I hate to say this, bud, but if someone finds you— leave her behind. They aren't going to hurt her, but we can't say the same for you."

———

Ella could hear Cash talking on the other side of the door, but she couldn't hear what he was saying. She'd crept over to the window when she'd first heard him, because she'd been alarmed at the sound of him talking, but he was standing with his back to her, one arm crossed over his body and the other holding a phone to his head.

She waited for a long moment, and then she retreated to her chair and picked up the book again. But she couldn't concentrate. It was impossible. She focused on the door. Waiting for him to return.

Finally the door opened and he came inside. A hard frown dominated his face and her heart skipped.

He stared at her for a long moment. Then he removed the jacket and hung it on a hook by the door. When he stalked toward her, her pulse skipped higher for long moments.

He stopped in front of her chair, glaring down at her, hands at his sides. She thought, vaguely, that if he worked for her uncle, she'd be afraid. But this was Cash and he'd been nothing but decent since he'd rescued her earlier. He'd cooked her dinner. Given her his clothes. And he'd sworn to protect her like a knight of old.

"Is everything okay?" she asked, strangely calm, though his manner was somewhat alarming.

"You tell me."

She frowned. "I think so. I feel fine. Do you?"

He turned and grabbed the television remote from a table nearby. Then he pressed the button and the screen flared to life. It took long seconds for the television to boot up. When it did, he pressed another button and the news came on.

She watched with interest. And then she was there, on-screen, her face flashing in front of millions. She cried out, rising from her seat as the story unfolded, but Cash gave her a hard look and she subsided again.

"You didn't kidnap me," she said, folding her hands on her lap so they wouldn't tremble. "You saved me."

"You're a princess," he said. "You failed to mention it."

Her heart hammered. She hadn't told him, no. When he'd asked who she really was, it had seemed so difficult to add that word to her name. It wasn't like she lived her life as anyone's idea of a princess.

"There is no longer a ruling family in Capriolo. It's merely a title. I inherited it from my father, but it's not something I think about."

"Seems important to your family—and not a good thing for me, I gotta add."

He didn't look happy. His brows arrowed down over his eyes and his mouth flattened in a hard line.

"It changes nothing. I'm still me and I still need your help." Another thought occurred to her. A dark, dangerous thought. "Do you plan to turn me over to them? Collect the reward?"

A reward she was pretty certain they had no intention of paying.

He managed to look insulted. "So the police can arrest me for kidnapping you in the first place? No, I'm not that stupid."

She resisted the urge to clutch her stomach as relief rolled through her. "So what do we do now?"

"We? I thought you had a plan—or would in the morning."

Ella closed her eyes as she dragged in a breath. He was watching her when she opened them again. "I don't have a plan. I never had one."

He snorted. "Didn't think so. Fucking hell, Ella the

princess—what did you think was going to happen when you ran away like that?"

His words stung more than she liked. Her aunt always told her she was stupid—maybe she was.

She bowed her head. "I didn't think. I'm sorry."

He knelt in front of her and tipped her chin up, forced her to look at him. The liquid swimming in her gaze threatened to spill over. His expression grew softer when he saw it.

"Hey, what's up with you?"

She knew he must think her crazy. Maybe she was.

"I'm not taking you back," he added when she didn't say anything. "I promise."

As if the idea of him taking her back was the problem.

Well, maybe it was *part* of the problem.

"Why not?" she whispered. "I'm causing you trouble. You would be happier if you got rid of me."

Those remarkable eyes searched hers for a long moment. She couldn't tell what he was thinking, and yet she knew. Of course he would be happier without her. But he was too nice to say it.

"Ella. I told you I rescue people. It's not all I do, but it's part of it. Would it have been easier to keep driving? Yeah. Would it have been right? Hell, no. I do what's right. Taking you back wouldn't be right, so it's not happening. You understand what I'm telling you?"

Her pulse zipped into the danger zone. Adrenaline spiked in her veins, made her almost giddy. She didn't know why. It was a ridiculous, over-the-top reaction.

Joy.

That's what it was. Joy that she'd met this man and he'd stood up for her. Was still standing up for her.

"Yes," she whispered.

He nodded. "Good."

He dropped his fingers from beneath her chin and stood. She could still feel the burn of his skin against hers. Worse, she wanted to feel it in different places. Secret places.

She cleared her throat. "When I stole the car, I wasn't thinking. One minute I was standing in front of a mirror and getting ready to walk down the aisle, the next I was sneaking outside and finding a car. I didn't really think I'd get as far as I did."

She dared to look up at him.

"If I'd thought about it, I never would have done anything," she continued. "Because I didn't know where to go or how I'd begin to live on my own when I had nothing." She shrugged. "I guess maybe I thought if I got away, if I got to the police or told someone what was happening, they'd stop it."

"You didn't want me to take you to the police."

"No, because by then I knew it wouldn't matter. I'm not American. Nobody could—or would—stop my aunt and uncle. Or Sheikh Fahd. I realized that after the security guard ran me off the road."

Cash frowned hard. "We're both in it now, Princess. No way out of this without help. Lucky for you, I've got help. They'll be here in the morning, so I suggest you get a good night's sleep. Tomorrow may be more intense than either of us realize."

Chapter Eight

CASH SLEPT in fits and starts. He was accustomed to it because he did it on missions. Snatching sleep in twenty-minute increments, waking to check his surroundings, sleeping again. He shouldn't have to do it on this trip, and yet here he was.

Protecting the princess.

He thought of the woman in the other room and his cock woke from its slumber.

Down, you fucking horndog.

He popped a hand behind his head and lay there, staring at the ceiling. She was a princess. Princess Antonella Maria Rossi. He could barely wrap his mind around it.

That slight, wispy, lovely girl was a princess—*and* a virgin.

And he was her knight in shining armor.

Cash rolled his eyes. *Yeah, right.*

Some knight. His fucking mother couldn't even hang around to see him grow up, and his father was the most uninvolved son of a bitch that ever lived. Only his stepmother was interested in him—and not in a good way. From the minute she'd married his father when Cash was eleven, she'd actively worked to let him know he wasn't important or necessary to their lives. And when she'd had a baby with his dad?

Yeah, he'd never had a chance after that. She'd shoved him as far away as possible, as if he'd somehow been competition for an infant. She'd pretended to care, but she hadn't. Passive-aggressive didn't even begin to describe that fucking woman. He'd worked for scraps of affection only to be kicked in the teeth again and again. By the time he was fourteen, he'd realized the truth and he'd stopped trying.

He'd effectively checked out at sixteen, not caring if he finished school or not. He'd only graduated because his track coach kept on top of him to do so. The second he was eighteen? Navy, baby. Best decision he'd ever made.

He turned over and punched the pillow. When next he woke, it was five a.m. Cash blinked into the predawn darkness. The house was quiet. After a few minutes, he flipped the covers back and went to make coffee. After that was done, he went outside to check the perimeter. There'd been no incursions, but he hadn't expected any. If there had been, they wouldn't have stopped at breaching the perimeter. They'd have blasted into the house and taken Ella—and they'd have probably killed him in the process.

Collateral damage.

He shook off the chill and went back inside. The house was warm and the smell of coffee was beginning to permeate the interior. He strode down the hall and toward the master bedroom. The door was closed and he put his ear to it. Listening.

There was no movement, no sound, so he turned and went back to the kitchen and the coffee. After he poured a cup, he headed for the shower. Fifteen minutes later, he was in front of the television, watching the news. A glance at his phone revealed no calls or messages, so he turned his attention to the screen.

The news about Ella wasn't foremost, but it was close. They'd tried to minimize the idea she'd been getting married. None of the photos showed her in a wedding gown or mentioned Sheikh Fahd. Instead, her family was worried about her and wanted her back safely and soon.

A man Cash presumed was her uncle stood at a podium and begged for her return while a hard-eyed woman stood in the background and frowned. Two young women were beside her, also frowning.

He didn't buy it. Partly because of her story and partly because her uncle reminded him a lot of his stepmother. Saying all the right things but not meaning them.

Fuck.

It was a mess, and he'd stumbled into it. Did he regret it? He thought about it, but the answer was not really.

Ella was cute. Sweet. All the things he didn't usually like in a woman. He liked them sexy and tough—even a bit jaded. Women who knew what they wanted in bed. Women who understood that sex was sex and nothing else.

Still, he liked Ella though she was none of those things. There was something about her. She was bold and vulnerable at the same time.

And so fucking lost. She reminded him of himself in a way. Well, himself a few years ago. She was young—twenty-two—and he was older and had learned that he had to seize his own happiness. Find his own way.

That's why he'd joined the Navy. And when he'd tried out for the SEALs? Oh yeah, he finally had a place to channel all that anger and determination he carried. Not that being an angry bastard would get you far as a SEAL.

No, it was more about making the anger carry him through the hell of BUD/S and then into the teams. It was about not giving in or giving up.

He'd thought getting into the SEALs was hard—and it was—but becoming HOT? That had been the most amazing fucking thing to ever happen in his life. He loved what he did, loved that he made a difference even if nobody really knew it.

He was on his second cup of coffee when there was movement in the hall. Her door opened and then she emerged. His belly twisted at the sight of her. So fucking sexy.

No, not sexy. NOT.

Cash hardened his heart as she approached. She was wearing his shirt again, but her legs were bare. Didn't matter because the hem hung to her knees. She'd rolled the sleeves, and her hair was piled on top of her head. Long strands spilled from a messy topknot, framing her face.

Her skin was creamy and smooth, and her lips drew his attention because they were so pink. He thought for a second she'd found lipstick, but then he realized it was just her natural color. Why he hadn't focused on that last night, he didn't know.

"Morning," she said as she shuffled over and sank onto the couch.

He muted the television, though he hadn't had it loud in the first place.

"Sleep okay?"

She pushed a stray strand of hair from her eyes. "Surprisingly." She frowned. "I woke up thinking I was married. Took me a few seconds to remember I wasn't."

"Want some coffee?"

"I would love some."

He pushed upright and she reached out to touch his

arm. The lightning bolt sizzling through him stopped him in his tracks. She snatched her hand back as if burned. Her dark eyes were wide and innocent when he gazed down at her.

"I can get it," she said.

"It's okay. I need another cup anyway. You take cream or sugar?"

"Just black."

He went over and poured coffee while she watched the news. When her face appeared on-screen, she didn't move a muscle. He brought the coffee over and handed it to her.

"Thanks," she said, taking the mug in two small hands. Elegant hands. The fingers were long and slender, the nails blunt and natural. He had a sudden vision of those fingers stroking his cock, and he shoved it away forcefully. But his balls ached anyway.

Her gaze didn't leave the television until the segment about her was over. Then she turned to him. "I'm sorry I got you into this."

He shrugged. "It's okay."

"You say that, but I feel like it isn't."

"Trust me, it is." He wouldn't elaborate, but knocking out the security guard and evading a pursuer was child's play compared to what he usually did.

His phone buzzed, effectively ending the conversation. It was Viking.

"Morning, sunshine," Cash said.

Viking snorted. "Dude, I've been up all fucking night researching your *problem*. Don't morning me."

"What'd you learn?"

"Enough."

There was the sound of a radio in the background. Maybe Taylor Swift, which would be fucking hilarious and something Cash would tease his SEAL team leader about for the rest of his life. Taylor had some kick-ass songs, but no SEAL would want to admit he sang about shaking off the haters, fakers, and takers in his bathroom mirror from time to time.

"What's the ETA?"

"We'll be there in twenty."

Cash's eyebrows climbed his forehead. Yeah, this was the shortest fucking fishing trip in the known universe. "We'll be ready."

The call punched out. Ella stared at him with wide eyes.

"Ready for what?" she asked.

"To leave. Need you to get your cute ass ready to go, Princess. Shower if you want, but we'll be leaving here within the hour."

She clutched her coffee cup. Her pulse throbbed in her throat. "Where are we going?"

"Not sure," he told her. "But we need to be ready."

———

There wasn't much she could do, but Ella went into the master bath and found a comb in the drawer. She combed her hair to make it presentable, then used the tie she'd found and put it up into a twist on her head. This twist was neater than the one she'd done to have coffee.

She pinched her cheeks for color, slipped into the sweatpants Cash had given her—tying the strings as tight as they'd go so the pants didn't fall down—and knotted the hem of his shirt at her waist. She had socks, but no shoes. There was no remedy for that. Cash didn't carry anything in her size. The socks swam on her, truth be told, but they were warm and she was grateful.

She cast a look at the wedding gown she'd laid over the

tub to dry. Poor thing—it was stiff and discolored from the weather and the splatters of mud she'd gotten on it. She went over and shook it out as best she could. She was torn on whether to leave it or take it, but in the end she decided to leave it where it was. It was simply too big to drag with her—especially when she didn't know where they were going.

Ella heard voices. For a moment, her heart leaped into her throat. But she strained to hear what they were saying and realized that no one sounded scared or angry. Cash's people had arrived.

She hesitated for a long moment before she drew herself up and went to join them. It took everything she had, but she channeled her aunt and glided into the room as if she owned it. Besides Cash, there were two big men. They all turned to her at once, and she felt like the smallest of bugs in comparison.

"Your Highness," one of the men said, and Cash started. She watched the look of shock cross his face and wished she could wipe it away. Yes, he knew she was a princess—but he hadn't quite processed it yet. Hearing her referred to so formally clearly jolted him in a way the news programs had not.

"Please call me Ella," she replied. "I prefer it."

"Ella, then. I'm Viking," the big blond man said, coming over and shaking her hand. "This is Cage." She must have looked confused because he grinned. "Call signs. It'll be easier for you since that's what we'll call each other. Though you likely know this guy as Cash."

"Yes," she replied, looking in the direction he'd tipped his head. "What do you call him if not Cash?"

Viking's grin didn't fade. "Money."

"Money," she said, trying it on. She shook her head. "I like Cash better."

"So what's the plan?" Cash asked, folding his arms over his broad chest and not making eye contact with her.

Why did that make her feel the tiniest bit frantic?

Viking turned his attention to Cash. "Need to leave your car for the time being. We'll come back for it in a few days."

Cash didn't look happy. "All right. Where are we going?"

"Dulles. Had to call Hawk in on this one."

"Not a bad idea," Cash said.

Ella had no idea what they were talking about. She wanted to tell them she was right here and not to talk over her, but they were both so big and tough-looking that she didn't quite have the courage. Not that they would hurt her. Still, they looked scary—and that was usually enough to silence her. Speaking out was impossible where she'd come from.

"You might not agree when you hear the plan."

The other man snickered. Or she thought he did. Ella studied him and... Yes, he was hiding a smile. Cash knew it too. He glared.

"What's so fucking funny?"

Viking cracked a grin as well. He spread his hands as the grin turned into a laugh. "Sorry, dude, really. But the plan—and no disrespect, Ella, I promise you," he said to her in an aside, "is that you're getting married."

Chapter Nine

CAGE GUFFAWED. Viking tried to look stern and failed. Cash glared.

"Fine," he said. "Wouldn't be the first time we did this shit for a mission."

Ella's gaze darted between the three of them, but she didn't say anything. Cash wanted to apologize for the idiocy of his teammates, but he was too busy frowning at them. Finally he shook himself and turned to her.

"It's okay, Ella. They're razzing me. Viking and Cage are both married and they think it's funny to yank my chain because I've told them I'm *never* getting married. Isn't that right, assholes?"

Viking sucked in a breath and wiped his eyes. Dude was so amused he'd been crying. Jesus.

"Not a joke, Money," he said. "You and Ella are getting married. For real."

Cash's guts turned to ice. They weren't kidding with him. "What the fuck?"

"Hey, watch your mouth around our guest. She's a princess, man."

Cash was ready to strangle somebody. "Then explain what the hell is going on. Married for real? Why?"

"It's the only way," Viking said, spreading his hands. "We've talked about it and tried to think of other options, but it's the only way to protect her. *And* you, you idiot. The story in the news is that you kidnapped her, though nobody seems to have provided you with a reason for doing so. They say you want a ransom, but how the hell did you know where to find her in the first place?" He shook his head. "Anyway, you're a kidnapper in the national narrative. No amount of explaining is going to fix this. But if the two of you were eloping? Yeah, explains everything."

A grenade detonated in his brain. His thoughts scrambled. He tried to examine the situation from all angles—but he couldn't figure out another way. Another explanation.

Oh holy shit, he'd doomed himself. He'd saved Ella from that goon and doomed himself. Because Viking was right. What other way could they deflect the attention from him? Her family had money. Sheikh Fahd had money. If they insisted that Cash had kidnapped their princess, who would believe he hadn't? His guys would. The colonel would.

But that wasn't enough, because they had missions to do and no time for the huge distraction his arrest would make. He could almost hear the staff meeting on this one yesterday. *Fuck...*

"So you're saying we get married for real, and that explains everything?"

"Almost everything. Sure."

"How did I meet her? How the hell did we form a relationship?"

"Not important right now."

Ella hadn't said anything. He turned to her. She was

watching them all with a frown on her face. She looked small and cute—and regal. How had that happened? She was a woman in a flannel shirt and sweatpants way too big for her, and she looked like a queen.

Or maybe that was his imagination running wild because she was a princess.

"Ella?"

Her expression hardened. He didn't know what that was about. Instead of telling him, she turned to Viking. "Is this situation only to protect Cash, or are you intending to help me too?"

"You'll be his wife. We'll protect you."

"For how long?"

"As long as it takes."

"Whoa, whoa, whoa," Cash said, hands in the air. "I'm not getting married forever. There has to be an end to this scheme. A target date for a divorce or annulment or something."

"We'll figure that out as we go," Viking said. "It's too soon to set an expiration date. First we have to get you two married and get the cops off your trail. Then we have to make sure Ella's family doesn't try to interfere."

"They will never give up," Ella said, and Cash's blood ran cold. He'd worry about that later.

"And where are we eloping to?" Cash asked, stamping his fury down until it glowed white-hot inside him.

"Where do you think? Vegas, baby."

"There is a problem," Ella said, and they all swung around to look at her.

Her soft pink lips were parted slightly. The lower one trembled and she licked it. Cash hated the way his balls tightened. He shot a look at the guys. If either of them had the same reaction, he'd stomp them into the ground. But they merely looked politely interested in what she had to say.

"I have no identification," Ella said. "No passport. How can I get married?"

Viking snorted. "Don't worry, Ella. We've got that covered."

"I don't understand."

Cash shook his head. He had to get into this game or he'd be standing around like a fucking idiot for the rest of the day. "Fake IDs, Ella. We'll make you one."

HOT made counterfeit IDs so damned good they made the real ones look fake.

"But the marriage won't be legitimate. My aunt and uncle will know it. So will Sheikh Fahd."

"No, that's not quite right. We're replacing any identification you had," Viking said. "Whatever your aunt and uncle are holding will be illegitimate. Colonel Mendez will make sure your prior credentials are declared lost. What we produce will be the real deal."

Cage spoke up in his Cajun accent. "We need to get going, *mon amis*. We can keep discussing it in the car, yeah?"

Cash grabbed his duffel. Ella stood with her hands clasped in front of her, her eyes downcast. He let his gaze drift down to the floor—and realized she had no shoes. Hell, she had no clothes other than his. It made him angry for some reason.

"We're going to need to get Ella some clothes," he said. "So plan a stop along the way."

Cage shook his head. "No can do, man. But we'll have something waiting for her on the plane."

Cash frowned. "Plane?"

"Did you think we were chauffeuring your ass to

Nevada? Hawk's wife is performing in Vegas. You're catching a ride with them."

Of course. After Hawk had married his pop-star wife, he'd eventually left HOT to start his own security business. They provided security services to high-end customers, but Hawk was still HOT to his bones.

Once HOT, always HOT. When Colonel Mendez had been on the run from the US government, it was Hawk and his resources that allowed HOT to help their commanding officer. They'd been stood down, their missions ended across the globe, but Hawk had provided them with what they needed. That he was helping out now was no surprise—but it also got Cash a bit in the feels.

HOT was the best family he had. He'd say the only family, but he had a half sister who'd somehow managed not to inherit her mother's dislike of him. He didn't talk to her often, but when he did, she was bubbly and sweet.

Viking's phone pinged with a text. "Let's roll," he said. "We've got to hustle to make it to Dulles."

Cash frowned at Ella. "Where's the dress?"

"I left it in the bathroom."

"You didn't want to harm the dress, but you're leaving it behind? After all that angst over it?"

"I didn't think there'd be any room."

Cash tipped his head at Cage. "Can you get her wedding dress?"

"Sure."

Cash closed the distance between him and Ella. She had to tilt her head back at a sharp angle to look up at him. He wanted to kiss those pretty lips, but he wouldn't. If she weren't so young and inexperienced, maybe he would.

Maybe.

"I'll carry you to the car," he said, and her eyes widened.

"I can walk."

"It's wet out and you don't have any shoes."

She dropped her gaze, and he found himself wanting to tip her chin up again so he could see what was in those eyes. Was she frightened of him? Or just shy? It bothered him that it could be the former. He just didn't know. And now wasn't the time to ask.

Jesus. He was marrying this woman. For real. It staggered him. No wonder his teammates were so damned amused.

Viking took the duffel from his shoulder. Cash could have carried it and her, but he appreciated the gesture. He swept her up. She was so damned light. He had a moment of raw anger at the bitch of an aunt who'd controlled Ella's food intake so severely.

Ella was small, but she was all angles. She should have more meat on her bones. Her arms went around his neck, but she wouldn't look at him. His gaze dropped to her throat and the pulse hammering there. Wouldn't take much to put his lips against that pulse. Caress it with his tongue.

Cage returned with the dress, and they went outside to the big black Suburban. Ella and Cash sat in the back while Cage and Viking went up front.

It would take about two and a half hours to reach Dulles. Then a few hours to Vegas. They could be married by nightfall. Cash shoved a hand into his hair and propped his head on his hand with his elbow against the window.

Not exactly how he'd planned to spend this weekend. And definitely not how he planned to spend the rest of his life. It was temporary. An arrangement. It'd be over before he knew it.

Chapter Ten

I T WAS around noon when they reached the airport. A man was waiting for them at the first checkpoint. She had to scoot over when he joined them in the back seat. After the way her body had burned when Cash carried her to the car in the first place, she wasn't ready for another round of boiling in her own skin just yet. Too bad though, because she was going to get it anyway.

"Thanks for the help, Hawk," Cash said to the newcomer.

He turned to them and smiled. "No problem. You know how Gina loves weddings." He held out his hand and Ella took it. "Pleased to meet you, Your Highness. I'm Jack. Or you can call me Hawk. My wife is looking forward to meeting you."

"I'm pleased to meet you as well—and please call me Ella."

He nodded. "Ella. I passed your sizes on to her. She has a few things for you. We'll pick up more in Vegas."

Ella didn't know what to say. *Thank you* didn't begin to cover it—but what else did one say? When she'd given

Viking her sizes while he'd been on the phone with this man during the ride here, she'd had no idea how much trouble he would go to for her.

"Thank you so much. I will pay you back." She didn't know how, but her pride dictated she say it. How could she be a royal princess and have nothing? It was the truth, but she'd figure something out. She'd get a job. Somehow.

"It's not a problem," he said. "Gina loves shopping. And I'm pretty sure she won't allow you to pay us back, so don't worry about it."

Before Ella could object, they pulled up beside a plane. There was a set of stairs pushed up to the open door at the front of the fuselage, and Ella felt her jaw dropping open. She closed it before anyone noticed.

It was a big plane. When these men had said that she and Cash would be traveling on someone's plane, she'd been thinking Learjet. Not a huge plane like people rode in every day. Her uncle used to have a jet, but he'd had to sell it. And it had been nothing like this one.

Everyone piled from the vehicle. Cash wouldn't let her set her bare feet on the tarmac, so she had to wrap her arms around his neck and let him hold her close once more. Oh, the things it did to her heart to be held like this.

And not only her heart. Her insides tingled, and her sex ached with the beginnings of arousal. Embarrassment flooded her, creeping on hot feet across her skin. She kept her eyes downcast, afraid that someone would see how silly and virginal she was.

"This is where we leave you," Viking said. "Good luck in Vegas. And Ella…"

She lifted her eyes to his and tried to smile.

"I know all this seems a bit crazy, but you're one of us now. We've got your back."

"Thank you."

"Wish we could be there to see you take the plunge, Money," Cage said.

"Shut up," Cash replied, his chest rumbling. "And tell Cowboy to go to hell when you see him. I know he's laughing his ass off right now."

Cage laughed and reached out to shake Cash's hand. "You know it, brother."

The men said goodbye and got into the Suburban to go, but not before handing off Cash's duffel and her wedding dress to someone waiting to take them onto the plane. Hawk nodded toward the gangway. "Go ahead and take her up. I'll be there in a second."

He went over to talk to some men standing nearby. Ella shifted in Cash's arms as he headed for the steps. "I can walk up on my own."

"The stairs are rough," he told her without breaking stride. When they reached the top, he set her down so she could at least enter the plane on her own power. She appreciated that.

She stepped inside and a flight attendant appeared, smiling broadly.

"Please continue into the main cabin," the woman said. "There are some light refreshments available, but if you need anything, don't hesitate to ask."

Ella murmured her thanks as she held tight to the ends of the shirt she'd tied at her waist. She felt like a beggar instead of a princess—which was nothing new, unfortunately. She had never felt like a princess in her life. She felt even less of one as she passed into the spacious and richly appointed main cabin. The seats were gray leather, club chair style. The walls gleamed with chrome and polished zebrawood accents, and there were murals of album covers. Oh my God, she recognized those covers...

Ella looked away and her gaze landed on a blond-haired woman standing with her hands on her hips as she faced down a small boy who gazed up at her with apple-red cheeks and flashing eyes.

Gina Domenico?

"No, Eli, you are not getting any more M&M's right now. Stop asking."

"But Mama," the boy whined.

"No, sir."

"Daddy?" he asked hopefully as Hawk strolled in behind them.

Daddy?

Ella might be sheltered, but she had a digital music account. And Gina Domenico was one of her favorites. Right up there with Taylor Swift, Selena Gomez, Demi Lovato, and Beyoncé.

"Are you seriously asking me if you can have something after your mama told you no?" Hawk asked the little boy in a gruff voice.

Eli thought about it a second. "No, sir."

"That's what I thought. Now go play with your nanny and stop giving your mama a hard time."

A young woman stood in the hall behind Gina. She took Eli's hand as he tromped over to her, and ushered him away. Gina turned with a bright smile.

"Hi there," she said, coming over and enveloping Ella in a hug before she knew what was happening. "You must be Ella. I'm Gina."

Ella was a bit bewildered, but she returned Gina's smile. Gina was famous, yet she seemed so genuine and happy. Not at all the mega talented pop star with the world at her feet.

"Yes," Ella replied, happy with herself for not stammering. "Thank you for having me."

"Honey, it's no problem. Glad we can help." Her gaze

drifted to Cash. "Nice to see you again, Cash."

"You too," he replied. "Thanks for letting me hitch a ride again."

Gina's smile was bright. "Oh sweetie, you know I'd do anything for a wedding."

"That's what I'm afraid of," Cash grumbled. "This whole thing was probably your idea."

Ella tried not to be starstruck while they bantered, but it wasn't easy.

Gina laughed. "I can't take credit, no. But it sounds to me like the boys know what needs to happen to keep you out of trouble and protect Ella from her deranged family. Sorry, honey," Gina added with a look at Ella.

For the first time all morning, Ella laughed, though it was a small sound. "It's okay. They are deranged."

Gina studied her. "I'm thinking you're ready to trade those hideous sweatpants in for some real clothes, am I right?"

Ella nodded. It wasn't that she didn't appreciate Cash's generosity in loaning them to her, but she felt self-conscious in his clothes.

"Then come with me. I've got a selection of stuff in your size. We'll find just the thing to get you started. Soon as it's settled, we'll be on the way."

Ella let Gina usher her toward the back of the plane. But she couldn't stop herself from looking over her shoulder at Cash. Just for a second. Her heart throbbed as their gazes met. His was intense, probing.

She couldn't tell if he was merely angry about the situation—or if he regretted he'd ever met her.

"Quite the mess," Hawk said after Gina and Ella were gone.

Cash gave himself a mental shake and turned away from his contemplation of the hallway they'd disappeared down. "Yeah."

"Drink?"

"Beer?"

"You bet." A few moments later, a flight attendant appeared with two beers. Hawk handed one to Cash and then held out his bottle to clink.

Cash took a long drink. "Not what I expected when I drove out of town yesterday. I should be standing in a trout stream today. Up to my ass in cold, clear water, casting my flies and waiting for a bite." He shook his head. "Dammit, why'd I stop?"

Hawk snorted. "Because it's how you're wired. Because there's no way in hell you could have kept on driving when she needed you. If you'd let it happen the way it was going down, you wouldn't have a right to call yourself HOT."

The truth of that statement squeezed his throat. He took another swallow of beer. "Yeah, I know. Damn."

"Come on, Cash. It's a mission. You're marrying the woman for a mission. Might be a real wedding, real paper, but it's all in the pursuit of keeping her safe from those assholes who tried to force her into marriage. And then there's Fahd— need I remind you what that fucker has his fingers in?"

"No, I know he's a trafficker. Arms, women, drugs. Oil isn't enough for him apparently."

"And neither is the other stuff. He wants to be king of Qu'rim." Hawk nodded in the direction that Ella and Gina had gone. "She's a princess, even if she's a princess in exile. He wants that tie to an old monarchy to boost his claim when the rebels overthrow the current regime."

The rebels in Qu'rim had been trying for a while—hell, they'd even taken the capital city of Baq for a couple of months before they'd been routed and pushed back. The situation was ongoing and not likely to be solved anytime soon. King Tariq bin Abdullah was still king, though the rebels fought to end his tenure daily. If they had a viable candidate in Sheikh Fahd? They'd fight harder—and they might succeed.

Cash couldn't imagine Ella as a part of that world. She was too sheltered. Too gentle. "Seems like he might find it easier with a princess from his own part of the world."

"True. But Capriolo lies in the Mediterranean, directly in the path of the shipping lanes for Fahd's oil. I'm sure he envisions favorable trade conditions, perhaps even the possibility of a refinery."

"I thought her family was in exile." None of this made any damn sense.

"They are—but if she were to become queen of Qu'rim? Capriolo would have incentive for trade, certainly. Especially if Fahd were to unite the tribes and put a stop to the instability in the region."

Cash blinked. "You don't really think that's possible. Not with the Freedom Force still running rampant."

Hawk shook his head. "Nope. But I think it's what Fahd thinks—and he's willing to acquire her, same as he'd acquire a car or a racehorse. He has other wives—what's one more added to the harem?"

Cash didn't even want one wife. He couldn't imagine several. "How would Ella be queen if he has a harem?"

"He'd probably make her the first wife. There's a hierarchy, but he'd twist it to suit his own agenda."

Cash hated the idea of Ella married to Fahd. It bothered him that he cared, but hell, he did. "He's gonna be pissed when she resurfaces."

"Probably."

"I don't see an endgame to this one, Hawk. Men like Fahd don't give up easily."

Hawk's mouth was a grim line. "Exactly right. Which is why she needs us. The minute she ran away, she put a target on her back."

"She needs witness protection, not a marriage to me."

"Possibly," Hawk said. "But you're all she's got."

Chapter Eleven

THEY LANDED in Las Vegas five hours later. Ella had changed into a powder-blue sheath dress with a pair of black pumps. Gina had a makeup artist and hairdresser traveling with her, and they'd gone to work on Ella's appearance.

"You need to be a glamorous princess," Gina had said. "Jetting off to Vegas with your dear friend Gina and her husband so you can marry the man you love."

Ella had frowned. "I never left the estate in fourteen years without being accompanied by someone. Everyone will know it's a lie."

"No they won't, honey," Gina had insisted. "Because your aunt and uncle would have to admit they'd held you prisoner. Besides, you only have to make the media believe the picture you present them. They'll take it from there."

Now they were in Vegas and Ella climbed into the waiting limo as Cash took her hand and helped her down into it. Then he slid in next to her, his expression giving nothing away. Her heart pattered out a beat that threatened to make her dizzy. He'd said nothing about her appearance. From the moment she'd returned to the main cabin during the flight until now, he hadn't spoken to her.

The limo pulled away with only them inside. She spun to look behind them. Another limo sat on the tarmac, and Gina was making her way toward it on Jack's arm.

"Why didn't they come with us?" she asked, turning back to Cash.

He glanced over at her. It was a cool, detached glance. Not that she blamed him. She'd caused him a lot of trouble, and all because he'd tried to help her. She was still causing trouble.

"Because Gina attracts a lot of attention wherever she goes. We're going straight to the hotel and up to our room. Hawk and Gina will join us a little later, and we'll get married. After that, we'll hang out with them and be seen. The media will pick up news of our marriage, and your family will find out. You'll have to express shock at their version of events, especially at the fact they've reported you missing."

Ella wasn't so sure about her ability to do that, but she nodded. This whole situation—God, it was out of control. But if she hadn't walked away, hadn't stolen that Mercedes and tried to escape, she'd be heaven knows where right now. But wherever it was, it would be with Sheikh Fahd… and she would no longer be a virgin.

Ella shuddered. Just the thought of lying beneath him while he stuck his penis in her body was horrifying. But if she replaced him with Cash?

Shivers cascaded up and down her spine. She clasped her hands in her lap and concentrated on breathing.

The limo left the airport and headed for the hotel. Ella had never been to Las Vegas, so she craned her neck and tried to see everything as they rolled along. It was so flat and brown. But in the distance there were mountains. The sky was blue and clear, and the traffic was thick. When they finally turned onto the Strip, they weren't on it long before the limo glided up the driveway of the Bellagio. A bellman opened the car door.

"Welcome to the Bellagio, sir. Madam."

Cash climbed from the car and helped her out. She thought he would let her hand go, but he didn't. They strolled into the hotel and up to the desk. It didn't take long to check them in. Soon they were on their way up to the room. Ella was trying not to freak out, but she quietly was. There was so much noise, so much life and activity in the hotel. The colors, the people, the smells—it was overwhelming compared to what she was used to. It wasn't that her aunt and uncle never went anywhere. They did, and they took Ella and her cousins with them. But in the past few years, they didn't travel the way they once had. And they'd never brought anyone to Vegas.

Cash held her hand in the elevator. There were other people with them, so she couldn't say anything. But her system was short-circuiting. All she could concentrate on was the feel of her palm against his, her fingers twined with his much larger ones. His hand was big and warm, a bit rough on the palms. She liked it.

When they finally reached their floor, they had a short walk to the room. Cash opened the door and let her go in first. Ella gasped. There was a small foyer, but when you got beyond that, the room was spectacular—plush furnishings in the living area, upholstered with gorgeous turquoise fabrics, and a king-sized bed with a tufted satin headboard and lush linens that she could see through the open bedroom door.

But the view was what drew her eyes.

Ella hurried over to the window and gazed out at the activity so far below. There was a small lake down there and fountains that shot into the air all across it. People crowded the sidewalks lining the lake, watching the fountains.

Cash loomed beside her and her breath shortened. He sucked all the air from the room. Made her hot and achy at the same time. She wanted to run from him, and she wanted him to hold her again.

"It's pretty amazing, right?"

She turned to him. His face was in profile to her as he stood with his hands in his jeans pockets and gazed at the view. He looked thoughtful. Or maybe it was sad. She thought again of how upset he'd been that morning when his friends told him he had to marry her. She'd been embarrassed and angry, but what could she say?

She'd thought about it all day, and she'd realized there was only one thing he'd want to hear.

"I'm sorry I've caused you so much trouble."

He didn't respond at first, and her stomach bottomed out. But then he turned to her, slowly, and those eyes were both fierce and tender as they raked over her.

"It's not your fault, Ella. If anyone's to blame, it's the people who tried to force you to marry against your will."

"But now you're marrying me against yours," she said softly.

"I am, but that's still not your fault."

"I feel like it is."

His expression was fierce one moment and kind the next. "Then you need to get over that, Princess."

"I'm trying."

"Try harder."

As if it was so easy. She swallowed the knot in her throat and watched the fountains throwing water into the air in synchronized splendor. Cash's phone disturbed the silence after a few moments. He turned away to answer it.

"Yeah. … Yeah. Great. … We'll be there."

He pocketed the phone. "We need to go to Jack and Gina's suite. The preacher—or whatever Gina got to do this—will be there soon."

Ella had thought her stomach couldn't drop any lower. She'd been wrong. "I can't believe this," she said as panic rose in her throat like one of those fountains down below. "I'm about to be a married woman—and I've never even been kissed."

———

Cash stiffened. *What the hell?*

He'd had a hard time looking at her from the moment she emerged from Gina's care hours earlier. Her long, dark hair was combed straight. It fell like a silken cloud over her shoulders, tumbling down her back.

Some idiot had put makeup on her. He didn't say that because he disapproved of makeup. What he disapproved of was a makeup artist with a talent for highlighting what was already there.

Ella was gorgeous. Dark, flashing eyes that contained more than a pinch of vulnerability, along with strength in abundance, had been turned up a thousand degrees. Now she had what Cage's wife had informed him was a smoky eye, with whatever it was artists did to make that happen. Eyeliner, mascara, eye shadow—all that shit. Her lips were colored a deep pink, and her cheeks glowed.

But it was the dress that had been his undoing all those hours ago. The palest of blues, it set off her creamy skin and dark hair to perfection. It skimmed her figure, not clinging, but definitely highlighting what was there. And then there were those bare legs. She was short compared to him, but she still managed to have legs that went on for miles.

He'd spent the better part of an hour imagining those legs on his shoulders. His dick had strained against his fly so hard he'd worried he might embarrass himself. He'd sat far longer than he normally would before he'd gotten up and moved around the cabin.

He'd deliberately ignored her. Not talked to her. And he was paying for it now by being alone with her in a suite with a massive king bed that was just made for hot, slow, sweet fucking all night long.

Except that she was a virgin. And Cash did not do virgins.

Even a virgin he was about to marry.

Still, what she'd just said. Holy cow. It socked him in the gut. Not because he ascribed deep emotions to kissing, but this gorgeous woman had never kissed a man? It wasn't right. She wasn't a teenager but a woman. A beautiful woman who'd never even been kissed.

He told himself that wasn't his fault. That he didn't owe her a kiss. Hell, he was marrying her to keep her safe —what more could she want? Because he damned sure wasn't going to have sex with her. If she thought that, she was mistaken.

Stop being an ass, Cash. Just kiss the girl.

"Do you want to be kissed?" he asked.

She met his eyes. Hers sparked with heat and his groin tightened. *Not now.*

"I have always thought so, yes."

He might have laughed if it weren't so serious. Sweet Ella, she was trying to think logically about the whole thing. But some things weren't logical at all.

"And now?"

"Now?" Her gaze dropped, her lashes hiding the

expressions in those eyes for a moment before she lifted them again. "Yes, I would like to try kissing before I have to kiss you officially. What if I mess it up?"

"You won't. We can agree to a kiss on the lips, no open mouth, no tongue. It'll be easy."

"Easy for you."

"If you want me to kiss you now, I can show you a thing or two. So when you date men later, you'll know what to do."

"That would be lovely."

Cash turned her gently until she faced him. Her lashes lifted and she gazed at him expectantly. He let his eyes wander over her face, taking in every line and curve. Then he slipped a hand into the small of her back and tugged her close.

She gasped as her palms shot up to press against his chest.

"If you want to do this right, you have to get close," he told her.

She nodded, chewing the inside of her lip. Cash slid his palm along the side of her jaw, just to feel her silky skin. His thumb glided over the pulse in her neck—and he nearly growled in satisfaction. It throbbed against his thumb like a trapped bird.

A voice in his head asked him what the hell he thought he was doing, but he stepped into her, even closer than before, though it should not have been possible, until her body melded to his from breast to hip. He brought his other hand up to cup her jaw so that her face was between his palms.

Then he tipped her head back and dropped his mouth to hers in slow, painful increments.

Chapter Twelve

ELLA'S EYES FLUTTERED CLOSED, though she wanted to watch the whole thing. But it was instinctual, this eye-closing. Parting her lips must have been a part of the instinct thing too, because she didn't recall telling herself to do it.

The heat of him slammed into her body. She was still trying to process the breast-to-hip feeling of being melded to a man—and the bulge of something pressing against her belly was ultra distracting—when she felt the first brush of his mouth against hers.

Ella whimpered and then hated herself for making a sound when he hesitated. The overwhelmingness of him, right there in her space, eased. She opened her eyes, blinking up at him. Was that it? Just a brush of lips against lips? Was that all he planned to do?

"You okay?"

"Yes. Of course."

He frowned, his gaze heavy-lidded and sensual. "You don't need to be afraid, Ella. I won't hurt you."

"I know that."

And she did. He'd been nothing but honorable since

the moment she'd met him. And if he was the kind of guy to take advantage of being alone with her, he could have done that yesterday. Nobody would have heard her scream for help if he'd attacked her.

But she'd known he wouldn't. She'd just known it from the instant he'd stood up for her with the rain beating down and her uncle's security man telling him it was none of his business.

"Good."

She curled her fingers into his shirt. He was wearing a black T-shirt and jeans, and his arms bulged from the sleeves as he cupped her face. The thought of kissing him made her pulse fly—and other parts of her ache.

"Please kiss me, Cash. It's okay."

He dropped his head toward hers, and she closed her eyes again. She found herself rising on tiptoe, seeking his mouth.

And then their lips met again, but this time she didn't make a sound. His mouth ghosted over hers, so sensual and light, his lips teasing and tormenting her. It was thrilling and painful all at once.

Ella strained toward him, her fingers curling harder into his shirt as if she could tug him down to her with sheer strength.

"Eager?" he whispered against her mouth, laughing.

But he didn't let her answer. Instead, he took her mouth harder, lips meshing together, his tongue sliding against the seam. Ella opened her mouth—and his tongue slipped in to join hers.

It was the most exciting, the most sensual thing she'd ever experienced. His tongue didn't devour hers. No, it teased and stroked and tormented. His hands dropped from her face to slide down her back and hold her against him.

The hardness pressing into her belly grew bigger. He shifted, taking the pressure away, and that disappointed her. She wanted to feel him there. Feel him growing bigger. She knew what was happening even if she had no practical knowledge of it herself.

Right now she wanted that experience pretty badly. But he wasn't going to give it to her.

He kissed her deeply, again and again, and she clung to him, savoring the sensation. At some point her arms had gone around his neck, and when he pulled away she tried to bring him back.

He gently unwound her arms and set her away from him, laughing softly. "Honey, if we keep doing that, I may have to forget every rule I ever made for myself."

Ella blinked. She could still taste him on her tongue. Her nipples tingled, her sex ached, and she wanted more of the same.

"You have rules?"

He stepped away and scrubbed both his hands through his hair as if trying to scrub away his thoughts. "Yes, I have rules." He stared at her pointedly. "Never getting married is number one on the list, but I'm about to break that one."

Ella's heart flipped. "What else?"

"No virgins. And since I'm breaking number one, I'm not about to break that rule too."

"I see."

"It's not personal, Ella. One day, when this is over, you're going to find the right guy. And you'll want to give yourself to him. If you give yourself to me, you'll regret it."

Ella folded her arms over her chest, hurt and embarrassment warring for first place. A tiny flame of anger kindled, flickering stronger with each passing second.

"Is that what you did? You waited to give yourself to the right woman?"

He had the grace to look sheepish. "It's different for guys."

"Really? And who told you that?"

He was frowning now. Hard. "It's been my experience—"

"Oh? How many times? How many virgins? One? Two? Ten? How is that representative of every single woman in the world?"

Okay, so she was surprising herself by arguing with him, but really, it was a ridiculous notion that she needed to wait and *give* herself to the right man. When she'd been sold to Sheikh Fahd for her virginity, it was truly the last thing she treasured. The sooner it was gone, the better. Men like Fahd would no longer want her, and her aunt and uncle would have no reason to want her back.

Though marrying this man was going to ruin her value anyway. Her virginity wasn't even an issue. Except to him, apparently.

He looked about as surprised as she felt. "Ella, I'm pretty sure, no matter how fierce you are about this, that you *will* get emotionally involved with the man who initiates you. You might not intend to, but it's going to happen. That man will not be me."

"I hate that you think you know me."

He grinned. "Not even married yet and we're having our first fight."

She was not appeased. "For your information, it doesn't thrill me to have to marry you either. I don't know you—and I don't like knowing you'd rather have a root canal than marry me. But this is the situation, is it not? So now we deal with it."

"We *are* dealing with it. We just aren't dealing with it by having sex."

Ella turned her back and started toward the door. Tears pricked her eyes, which annoyed her, but he made her so mad. Not because she expected sex, but because he'd totally dismissed the idea simply because she'd never done *it* before.

She stopped and whirled. "Tell me something—if I weren't a virgin, would we be having this conversation?"

He stalked toward her, all pretense of humor gone. "Probably not. Because we'd both understand what the score was."

Oh, he was infuriating. "Do you have any idea how ridiculous that sounds? What if I'd had sex exactly *once?* Would that magically make me able to avoid emotional involvement with you?" She waved a hand. "You think you know everything, Cash, but you don't. And you most certainly don't know me."

He was staring at her as if she'd sprouted another head. She didn't give him a chance to speak. "Now please stop wasting my time with your stupid arguments, and let's get married."

—————

Cash didn't like the way this situation was going. And he didn't mean the marriage.

No, he meant *her*. Princess Ella, who'd just princessed all over him. He knew when he was being told off. Worse, he knew when the other person was mostly right.

And she was right to point out the ridiculousness of his arguments. Hell, he had no idea what she would do if he fucked her. He'd never actually initiated a virgin himself—

but his best buddy in basic had, and it had crushed his dreams of being a SEAL right out of existence. Charlie had ended up married, pussy whipped, and supporting three kids in three years. He'd also never made it onto the teams. He was regular Navy, which was fine, but when you'd always wanted to be a SEAL, it was a bit of a letdown.

Charlie had never rescued a hostage or taken out a pocket of terrorist assholes, and he was somewhat bitter, though he tried not to let it come through whenever he and Cash talked. But it did. Cash had told him that he could still be a SEAL if he wanted, but Charlie always had a reason why Deidre and the kids wouldn't like it.

Cash had thought about quietly backing away, but whenever Charlie called or they were in the same town, Cash couldn't refuse the contact. They'd been best friends when they were young and new to the military, and they'd helped each other.

But seeing Charlie now was painful. His marriage had been rocky as hell, though the last time Cash had spoken to him, he and Deidre were in counseling and things were going well.

Ella stomped over to the door and threw him a glance over her shoulder. "Are we going or not?"

Oh yeah, the wedding.

"We're going." He went over and opened the door, preceding her as was his habit. To hell with letting a lady go first. You couldn't protect the lady if you sent her out in front of you when you didn't know the territory. But there was no one waiting for them as they made their way down the corridor.

They reached Hawk and Gina's room without speaking to each other again. Cash was still trying to process the way his guts had twisted the second he'd touched his mouth to hers. Not to mention the way his blood had pounded in excitement when she glared at him and told him off.

He rapped on the door and it opened instantly. Gina beamed at them both while Hawk groaned in the background.

"Baby, what have I told you about opening the door?"

Gina waved him off. "You said to let you do it—but sweetie, I'm not an idiot. I used the peephole and verified it was our happy couple."

Not that happy, Cash thought.

Gina frowned at them both. "Now what is going on here? Y'all didn't look so glum on the plane." She reached past him to hook her arm into Ella's. "Come here, love. Tell me what bad ol' Cash did to you."

"Hey," Cash protested as he followed them inside. The suite was predictably lush and expansive with a view of the Vegas Strip and the lake below. "I'm right here. And I didn't do anything. Ella and I are feeling the pressure, that's all."

"Well, y'all need to look happy for the pictures—"

"Pictures?" Cash burst out. "What the hell, Gina?"

Hawk was too busy laughing to get mad about Cash demanding answers from his wife.

"Oh honey," Gina said as she threw him a look. "You really aren't using your head with this one, are you? The whole idea of getting married has got you so twisted up—" She cocked her head. "Do you need a massage? I can get someone up here in no time flat."

Cash held up his hands. "No, thanks. I'm fine."

"You don't look fine. He doesn't, does he?" she asked Ella.

Ella looked about as happy as he did. Which, he suspected, was something akin to a cornered bear.

"I think it's still a shock to us both," Ella said.

He liked that she didn't instantly start complaining about him. That she actually tried to share the blame for the tension between them.

Gina put her hands on her hips and faced them both with a stern look on her face. "Now look, you two, this is important. If we're going to pull this off, you have to look like you like each other. Even better would be if you can't seem to keep your hands off each other, though I'll accept looking at each other with longing. We're going to have a wedding, *with pictures*, and then we're going out on the town for a little while. The point is to be seen and to dispel the notion that anybody was kidnapped."

Cash looked to Hawk for help. There was nothing forthcoming from that quarter. No, Hawk was too busy laughing.

"She's right, Money. This may not be an official op, but you've got to get in the game like it is. Play the part for the media and then go to your room and refuse to speak to each other if you like."

It was Gina's turn again. "I had some more clothes sent up, Ella. I think you should wear white, even if it's not a formal dress like the one you brought on the plane. I have a few options to try." She glanced at her watch. "The minister will be here in fifteen minutes."

"What about her documents?" Cash asked when Ella and Gina disappeared into one of the bedrooms.

Hawk picked up a packet from the table nearest him. "Delivered."

He handed Cash the packet, and Cash opened it to reveal a black Capriolan diplomatic passport and a Virginia identification card. He opened the passport.

Princess Antonella Maria Rossi of the royal family of Capriolo

There was a picture of Ella, her birth date—she would be twenty-three in another month—and her address. A stone formed in his stomach as he thought about what would have happened if he hadn't intervened when she needed him.

Didn't matter that he'd gotten himself tangled up in Capriolan politics. Cash had done what was right, and he'd given Ella a chance.

"There's something else you should know," Hawk said, and Cash lifted his head.

Hawk looked mighty serious.

"What's that?"

He nodded at the passport in Cash's hand. "I don't think she knows it, but Ella isn't just a princess. If the Rossis hadn't been exiled from Capriolo, she would be their queen."

Chapter Thirteen

ELLA STILL COULDN'T QUITE BELIEVE she was hanging out with Gina Domenico, the golden-voiced singer who'd sung in her ear when she holed up in her room and wished she were living a different life than the one she had. Gina's songs were about strength and purpose and heartbreak. They were about life lived to the fullest. Ella could hear the refrain from one of her favorites, "Get It, Girl," playing in her head as she surveyed the dresses hanging from a garment rack in Gina's bedroom.

Gina was strong and amazing. She had a gorgeous man, two adorable children, and the world at her feet. Ella wished she was half as strong and accomplished.

"You okay, hon?" Gina asked.

"Yes." Ella cleared her throat. "Just thinking. So much has happened."

"Do you wish you'd stayed where you were?"

"No, definitely not." There was nothing for her in the life she'd left behind.

"I know Cash is a bit gruff and pissed off right now, but he'll come around. He's a good guy, Ella. I know the type because I married one. But let me tell you, it wasn't all roses and sunshine. It was hard, and I had to fight for what I wanted."

Ella's brows drew together. Gina and Jack seemed so happy. "He didn't want to get married?"

Gina snorted. "He didn't want anything to do with me. It's complicated, but the short story is that we didn't see each other for four years after the first time. I had Eli, our son, but I didn't tell Jack because he'd told me he didn't want children." Her expression pinched. "Well, it was more than that—but anyway, it took four years. And he was furious with me. Truthfully, I thought he hated me—but it worked out. Everything happens for a reason."

"I don't even know Cash. I don't know that I *want* to be married to him. But I'm grateful for him, and I'll do whatever it takes to be free of my aunt and uncle."

Gina reached out and squeezed her hand. "Cash was there for a reason. I believe that. Whatever happens between you is meant to happen." She shrugged. "Nothing to do but wait and see. Now, tell me which of these dresses you want to try on first."

Ella chose a long strapless white dress with a sweetheart neckline. The dress was silky and glowing, the skirt falling to the floor and trailing behind. Gina had underwear to go with it, and Ella changed in the bathroom, gasping at the sleek lines of the dress in the mirror. When she walked out to show Gina, the other woman put her hand to her mouth with a soft *oh*.

"That's lovely, Ella. I don't think you should try anything else." She pulled a black ribbon off the rack and came over to wind it around Ella's waist. "Just a little contrast. What do you think?"

Ella turned to the mirror and stared at herself in

wonder. This dress was more her than the lacy, bejeweled thing she'd worn yesterday. It was perfect.

"And one more thing," Gina said, going over to the dresser and retrieving something. When she returned with a tiara, Ella started to shake her head. It was too much like yesterday, too much making her into what she was supposed to be rather than what she felt like.

"Oh honey," Gina said. "It's okay. It's meant to drive home the idea that you *are* a princess to the media. If they don't see a tiara, they won't quite emphasize that fact. And we want them to. We want them to run with the narrative that a royal princess has found her American prince. It will make your aunt and uncle's story much less appealing."

Ella bowed her head while Gina put the tiara into place. When she lifted her head and gazed in the mirror, it wasn't as out of place as she'd feared. The tiara was small, tasteful, nothing like the bejeweled crown of yesterday. It perched on her hair like an airy confection. Enhancing but not dominating. It worked.

"See?" Gina said.

"Yes."

"I know it's common to put your hair up with a strapless dress, but I think leaving yours long is the right answer." She lifted a lock of Ella's hair. "You have beautiful hair, and leaving it long emphasizes innocence and virginity."

Ella was a little shocked. "You've thought about this a lot."

Gina laughed. "I love weddings. I admit it. Honestly, if I weren't an entertainer, I'd be a wedding coordinator. There's just something about watching a girl walk down the aisle—and seeing the groom's reaction to her—that makes me happy. When the groom has no idea what's going to happen—and even sometimes when he does—the look on his face is just… Oh…"

Ella couldn't help but laugh a little bit. "Cash won't be looking at me that way. It's like that reality show where they got married at first sight. That's us. Most of those didn't work out, right?"

"Yes, but you're playing a part here. For the media. So we're going act like this is a love match."

Ella gulped. "I can do it."

"I know you can. Ready?"

Ella nodded and Gina led her back out to the living room. Jack and Cash weren't there, but someone rapped on the door, and a servant appeared out of nowhere to open it. Ella wondered why Gina hadn't let the man open the door earlier, but maybe he hadn't gotten a chance. In fact, the man had pretty much rushed the door like he was attacking it. Quite possibly on orders from Jack Hunter.

It wasn't anyone dangerous on the other side though. It was a man in an Elvis costume, along with a woman who carried a briefcase. Ella blinked and Gina clapped, laughing.

"Perfect," she said. "Absolutely perfect."

"Is this little lady the bride?" Elvis asked with a curl of his lip.

"She is indeed."

Ella thought it was a little obvious, but whatever.

"Thank you. Thank you verra much." Elvis swaggered inside and then dropped on one knee in front of her. When he broke out into "Love Me Tender," Ella's eyes widened in shock.

He took her hand, singing that he wanted her to love him tender, love him true. All his dreams fulfilled. It was silly and poignant at the same time, because the man she was marrying felt *none* of those things.

As if on cue, Cash appeared with Jack. He'd changed into a black tux, and her heart did a flip in her chest. My God, how did he manage to look so handsome and so tough at the same time?

He glared at Elvis for a long minute, but Elvis didn't seem to care. She thought that Cash shot her an odd look, but she wasn't sure. Probably he had. He didn't want to get married, and now this.

Freaking Elvis.

When Elvis finished his song, he got to his feet with a flourish, kissed Ella's hand, and straightened the lapels of his white sequined jumpsuit. "Y'all ready for some tender lovin'?"

Gina was laughing. "We certainly are."

Cash's frown was heavy, but he strolled over and stood beside Ella. "So where are we doing this?"

"Right there's good," Elvis said.

He turned to the woman with the briefcase. A moment later, he was wearing a shawl and holding a Bible. His expression grew serious.

"Dearly beloved," he began.

It didn't take long to run through the ceremony. Ella kept expecting her aunt and uncle to burst into the room and put an end to the whole thing, but it didn't happen. Before she knew it, she was saying, "I do."

"You may now kiss the bride," Elvis said, and Cash turned to face her.

He looked awfully angry. Or maybe it was despair. Because he was trapped.

"Sorry," she mouthed.

He frowned harder. And then he reached for her. Her heart thudded a dizzy drumbeat in her ears as he wrapped her in his embrace. His mouth lowered to hers. She braced herself for a whirlwind of sensation, like earlier—but it didn't happen.

He treated her like he had the first time he'd kissed her. A brief touch and then it was over and he was looking down at her. She blinked up at him. Before she could gather her thoughts, he set her away—gently—and turned back to Elvis.

Elvis was smiling, his thick black hair and bushy side-burns almost comical as he shoved on his sunglasses and clicked his teeth. "Thank you. Thank you verra much, Cash and Ella. Congratulations. I hope your life together is long and fruitful. Now, if you can sign these documents, we'll be done."

Ella and Cash both signed, and a waiter appeared with champagne flutes. Ella took one. So did everyone else. Gina stood with Jack, a tear in her eye.

"Oh my gosh, y'all," she gushed. "I'm just so happy for you both. May you be as happy as Jack and I."

Jack put an arm around her and kissed the top of her hair. He murmured something to her that made her smile and swipe a finger beneath her eyes. Then she turned to him and cupped his jaw, kissing him swiftly and hotly.

Ella burned with envy. That's what she wanted. What she'd always wanted. To *belong*. To know she had a home with one person who cared.

Gina lifted her glass. "To Cash and Ella."

Ella touched the glass to her lips. She'd had champagne, so it was nothing new, but this version tasted so much better than the one her aunt and uncle served. It tasted expensive, and she found that it went down much easier than anything she'd ever had before.

Her insides warmed as the wine hit and burst into tiny bubbles in her belly. She felt mellow, calm, and she smiled as a photographer appeared and took pictures of them together—and with Elvis. Ella didn't find it hard to smile with a glass of champagne in her. She threaded her arm into Cash's and smiled big as the photographer snapped photos.

Cash twirled her into his arms and held her close. Her heart pounded and her belly flipped as she laughed. Jack and Gina joined them, the four of them hamming it up for the photos. In another picture, it was just her and Gina. It felt so natural, so ordinary, that Ella had no trouble smiling and laughing.

When Elvis, his assistant, and the photographer were gone, her veins still hummed from the champagne. She wasn't drunk, but she was happy.

"Well, that went over rather well," Gina said. And then she sighed. "Not the ideal wedding, but good. Ella, if it doesn't work out with this clown, let me know. I'd love to coordinate a real, big gala wedding."

"I will," Ella replied. But in truth she couldn't imagine it. She'd nearly had the big gala wedding, and it had unnerved her to the point she'd run. And thank God she had.

She glanced at Cash. He'd accepted a second glass of champagne, but he was frowning. She took another one too. She was going to need it if she had to endure his frowns.

Gina clapped her hands. "All right, I know this is the time when you'd run off to the reception in a typical wedding, but I need an hour to take care of some prior commitments before we go out on the town. Can you two amuse yourselves?"

"Yeah, we got it," Cash said.

She didn't know what that meant, but after copious cheek kissing and plans to meet downstairs in an hour, Ella and Cash left the suite and strode silently toward their room. Cash didn't say a word, and the longer it went on, the more unnerved she felt.

They reached their room and he swiped the keycard.

Ella drifted past a mirror on her way inside and started. "I left my clothes!"

The white dress was stunning, but it wasn't something she should wear out on the town. Cash flicked a glance at her. He glanced down and realized he was still in his tuxedo.

"Fuck. Damn that Gina."

Ella felt a little bit offended on Gina's behalf. "She's nice. I like her."

"She is nice. She also meddles."

"She means well."

"She thinks every damn wedding leads to happy ever after."

"I don't think she thinks that at all. She's happy in her marriage. She hopes other people will be as well."

He considered her before he jerked his tie loose and went over to pour a drink from the liquor cabinet. "Want anything?"

Ella shook her head. She was still swimming from the last one.

She was surprised when he handed her a glass of white wine. She thought about refusing, but she took it anyway. He took a sip of his drink—whiskey, she thought—and she did the same.

"Tell me more about Capriolo," he said.

Ella blinked. "More? I have never been there."

"How was the monarchy set up? Who was the king? That kind of thing."

Ella frowned. She honestly didn't remember much about what she'd been told. "I don't know. My grandfather was the king—but there was a coup, and we were sent into exile. My parents lived in Europe. Italy. I think I spent the first eight years of my life in Tuscany and the Amalfi Coast. I loved it there."

"How did your parents die?"

Her heart pinched. It always hurt to think of Mama and Papa. They had loved her. When she'd gone to Aunt Flavia and Uncle Gaetano, she'd thought she'd get more of the same. She'd been terribly wrong.

"A car accident. The Amalfi Coast is very twisty and turny. They were out driving—and something happened. Failed brakes, a car running them off the road—I don't know precisely. All I know is they never came back. And I was sent to America."

Chapter Fourteen

CASH WAS HAVING trouble processing what Hawk told him earlier. Ella was a queen. Or would be, if Capriolo still had a monarchy. She hadn't told him she was a princess—had she also hidden the fact she would be a queen, or did she truly not know? Not that it mattered really. She wasn't a queen—and never would be unless Capriolo suddenly decided they wanted to invite her back.

But it might explain a lot about her aunt and uncle. The way they'd treated her, the way they'd sold her into marriage to Sheikh Fahd. It would explain a lot about Fahd as well. Why he wanted her, why he was willing to pay to marry her. A queen—even an exiled queen—would go a long way toward cementing his claim in Qu'rim.

"Who would the king be today, assuming you still had a king there?"

She frowned. "My uncle, I think. He is a Rossi."

"But who was the eldest Rossi? Your uncle or your father?"

"I don't know."

"You've never googled these things?"

"No. My aunt and uncle restricted what we could search for. If I wanted to keep my privileges—downloading music, reading books—then I knew not to violate the restrictions."

Ella Rossi—hell, Ella McQuaid now—was a goddamned queen, and her relatives had hidden it from her. Hidden it from the world, apparently. Because like Hawk had said, it was buried deep. The line of succession went from her grandfather to her father to her. She'd effectively been the exiled queen since she was eight years old—and she apparently didn't know it.

It was clear to him she didn't. So did he tell her? Or did he keep it from her because it didn't matter?

He wasn't certain—but he was certain that now was not the time to discuss it.

"Why are you asking me this?" Her head was tilted as she stared at him. He couldn't help but notice the pinkness of her mouth, the smokiness of her eyes. Her hair was a lush waterfall of silky darkness. Her eyes were pools of sepia ink. The urge to kiss her smashed through him like a nuclear detonation.

A little voice whispered that he had the right. He could kiss her. He could undress her, explore her, make her come. It was his *right*. She was his wife. *His wife.*

Cash shook himself and turned away, taking a gulp of the whiskey he'd poured. It scalded his throat. He needed to remember. Remember that she was a virgin and he shouldn't touch her. Because this wasn't real and it wasn't going to last.

It was a job. She was his job. Protect her. Keep her safe. Let her go at the end of it so she could make her own life.

"Just wondering," he said. "Figured I should know more about you."

He tried not to let his gaze wander down her body.

Damn that Gina. She knew how to dress a bride. It had taken everything he had not to let his tongue fall out earlier when he'd walked into the room and seen Ella in that white dress. It was strapless, and the white of it set off her creamy olive skin and made her glow. The bodice was fitted, and the skirt clung to her hips before flaring below the knee and dragging in a silky puddle behind her. There was no ornamentation, unlike the dress she'd been wearing when he rescued her yesterday.

But this dress suited her so much more. In that dress, she'd seemed untouchable, armored. Like a doll instead of a woman. In this dress? She was feminine and appealing. Touchable, though he couldn't touch her. Not ever.

He wanted to. More than ever, he wanted to. He tossed back the whiskey and chalked it up to the perversity of the situation. He, Cash McQuaid, the avowed bachelor, was *married*. A thing he'd sworn he'd never do. It was as if fate were laughing at him. Fate had found Ella, put her in his path, and was currently laughing her ass off at him. Or was it asses? He seemed to remember that the Fates were plural in Greek mythology.

Whatever.

"And what about you?" Ella asked, her dark eyes liquid pools of curiosity. She held the wineglass in delicate fingers, taking periodic sips of the golden liquid. Was it his imagination, or did she sway a tiny bit on her feet?

"What about me?"

"You asked about my parents, my past. What about yours? I know nothing about you."

"You know enough. I'm a Navy SEAL. I protect people. I'm protecting you."

She took a delicate sip of wine. "I thank you for that. But who are you, Cash McQuaid?" She frowned and shook her head as if to clear it. "That is such an odd thing to say. Cash McQuaid—I am Mrs. McQuaid, am I not? My last name has been Rossi for so long."

"I think you will always be a Rossi," he said. "And this is America. You don't have to take my last name."

"But I did. It was on the forms."

He shrugged. "That was done to protect you. When we divorce, you can change it back."

She frowned and dropped her gaze to her drink. "Of course."

"Don't be offended, Ella," he said. "I'm just telling you the truth. You won't want to stay married to me."

Her eyes flashed as she lifted her gaze. "I didn't say I did."

Jesus, did she have to be so pretty? "Didn't Gina give you any other clothes?"

She frowned. "I selected an outfit on the plane. That was all. Besides, I don't want her to *give* me clothes."

Cash blew out a breath and went to pour another whiskey. *Damn.*

"I don't think you want to go out on the town wearing a wedding dress. That's all I'm saying."

Her lower lip stuck out for a second before she sucked it back in. "I don't want to go out on the town at all."

"That makes two of us," he grumbled before sipping his whiskey.

She went over and sank down on a plush Queen Anne chair. Her dark eyes studied him. "You have not answered my question. Who are you, Cash? Besides a Navy SEAL. Where do you come from? Who are your parents?"

He frowned. He didn't like talking about this stuff. But she kept looking at him expectantly and he thought, *What the fuck.*

"My dad is an asshole. A misogynistic, womanizing bastard who thinks women are possessions. My mother left him years ago. I haven't heard from her since. I have a stepmother though. She hates me. My half sister is a sweetheart who adores me. I don't go home much other than to see friends."

Ella's lip trembled and then stopped. She sipped her drink and tried to look cool. "I'm sorry."

He shrugged. "Don't be. I knew the score years ago. I couldn't leave fast enough."

"You sound like me in a way. I wanted to leave but could not. They wouldn't let me."

He did feel sympathy for her. "And now you have. How do you feel?"

"Strange. I ran away from a marriage and now I'm married. I wanted to make my own decisions, but so far they have all been made for me. I don't see that changing soon."

He shook his head. "No, I'm sorry, but I don't either. It's the nature of the business. To protect you, we have to create and control the situation. Eventually you'll be free."

"Yes, I'm sure I will."

"Are you hungry?" he asked after a few silent moments. "We can order something from room service. Hell, we can tell Gina we aren't going anywhere if you wish. She has pictures of the ceremony. That should be enough."

Ella looked relieved for a moment, but then her expression hardened as if she was summoning all her willpower. "No, I think we have to stick to the plan. I can wait for dinner."

He glanced through the open bedroom door at the king-sized bed and cleared his throat. There was still that hurdle to cross, wasn't there?

Ella glanced at him. Her gaze followed his, and he was certain a red flush crept up her throat. He hurried to reassure her.

"I'll get the hotel to bring up a cot," he said. "You can have the bed."

"That's kind of you," she murmured.

Kind? He didn't think it was kind at all. Instead, he thought it might be an act of self-preservation.

He took another slug of whiskey. It was starting to send warm fire snaking along his veins. The temptation to down it chipped away at him, but he refused to lose control. He had too much discipline to do so.

"No problem," he said.

"But Cash," she replied when he strode to the phone on the table and started to pick it up.

"Yes?"

"Will it get out to the press that we had a cot brought up? Should we perhaps think of something else? Gina says that what the press reports is very important to my future."

Shit.

He laid the phone in the cradle and drew in a deep breath. "I'll sleep on the floor."

"You could sleep in the bed," she said. "With me. There is plenty of room."

Something of what he was feeling must have shown on his face, because she rose and held out her hand in apology. "No, that is not what I mean. I simply mean the bed is large and there is room for us both."

He wanted to growl and then he wanted to tug her into his arms and bite her. In the best possible way, of course.

"Ella," he said tightly. "There may be room, but it's not a good idea. Trust me on this."

She seemed shocked. And then she seemed pleased. "Do I excite you, Cash McQuaid? Is that the problem?"

He was planning to deny it. But when he opened his mouth, he didn't.

"Yes, Ella. That is exactly the problem."

Chapter Fifteen

ELLA KNEW she was playing with fire, but there was something about the way he looked at her, green eyes flashing, that excited her beyond reason. She shouldn't push him. He was helping her out, doing her a favor, and she was needling him about attraction.

Specifically, their attraction to each other. Because she was attracted. So very attracted. Her nipples drew into tight little buds, and her center grew wet and swollen at the idea of sharing a bed with him.

Oh, that stupid porn she'd viewed. It had put ideas into her head. Ideas she'd never had with Sheikh Fahd. But Cash McQuaid? Her husband?

Husband.

The word made her shiver deliciously. It conjured up all sorts of wonderful pictures in her mind. She did not know what he looked like naked, but she imagined he was spectacularly beautiful. She did not see how he could be otherwise. His body was lean and hard with muscle. She knew that from being pressed up against him.

But what would he look like unclothed? His penis hard, jutting from his body? And how would it feel when he slid it into her body? That she did not know.

She'd masturbated, of course she had, but she'd never had a man—or anything resembling a man—inside her. She had, however, read romance novels. And oh my goodness did they make it sound wonderful.

So had the porn she'd viewed. Well, most of it. A couple of the videos were clearly geared toward men. She, for instance, had never considered kissing another woman or grinding her lady parts with someone else's. And yet that was often a feature in the male-oriented ones.

But it was the man-on-woman action she'd loved the most. And when the man was considerate of his partner? Amazing. It was clear to her that some porn was made for women and some for men. She far preferred the woman porn because of the emphasis on mutual pleasure and not on titillation for titillation's sake.

Cash was watching her with narrowed eyes. He threw back the whiskey—the second glass since they'd returned to the room—and slammed the empty on the bar.

"Yes, you fucking excite me," he growled. "But it's not happening, sweetheart. Not at all."

A thrill shot through her. It was intoxicating to hear him admit it. Even more so than the wine she'd been drinking.

"I don't mind if it does. You'd be helping me take care of a problem." Because virginity was a *huge* problem for her. Get rid of it, end the appeal to sheikhs and other rich men who were willing to buy her hand in marriage from her aunt and uncle. It was the answer to her prayers.

"It's not a problem anymore, Ella. We're married, and there's not a soul on earth who's going to believe you're still a virgin after tonight."

That was probably true. She had to admit it was—in fact, she'd thought it herself earlier. And yet it disappointed her. She wanted more. She wanted to know what it felt like to belong, even if only for a night. Worse—she wanted to know what it felt like to belong to *this* man.

After everything he'd done for her, she knew he would take care of her. He was wired to do so. It wasn't in him to be selfish when it came to how he treated her.

"I know more than you think," she said, swaying a little on her feet. She wasn't drunk, but oh, she was warm. Glowing from the inside out. And she was strangely willing to talk about things that would have embarrassed her only a short while before.

It's the champagne and the wine. Shut up, Ella. Just stop before you make a fool of yourself.

But she couldn't. She'd been silent for so long. About so many things.

Cash was looking at her with a hard frown on his face. "What does that mean?"

"About sex," she said. "About what happens. I've watched porn."

His eyes widened. If she wasn't mistaken, he sucked in a deep breath and let it out slowly. She was emboldened to continue.

"I know that a man likes it very much when a woman licks his penis and tugs on it with her hand at the same time—"

"Ella."

"It's true! I know it's true—"

"Ella, for God's sake."

"I know how it works, Cash. I know where a man's dick —or cock. They call them cocks sometimes—goes when a woman isn't sucking on it. I know I'm supposed to feel immense pleasure when it's inside me, though I can't quite figure that out because my finger didn't have the same effect—"

"Jesus," Cash said. "Stop. Just stop."

"I want to know, Cash. I want to feel what it's like." She sucked in a breath and then put a fist beneath her breasts, pressed it there. "I want to feel what those women felt deep inside. I want to be so lost in what a man does to me that I forget everything else, that I understand what pleasure is…"

Her voice faltered as he started moving toward her.

"…I want what those women had. Not all of them…"

He was still moving.

"…Some of it was fake, I'm certain, so not that…"

He was a wall of muscle that swept into her, swept over her, pushing her back against a long table sitting against the wall. He overwhelmed her with his size, but he didn't do it in a way that was frightening. No, he did it in a deliciously territorial way.

She tipped her head back to look up at him, her hands automatically reaching for the table's edge behind her. Her heart slammed her ribs. He caged her in, arms on either side of her head, hands pressing into the wall behind the table. His nostrils flared.

"Ella, you have to stop talking about this shit."

"But I don't want to," she whispered.

"You want to kill me, don't you?" He shoved the fingers of one hand through his hair. He might have growled. She wasn't certain. Her heart still throbbed and her sex ached with want. She was wet and swollen. He could fix that.

"I don't want to kill you. Honest. I just want you to touch me."

His eyelids dropped. His shoulders seemed to sag. When he met her gaze again, his eyes blazed. "I know what you need, Princess. And I'm going to give it to you—but no more of this, okay?"

She nodded, unable to speak because her lungs had stopped working. He fisted her silky gown in two hands and began to slide it up her thighs. His mouth came down on hers, lightly, sweetly, and she found herself reaching up to wrap her arms around his neck. When he reached for the elastic of her panties, her heart shot skyward.

Oh God, could she do this?

The answering voice in her head was stern. *You asked for it, Ella. Stop being wishy-washy.*

His thumbs hooked into the waistband and dragged the skimpy fabric down. It didn't want to go anywhere at first, but at a certain point gravity took over and he let go. The panties slid down to her ankles. She didn't have time to think about it as his fingers feathered into the curls between her legs.

His tongue delved deep into her mouth and she moaned, taking everything he had. Part of her wished his tongue was where his fingers were—oh yes, she'd seen that too.

He skimmed a finger down the seam of her body, sinking into the wetness there. Ella gasped, her grip on him tightening. He broke the kiss to gaze down at her.

"Change your mind, Princess?" His voice was husky, his eyes gleaming.

"No…"

"Say no at any time. I'll stop."

"I know."

He kissed her again, and she lost herself in it. His fingers skated over her sensitive flesh, light, teasing. Part of her was scandalized at herself. Part wanted to rip this dress off and bare her body for him—and then beg him to do all the things she'd dreamed about since watching them in videos.

He pressed a little harder now, his thumb taking up a rhythm on her clit that made her gasp.

"Open your legs," he murmured.

She did, and he was free to move his fingers faster. More skillfully. He pinched and rubbed, and her breathing quickened as her body spiraled toward release. She didn't know what he had planned, but she didn't want to stop him. Perhaps he would do this first, and then he'd strip her naked and slide his penis into her.

But right now all she could do was ride his hand, her hips jerking against him, her body tightening with pleasure. She wanted to be naked, wanted to feel more than this, but it was a start.

She gripped his shoulders, arched herself into him, sucked his tongue deep—

And exploded.

Ella ripped her mouth from his, crying out, riding the wave as long as it carried her. It was more intense somehow. More exciting with him than alone.

His lips were at her ear. "That's it, Ella. Beautiful, beautiful Ella. Let go. That's it. Damn, that's so hot, baby. You make me harder than stone. So fucking hard."

He stroked her until she shuddered, until she went limp in his arms. She thought he might pick her up then. Might carry her to bed and finish what he'd started.

But he didn't. Instead, he let her dress slide down her hips. Then he stepped away, adjusting himself. It took her a moment to realize that it was over. That there would be no more.

A man had finally touched her—but she was still a virgin.

"I don't understand," she said, her chest aching, her body throbbing with release—and somehow still with need.

"I don't either," Cash muttered. "But that's how it's going to be."

———

He was dying here. Ella was so damned innocent and sweet—yet still dirty enough to confuse the shit out of him. Porn? What the fuck?

Cash's dick throbbed. His heart beat faster than he liked. The urge to bend her over and slam into her was strong. He wouldn't, but he wanted to.

Virgin princess. Virgin *queen*.

God, what a nightmare.

She was watching him with wounded eyes. Her cheeks were flushed, the only hint of what had just happened. Otherwise she stood there so serenely, her gown covering her, all evidence of her desire hidden from view.

She wanted him, would have spread her legs eagerly, but he couldn't do that to her. It wouldn't be just sex for her, no matter that she wanted to pretend it would be. She already trusted him far too much. If he took her over that hurdle?

He shook his head. No, he couldn't do that. She needed to make a clean break from him when it was time. If they were involved? Too complicated.

"How is it you've been watching porn? I thought your aunt and uncle restricted what you could see online."

She dropped her chin, clasped her hands in front of her body. "My aunt thought I should know what to expect."

He reeled. Fucking reeled. Her aunt had given her

access to porn to teach her about sex? As if what happened in porn was real sex. As if the ridiculousness of fake-breasted women humping the pizza-delivery guy within seconds was normal. Or, worse, some of the shit that happened in those things. Women taking guys in every orifice at the same time as if it were ordinary. Not that he cared what the hell people did in the privacy of their own bedrooms, but he was a one-on-one kind of guy. No way in hell was he sharing a hot babe with another swinging dick.

One-on-one.

"I hope you know that most sex doesn't happen like that."

She lifted her gaze to his. "It seemed straightforward enough."

Somebody kill him now. "That's not what I mean. The mechanics, yes. But the artifice, the way people always seem to do a hundred positions all over the house before anybody comes—that's not great sex."

She was listening intently. He was beginning to think he'd made a strategic error in judgment.

"What is great sex?"

His dick was not going down. Not at all. "Great sex is two people being into each other, touching and feeling and doing what gives them pleasure. If it feels great, it is great. If it doesn't feel good, don't do it just to please the other person."

She nodded, her expression so serious. "I will remember that."

"Your aunt should have told you these things. She shouldn't have given a virgin porn and expected her to figure it out for herself."

"But maybe she doesn't know what it is either."

He blinked. Wise girl. "Yeah, that's entirely possible."

"But it was still helpful. And then there were the romance novels. Sex is always so wonderful in them."

Cash didn't know what he'd done to piss off Lady Karma, but she was gunning for him hard right now. Ella's slick heat was seared into his memory banks, and here they were discussing what made sex great. Torture was a mild word for it. "Is it? I've never read one."

"You should."

He didn't think that was likely, but he wasn't going to tell her that. "Yeah, maybe so."

There was a knock at the door. He reached for the Glock he'd tucked behind his back and motioned to Ella to stay where she was. When he got to the door, he looked out the peephole—and relaxed. Thank God for the interruption. It was just one of Hawk's guys carrying garment bags over his arm. Cash jerked open the door, though he kept the Glock hanging at his side. Just in case someone was out there.

"Clothing for tonight," the guy said, holding out the bags. "Hawk says they'll be ready to go in fifteen minutes. He'll text you before it's time to go downstairs."

Cash wanted to beg the guy to stay until then, but how could he reasonably do that? He couldn't, so he took the bags and thanked the guy. When he was gone, Cash locked the door again and carried everything into the bedroom.

Ella was sitting on the end of the bed. The bed was huge, and she was a vision in white. She looked so demure sitting there. And she also looked sweetly sensual, because he knew what he'd just done to her. How she'd orgasmed, clutching him and crying out while she came for the first time ever with someone else touching her.

Christ.

It hit him then how significant that was. Ella had never been touched by another man. No one had ever made her come before today. Any orgasms she'd had up until now were given by her own hand.

Anger punched him. He'd made her come while backed up against the edge of a table. Her legs barely spread, her skirts hiked up, his need to keep her at arm's length driving him to give her something impersonal, something easy. Something requiring no commitment or, hell, finesse.

He was an ass. "I'm sorry, Ella."

"Why?"

He tossed the bags onto the bed. "For what just happened. I shouldn't have done that."

Her lashes dropped, covering those dark eyes of hers. "I liked it."

A shiver went through him. "I'm glad. But I still shouldn't have done it. Your first time being touched by someone—it should have been better than that."

Her head lifted, her eyes widening. "How could it have been better?"

He had an urge to show her. To go over and ease her back onto the bed, strip her slowly, and show her everything she should demand from her future lovers.

"I should have taken more care," he said roughly. "You deserve patience, not a quick and dirty encounter against a piece of furniture."

She tilted her head as she gazed at him. He felt like a bug under a microscope. It was an odd feeling, especially since he didn't typically give a shit what anyone thought about him.

"I think both ways have their time and place, yes?"

Holy shit. This woman.

"Yes, that's true."

She stood and reached for the garment bag labeled with her name. "I assume this is for tonight."

"I think you're right."

She picked it up and walked toward the bathroom. When she was nearly there, she turned back to him. "I liked the way you touched me, Cash. I would like it if you did it again."

Chapter Sixteen

ELLA DIDN'T KNOW what to expect during their night out, but she was still surprised at the amount of attention they got. Oh, most of it was directed at Gina, certainly. But once the reporters snapped pics of her and Jack and got answers to their questions, they'd turned to Ella and Cash.

And then, as the evening wore on, many of them came to her and Cash first. Because the news of her marriage to Cash, combined with the national story of her disappearance, was a hot topic.

It was so strange. She'd spent her life sequestered behind walls at her aunt and uncle's estate, for the most part, so this attention was astounding. And overwhelming. She began to shrink from it, to dread it. Cash seemed to realize it at some point because his arm around her waist tightened whenever a gaggle of reporters approached.

It only happened when they moved from one location to another, but it was enough she was beginning to fear it. They had dinner in one casino, drinks at another, played the tables at a third, took in a show—and now they were on their way back to the Bellagio in order to have more drinks.

It was grueling, and she was on the brink of an introvert meltdown. So many people for so long, when she'd only ever been around people in snatches. Maybe it was the fact she was the center of attention, or maybe she just couldn't handle people for very long. She didn't precisely *miss* her room on the estate in Virginia, but she missed the solitude.

Cash kept his hand on her back when they were moving. When they were still, he looped an arm over her shoulders. It made her feel safe.

"Princess Antonella," the reporters called as they left the safety of the limo and started across the carpet toward the casino entrance. "When did you meet Cash McQuaid? Was it love at first sight? Why didn't you tell your family about him? Did you really run away from a wedding to Sheikh Fahd?"

Ella kept her chin high, but she trembled deep inside. She could feel Cash stiffen. And then he stopped, anchoring her against his side as he faced the reporters.

"My wife isn't answering any more questions about our marriage. If you need to know something, you can ask me. We're married, we're in love, and her family will just have to get used to it. End of story."

He steered her toward the doors as the reporters clamored behind them. They were inside within seconds, the seething mass of questions left behind. When Ella glanced over her shoulder, she saw Gina vamping it up for the photographers. The reporters turned to questioning her while Jack stood there with a hard look on his face.

"How does she do it?" Ella asked.

Cash looked back. "Practice, I guess. She's been a star for a long time."

"I am not a star. I'm someone with a title that means nothing here—and nothing in Capriolo anymore either—and yet they hound me anyway."

Cash looked intense, as if he would say more than he finally did. "It's interesting to them. To America. You're a princess who eloped with a commoner. That's how they'll sell it and what their readers will lap up. You may not command attention like Kate Middleton, but you're probably a close second at the moment."

"But nobody knew who I was until today."

"Until you ran away from home and made it your uncle's business to try to get you back by any means necessary?"

Ella nibbled her lip. "Yes, that is true." Another thought hit her then. "Will it ever stop? Will they let us go about our lives?"

"I'm not sure. I hope so." He didn't look convinced though.

For the first time, she began to consider that this marriage could last longer than either of them had thought it might. Not that the idea of being with Cash bothered her—but she was pretty sure it bothered him. He played the happy husband better than she could have hoped for, but only she could feel the tightening of his fingers against her during the prolonged evening. Only she could see the lines of strain in the corners of his smile.

He ushered her into an exclusive club located in the casino. It was for high rollers, important guests. The two giant men at the door didn't even blink when they walked up. Perhaps that was due to Cash being every bit as tough-looking as they were. Or maybe it was the way Jack's people seemed to both precede and follow them everywhere they went. They were surrounded and well-guarded.

The doors opened and they walked inside. Cash led

her over to a cozy corner where plush couches flanked a low table on three sides. At another table, a dark-skinned man with copious amounts of gold around his neck looked up and gave them a nod.

Cash nodded back.

"Who is that?" Ella whispered. Or tried to whisper. The music was loud so she had to pitch her voice higher.

"A rap artist. Can't think of the name right now, but he's pretty famous. Gina will know."

She took a seat on the couch he indicated, crossing her legs and leaning back as if she were relaxed and having the best time ever. Gina had coached her on how to behave, and she was doing her best to emulate the grace and poise of the other woman.

Her dress was short, black, and sequined. It didn't fit like a glove, but it hugged in all the right places. Her shoes were black, with ties that wrapped around her ankles and ended in pretty bows. She felt sexy and beautiful—and foreign. So, so foreign. This wasn't like anything she'd ever worn. She loved it, and yet she couldn't be certain her lack of experience wasn't showing. Like a little girl playing dress-up with her mother's clothes.

Cash sank down beside her, his expression strained. He hated everything about this night, she was certain. The endless parade around Vegas, the pretense of being a happily married couple, the staged photos for the media when he bent his head to her and whispered in her ear, telling her to smile as he ran his fingers along her jaw and made her shiver.

She glanced at the plain wedding band on her finger. He had a matching one. It wasn't anything either of them had picked out, and yet it felt as real as if they had. The rings were platinum but unadorned. Gina had apologized when she'd presented the jewelry to them. Ella hadn't even

thought about rings. They hadn't had them for the ceremony, but Gina said they needed them before they went
out. A jeweler had sent up different sizes and they chose
what fit. The end.

A cocktail waitress in a skimpy costume that barely
covered the important parts sashayed over. "Can I get you
anything, sir? Madam?"

"Club soda for me," Cash said. "What would you
like, Ella?"

She'd been drinking club soda as well, with a lime so it
looked like she was truly having a drink, but she was weary
and she wanted something to take the edge off.

"Champagne," she said.

"Does madam have a preference?" the girl asked, pen
poised over her pad.

Ella shot a panicked glance at Cash.

"She'll have Dom," he said. "In fact, bring a bottle
with extra glasses."

The waitress disappeared in the direction of the bar.

"Who will drink all that champagne?" Ella asked.

Cash shrugged. "Does it matter?"

"No, I guess not."

Jack and Gina came through the door to the club then.
The music didn't stop, but everyone seemed to go still for a
second. And then the chatter ratcheted up as Gina strode
over on platform heels. She took a moment to wave at
someone, and then she sank down on one of the couches
opposite. Jack joined her. But if the attention in the room
was for her, her attention was on him. He bent her back
against the cushions and kissed her. Her arms went around
his neck almost helplessly.

It wasn't an obscene kiss, wasn't anything inappropri-
ate, but Ella suddenly felt as if she were intruding on a
private moment. They stopped kissing and merely sat with

their foreheads touching and their mouths moving as they whispered words to each other that no one else would ever know.

Ella glanced away—and locked gazes with Cash. His eyes glittered as he slumped decadently against the cushions. He looked relaxed and lazy, but she was certain it was a myth. This man was not as unaware of everything going on around him as he pretended to be.

His face was a study in perfection as he watched her. In the dim light of the lounge, his gaze was dark and brooding. His mouth was set in a firm line. The knuckles of one hand rolled back and forth beneath his bottom lip, a gesture that said he was thinking deeply about something.

About her? About them? About what she'd said to him earlier?

She'd told him she liked the way he touched her, that she wanted him to do it again. She didn't expect he would, but just in case, she'd wanted him to know it was okay.

Two days.

Two days was all she'd spent with him, and here she was fending off a hot need to straddle his lap and grind her body against his. As if she'd known him for years. As if she trusted him to take care of her.

But she did.

She did trust him to take care of her. And, no matter that they were married and her family would know it by now, she was also more than a little bit panicked that she was still a virgin. As if her aunt and uncle would find her, kidnap her, have the marriage annulled, and force her into Sheikh Fahd's arms after all.

Because that's the kind of people they were. Hell, they'd do it whether she was a virgin or not if they got the chance. Which was why she wanted to at least know what it felt like to be with a man she wanted to be with. If her relatives succeeded, she could take the memory of a night with Cash with her and use it to wall herself off from a man who used her body because he'd bought it.

The waitress arrived with the champagne and glasses then. She popped the cork while they looked on, then poured four glasses.

Gina picked hers up. "To Cash and Ella," she said, lifting the glass.

It wasn't the first time tonight, but it still felt as awkward as it had earlier.

Everyone took a drink. The men, she noticed, put their glasses down and didn't touch them again. A thumping song came on and Gina squealed.

"Oh, I love this one. Let's dance, baby," she said to Jack.

"No way, honey. You know I'd rather watch you."

Gina popped her hands on her hips. "Fine. Ella, you want to dance?"

Ella's initial reaction was to say no—but instead she took another gulp of champagne and stood. "Why not?"

Gina didn't lead her far away from the men, but when they reached the spot she'd decided was the right one, Gina began to dance. Her body was sensual, fit, and she rolled through moves that Ella had no idea how to do.

"Let me show you," Gina said, putting her hands on Ella's hips and showing her the rhythm. "Like that, yes. Be sexy, Ella. Be seductive. Show that man what he's missing tonight if he doesn't take you into his arms."

Ella thought she should be embarrassed, but the little bit of champagne gave her courage. She found her rhythm, rocked her hips, followed Gina's lead—and started to have real fun for the first time that night.

"That's it!"

They danced through two songs, laughing and talking

from time to time as Ella felt looser and freer than she had at the beginning. She got the idea how to move, copied Gina shamelessly, and let herself go.

She let her hair swing around her, wild and free. She spread her arms and rocked her hips from side to side. Whenever she cast a glance around the club, men were watching her and Gina. They weren't the only two dancing anymore, but many eyes stayed locked on them.

And then there was Cash. His eyes didn't leave her—at least not when she looked at him. He still slouched, but he wasn't talking to Jack. He was watching her intently. Jack watched Gina, but his expression was happy. Oh, there was lust there as well, but there was also contentment. Ella wished she knew what that felt like. Being content with someone. Being happy and safe and certain they were there for you no matter what.

Cash was there for her because he had to be. She appreciated it, but it wasn't quite the same thing.

She turned her back to him, undulated her body to the music. Closed her eyes and lifted her hands over her head, snapping her fingers as she danced. A laugh escaped her. A wild, free sound that startled her at first. But Gina laughed with her, her eyes sparkling.

"That's it, honey. Have a good time. Don't let Cash ruin the fun for you."

A moment later, Jack was there, tugging Gina into his arms. She threw her head back, laughing as she went. He didn't dance, but he held her and said words to her that made her expression melt into a sensual look that said everything.

"Yes, baby, I agree." Gina shot a look at Ella as she twined her hand with Jack's. "We're going now. You and Cash be good. See you in the morning."

She left the floor with Jack, holding hands, her body clinging to his as they walked out of the club together.

Ella kept dancing, though it was a little odd to do so while alone. She turned away from Cash's hot gaze, unwilling to stop just yet. A man approached from the other side of the club. His eyes rolled down her body, back up again. There was intent in his gaze. He wasn't unattractive, but he wasn't Cash either.

She didn't have to worry. A solid body pressed to her back, a hand going possessively around her waist. The lips at her ear made a hot shiver crawl down her spine and between her legs.

The man approaching her halted in midstride. Then he turned and walked away. Cash spun her in his arms just as the music slowed. His eyes were hot, intense. Fathomless. What was he thinking?

She wished he was thinking about her. About making love to her. Because that's what she thought about. What she'd been thinking about since the moment he'd kissed her before their wedding ceremony.

She stretched her arms up, put them around his neck. Her heart thudded at the feel of his hard body pressing into hers.

"You're playing with fire, sweet Ella," he growled. "Better be careful before you get burned."

She tossed her hair defiantly. "And what if I want to burn?"

His eyes narrowed. "How much champagne did you drink?"

"You were sitting right there. One glass."

"One glass. You're a lightweight, aren't you?"

"I'm not a drinker, if that's what you're asking." She sighed and swayed against him. One glass relaxed her. Made her feel warm and tingly inside. It was a good thing.

"Take me to bed, Cash. Take me to bed and show me how to give you pleasure."

"You're killing me, Princess. Killing me dead."

She gasped as he swung her up into his arms, tightening her hold on his neck as the world tilted. "What are you doing?"

"Taking you to bed."

Chapter Seventeen

BY THE TIME they'd reached the elevator, the thumping of the bar was muted. Cash didn't set her down, though Hawk's people were watching them from a short distance. When the doors to the elevator opened, he carried her inside and turned as if it was an everyday occurrence.

Hawk's men entered and turned away, studiously pretending nothing was going on. Cash was glad they were there. If this were any other night, any other woman, he'd have her up against the wall with his hands in her panties the second the door slid shut. He might even stop the elevator and fuck her in it, though that wasn't quite as likely here in Vegas since there was a security camera pointed at them.

Though, truth be told, the casino personnel had probably seen it all on these cameras.

The elevator rose silently. Ella's eyes were closed as she laid her head against his chest. He could only hope she really was exhausted and that she'd stay that way when they got back to the suite.

He didn't think he was that lucky, however. Ella Rossi

would come alive the second they were alone. He'd bet on it.

And he didn't know how he was going to keep resisting her. It was almost funny how this one small, virginal woman affected him. He'd had sex with innumerable women and he'd enjoyed it. He wasn't a man who lacked for pussy.

So why was he jonesing for this one? Why did he want to be inside Ella in the worst way?

He didn't do virgins. In fact, he'd had no desire to do virgins before, so why now? Why did he want to break her hymen so badly? There would be blood. She would cry. She would also be sore. There would be no long night of fucking, only one encounter that would leave her hurting in spite of how careful he was with her.

And yet the temptation was strong to do it anyway.

The elevator stopped at their floor. Hawk's men shadowed them back to their room. Cash would have cleared the room himself, but he had Ella in his arms. So he touched the card to the reader and let one of them go inside, weapon drawn. When he returned, he gave a nod.

"All clear."

"Thanks, man."

"Yes, sir."

"I'm not a sir," Cash said. "I'm a SEAL. Enlisted, not officer."

The other man nodded. "Former Air Force. We'll have a guard on the floor all night, by the way. She'll be safe."

Cash thanked them and carried Ella inside, kicking the door closed with a foot. He twisted the dead bolt with one hand while she held on to his neck, then took her in and set her down. She made a reluctant noise, but she let him go.

"I thought we were going to bed," she said, her lower lip sticking out in a pout.

God, he wanted to bite that lip. Suck it. Feel it on his dick.

"You're going to bed, Ella. Alone. It's been a long day."

She glanced at the clock. "It's only eleven p.m."

"Which is what time in Virginia?"

She frowned. "Oh, yeah."

"Right. Three hours difference."

"I'm not tired."

"You will be. Put your head on the pillow and see what happens."

She frowned. And then she snorted. "Listen to you. Treating me like a small child who refuses to cooperate." She shook her head, all that glorious dark hair shimmering as she did so. "I'm a grown woman, Cash. I'll decide when I go to bed."

There wasn't much he could say about that. "Fine. You decide."

He went over and flopped onto the couch, grabbing the remote and turning on the television. He could see Ella in his periphery. He could see her far too well, in fact.

That ridiculously short sequined dress, those long legs, and the damned bows at her ankles that he wanted to untie with his teeth before spreading her open and licking her into oblivion.

Things he would not do, no matter how badly he wanted to.

He flipped to the news channel to see what the story was about Ella. He didn't have long to wait before pictures of him and Ella flashed across the screen. The anchor read about their marriage in Vegas, about the nationwide hunt for her that had now been called off.

Ella walked over and stood a few feet away, arms

folded over her chest as she watched. Her uncle appeared at one point, a microphone thrust into his face —a red face with a prominent vein throbbing in his forehead.

"We are thrilled she is safe, yes. But Her Royal Highness has acted very irresponsibly. She's disappointed her family and the man she was contracted to marry. But she can still come home. She can still do her duty. We will always welcome her with open arms."

Ella scoffed. "With chains, more likely."

"The princess married a commoner. An American military man. How does that affect the succession in Capriolo?"

Cash changed the channel before something that would likely upset Ella got said.

"Hey," Ella said. "I was watching that."

"You heard the important part."

She frowned and tapped her foot. "I've no idea why they were talking about the succession. *If* the Rossis still ruled, my uncle would be king. And my cousins would be next in line. I'm fourth in line at least. And I would be pushed farther down when my cousins have children." She shrugged. "It's not important anyway. The people of Capriolo chose to exile us when they chose a representative government rather than a monarchy."

"Does that bother you?"

"Why would it? I have been raised in America. Capriolo has done well enough without us. I would not want to be queen anyway."

"You wouldn't?"

"It is simply another kind of prison, I think. I am tired of prisons. I want to be free."

"You're married to me," Cash said. "That's not freedom."

"Maybe not, but I am free of the Rossis. And that's what's important to me."

She laughed suddenly, a sound filled with glee. A sound that struck a chord within him. Had he ever been that happy?

"I'm finally free of them, Cash. And I have you to thank for it. If you hadn't stopped when you saw me…" She shuddered and wrapped her arms around herself. "Well, I can only imagine how I'd be feeling right now."

He could imagine it too. And he didn't like it. She would be terrified probably. He didn't think Fahd would hurt her, but he also didn't think Fahd would have taken care of her either. He'd have taken her virginity in the way that gave him the most pleasure and to hell with her feelings about it.

"I'm glad I stopped too."

She arched an eyebrow. "Even though you're saddled with a wife you didn't want?"

"If marrying you got you free of those people—and Fahd—then yeah, I'm glad. Besides, it's not permanent. We'll both be free again before we know it."

She didn't look at him. "Yes. We will."

Somehow she managed to be sexy and innocent at the same time. Vulnerable and strong. She confounded him in ways he'd never experienced. He wanted to get up and take her in his arms. Tell her it would be all right in the end. That she'd be fine.

Except he couldn't do it. Because if he did, if he wrapped her in his embrace, he was pretty sure he wouldn't let her go for the rest of the night.

———

Ella slept fitfully. She woke at odd hours, her heart

pounding a crazy rhythm, her ears straining to hear any movement in the darkness. But then she heard Cash's breathing and her heart slowed again.

He lay in bed with her, but so far on the other side of the mattress that he might as well be the next county over. The bed was huge and there was room for them both— plus four other people if they all lay still.

She was a light sleeper, and a still one. Cash didn't move much either. There was little chance they'd wake up next to each other.

By the time morning arrived, Ella was cranky from lack of sleep. When Cash woke her, she threw a pillow at him.

"Sorry, Princess, but we've got to get moving. Breakfast with Hawk and Gina and then a helicopter tour of the Grand Canyon. Real honeymoon shit."

Ella grumbled as she pushed herself onto an elbow. Cash was far too awake and far too beautiful standing over her. "Staying in bed *is* honeymoon shit. Not helicopters and stuff."

"I think both are acceptable. This morning it's a tour. You can sleep later."

"I wasn't talking about sleep," Ella muttered under her breath.

"What are you mumbling about?"

"Nothing." She threw back the covers, revealing her tank top and sleep shorts. Thankfully, Gina had sent a few things up to Ella's suite. She still didn't know how she was going to pay the other woman back, but she would. Somehow.

Cash's eyes narrowed. Then he turned and walked away. There was a coffee maker on the mirrored bar near the door. He went over and poured a cup.

"You want coffee?"

"Yes, please." She climbed from bed and shuffled into

the bathroom. When she was finished, she went out to join Cash. He held out a cup.

"Black, right?"

"Yes."

She took it and sipped, waiting for the liquid to make her come alive. Her head started to throb. Really? Great.

"What's wrong?"

She glanced up at Cash. He'd noticed? "Slight headache."

"Too much champagne, I imagine."

"I didn't have too much."

"You danced in front of a crowd."

She had, hadn't she? "I had one glass, Cash. I said so last night. Besides, it was Gina who got me out there."

He went over and rummaged through his bag. When he returned, he held out two caplets. "Take this. You'll feel better."

She swallowed them down with hot coffee and hoped he was right. He was staring at her when she looked up.

"What?"

He shook his head. "You're too trusting, Ella. You have no idea what I just gave you."

"Would you give me anything bad?"

"No."

"Then what is the problem? Should I have demanded an explanation before taking headache pills?"

"Maybe not with me, but when you're on your own, be more careful, okay?"

Her heart gave a throb in time with her head. "Of course. I'm not stupid."

She finished the coffee while he took a phone call. When she felt awake enough, she went and got dressed. She put on cropped navy trousers, flat sandals with little jewels on the leather straps, and a long white shirt with tails that she knotted at her waist.

She tied her hair up in a loose knot and grabbed the small handbag Gina had given her. She had lipstick and her new ID inside. Maybe she could get a phone next. The thought excited her.

Until she started thinking about who would call her. Precisely nobody. She had no friends, no colleagues. Cash might call. Gina. She sighed. Perhaps a phone wasn't all that exciting after all.

She went back into the main living area of the suite. Cash was sprawled on the couch, watching the news. She heard her name and then he pressed the button and the sound went dead. He was frowning and her belly sank just a bit farther toward her toes.

"What is it?"

He looked up. "Nothing."

"You don't look like it's nothing. Is Uncle Gaetano being an ass on television again? Did Aunt Flavia demand my return?"

"No." He sat forward, elbows on knees, and gazed at her. "You don't really know a lot about Capriolo, do you?"

He was beginning to worry her. "Why should I? I have never been there and will never go there since the royal family is exiled. Is there something amiss on the island?"

He levered himself up and came over to put his hands on her shoulders. "There's no easy way to say this, but… They lied to you, Ella. Your whole life, they lied."

It didn't surprise her that anyone had lied, but she still wanted to ask *who* he meant exactly. As if she didn't know.

"The news outlets have it now, so you need to know the truth. Before we walk out there and you have to face something you won't be expecting."

LYNN RAYE HARRIS

"What is it, Cash? Just say it, for heaven's sake." Her imagination was beginning to run wild.

She was already married to the sheikh because only a contract was necessary.

She was adopted.

Or illegitimate.

"Your father was the heir to the throne. Not your uncle."

She searched his gaze. Looking for deception. For humor—was he kidding her? But there was nothing like that. Just concern and, yes, anger. He tried to keep a lid on that anger, but she saw it flickering behind the concern.

The enormity of what he'd said rolled over her. Pressed down on her. If Papa had been the heir, then that meant...

No.

Yes.

"If we still ruled, I would be queen."

"Yes, you would be."

Her jaw opened and closed. Shock flooded her. She was a queen? All this time, and they'd told her nothing.

Fury kindled deep in her belly and flared hot. It wasn't that she wanted to be a queen. Not at all. But the way they'd treated her. The way they'd made her *feel*.

"All these years... The fear, the deprivation, the way they made me believe I was a burden to them..."

She closed her eyes and squeezed them tight. All she'd ever wanted was to belong. To be loved. Hell, to be *liked* would have been enough. Instead, they kept her with them, begrudging everything they gave her, telling her she cost them money and that she owed them. Owed them her virginity, her fealty, her very life.

She'd nearly married Sheikh Fahd. For *them*. For a group of people over whom she should be sovereign, were they still in Capriolo. They'd stripped her of her dignity and given her nothing in return. And all the while, she was the ranking royal family member in their midst. It was monstrous and vile.

And wholly like the Rossi clan she knew.

"I hate them," she said from between clenched teeth. She'd thought it many times, but she'd never voiced it. Guilt had always stopped her. The idea that she'd been foisted on her aunt and uncle and they were doing the best they could.

But no, it hadn't been that *at all.* They'd used her, denied her, ignored her.

"I know, honey," Cash said, wrapping his arms around her and pulling her in close. She spread her palms over his shirt, felt the warmth of his body beneath. Concentrated on his scent and his solidness.

"The money," she said as the enormity of it began to sink in. "The money they spent, the money they used to fund their lifestyle—it was probably mine all along."

"Probably. But it's gone, right?"

"Not all of it. There is still the estate. But how would I prove anything? It's not like there is a royal treasury anymore. I have no power here."

"We'll figure it out."

She pushed back, gripped his arms, stared up at him. "How? How can you do this?"

"I know people, Ella. No guarantees, but if anyone can figure it out, my boys can."

"Your boys?"

"The people I work with."

Another thought unfurled deep inside. An insidious thought. If her aunt and uncle were cornered, they would strike back. Besides, it wasn't the money she cared about so much as the freedom that money represented. She could buy a house. Go to college. Make her own way. But was it worth the risk to Cash and his friends for them to pry? Her uncle could be ruthless. What if he hurt Cash?

"Maybe we should leave it alone. I only wanted my freedom. If I have that, it will be enough."

He looked fierce. "They should pay for what they've done to you."

"They already are. Without the money they were to get from Sheikh Fahd for the marriage, they will soon be hurting. I won't be sorry about that."

He didn't like it. She could see that in his eyes. "You okay, Princess?"

Ella pulled in a deep breath. She was still reeling inside. Would probably reel for days. Nothing was as she'd thought. She was a queen. Or would be if there were still a monarchy. Without a crowning ceremony, she would always be a princess. But a princess who was first among Capriolan royalty.

It was a lot to take in.

"I don't want to go anywhere, Cash. Can we please stay here today?"

His fingers ghosted down the side of her face. "Yeah, we'll stay. I'll call Hawk."

Chapter Eighteen

CASH HAD no idea what came next in this adventure. He was already so far out of his depth that he couldn't begin to predict anything. But one thing he knew—he had to protect Ella. She wasn't precisely fragile, but she was feeling the psychological bruises today. That's why he called up Hawk and told him they were staying in. Cash didn't particularly want to spend an entire day cooped up with Ella, but it would be cruel to drag her out to deal with more reporters when she was still absorbing the fact that her relatives had lied to her for so long.

While Ella curled up in a chair by the window with a book she'd found on one of the shelves, he surfed through TV stations, looking for something mind-numbing. He landed on *NCIS* and kept it there. That show was fun even if it was cheesy as hell and inaccurate about a lot of shit that he and his kind did. Gibbs made him think of Colonel Mendez, except that Gibbs was a bit older. Still a badass though.

He kept the sound low so as not to disturb Ella. He couldn't remember the last time he'd seen anybody so engrossed in a book. She had no cell phone, so she wasn't constantly picking it up to check her social media accounts. It was strange and refreshing at the same time. He'd been out with women who were tethered to their devices, who had to glance at it every chance they got. Some even picked it up after sex. One had Instagrammed the rumpled sheets and her bare legs. When she'd tried to snap his abs, he'd taken the phone and tossed it onto the floor before giving her a reason to forget all about Instagram for a while.

A couple of hours into his *NCIS* marathon, his phone rang. A glance told him it was Camel.

"Hey, dude," Cash said.

"That was one hell of a fishing trip you went on," Camel said.

Cash snorted. "Caught something I didn't expect, that's for sure. If you'd come with me like I asked, maybe this wouldn't have happened."

Though that meant that Ella would currently be in Sheikh Fahd's harem somewhere in Qu'rim. She wouldn't be a virgin anymore. And she'd probably be crying.

"I'm allergic to fish."

"I've seen you eat shrimp and striped bass. You are not allergic."

"Fine, I'm allergic to fishing. Who wants to stand around and throw a line in the water all day? Give me a rifle and let me hunt."

"Is that really fair to your prey? You're a fucking military sniper. You don't miss. Bambi doesn't stand a chance with you."

"Hey, when I shoot a deer, I take it to be processed and donate the meat to the homeless shelters in town. It might not be fair to the deer, but it's good for people who need to eat."

"Fine, you got me there. So what's up back at HQ?" he asked, knowing this was more than a simple shoot-the-breeze call.

"Same shit, different day. When are you coming back?"

"We're supposed to head back tomorrow. But I don't know what happens after."

"So you really got hitched, huh?"

"You know I did. You motherfuckers have probably been laughing yourselves silly about it for the past two days."

Camel snorted. "Yeah, you bet we have. Cash "Money" McQuaid, the dedicated bachelor, hitched to a frigging princess. She's a hot little piece of ass too. You tapping that yet?"

Cash couldn't explain the wave of ice that crystallized in his veins. Or the hot anger that burned it up again. "No." He glanced at Ella. She was still face-first in her book. He pitched his voice lower anyway. "I'd appreciate you don't talk that way about my wife, man. Not cool."

There was a moment's hesitation on the other end. "Dude, you're serious."

"Sure am. Don't do it. You don't talk about Ivy or Christina or Miranda that way to Viking or Cage or Cowboy's faces, right? So don't do it to Ella."

"Copy that, and sorry if I crossed a line."

"It's okay. But now you know."

"You falling for her?"

Cash frowned. "No way. But she's been through a lot. I don't want to see her deal with more crap than she can handle."

"I guess my real reason for calling doesn't even need to be discussed now. The answer is clearly no."

"You can't say that for sure. What is it?"

"Women. Two of them who want to double-date this weekend."

"I just got married and you thought I'd want to go on a date?"

"Hey, we were told you had to do it in order to cover your ass. I figured you'd go your separate ways when you got home and you'd be back to your usual routine."

His usual routine. Missions, women, missions, women, missions. Lather, rinse, repeat. Didn't sound so fun at the moment, even though it was the way he lived his life on a regular basis.

"Probably be a while before things get back to normal."

There was amusement in Camel's tone. "So I gathered. Hey, let us know when you're back. And what we can do to help with the situation. If she needs twenty-four seven protection, the guys will make it happen."

"I don't know what's going to happen, but I appreciate the offer."

"Enjoy your honeymoon, Money."

"Don't be a dick, asswipe."

Camel laughed. "You know that's not going to happen. You've got an old lady now. It's fricking hilarious as shit."

"I'm hanging up now." Cash ended the call with Camel's laughter ringing in his ears.

A glance at Ella revealed that she'd fallen asleep in the chair. The book lay in her lap, her head was tilted to the side, and her pretty pink mouth dropped open the slightest little bit.

He thought about moving her to the bed, but touching her was an exercise in iron control. Not that he wasn't capable of maintaining control, but it hurt. Physically hurt in ways that could only be relieved in the shower with his hand wrapped around his cock and thoughts of her in his head.

There was time for that. He could sneak off to the shower, turn on the spray, and release some of this tension before she woke.

Cash shook his head. No, he wasn't leaving her here. What if she woke up while he was gone? What if she opened the door to the room and someone grabbed her while he was standing in the shower and beating off to the thought of her?

Nope, not the way he operated. He was just going to have to suffer for a while.

He went over to pick up the book and laid it on the table before it slipped to the floor. The book was jacketless. He'd expected one of her racy romance novels, but instead it was a nonfiction tome.

Body of Secrets: Anatomy of the Ultra-Secret National Security Agency.

Cash blinked at the woman asleep on the chair. Seriously? She was reading a book about the National Security Agency? She'd been engrossed for hours now. He took it over to the couch and flipped it open to the beginning.

Holy shit.

It was all about cryptography and code-breaking. National security. He flipped through it, careful not to lose her place. Fascinating shit. He'd loved reading as a kid. Still did, but he didn't get much time for it these days. Mostly he read mission briefs, studied intelligence reports, read the paper—things like that.

Cash didn't know how much time went by while he got sucked into the pages before he heard Ella stir. He glanced up, watched her search for the book.

"I've got it," he said.

She looked up. "You stole my book."

"You were about to drop it."

She stretched. "Well, then. I suppose you've done me a service."

"Why did you choose this one? Of everything on the shelf?"

"Have you been reading it?"

"Yes."

"Then you know why. It's fascinating."

It was indeed.

"You read many things like this?"

"I read a lot, yes. My aunt and uncle have a library filled with books. Fortunately, they never censored my reading. My access to the internet, yes. But not my reading."

"I thought you liked to read romance novels."

"I do. But I like to read a lot of different things, Cash. Greek mythology, science, economics, biographies. I especially love biographies. People live such fascinating lives."

And she hadn't. That was the implication. He heard it as clear as a bell. It angered him on her behalf. He closed the book and set it on the table.

"You want it back right now?"

She shook her head. "I'm hungry. Can we order something?"

"Yeah, we can order up."

He went and got the room service menu and took it to her. She studied it carefully, then chose the least expensive thing on it. He knew because he'd looked at it earlier.

"Get what you want, Ella."

"I want that sandwich."

"You don't. You want the steak. Or maybe the pasta with lobster in it. You don't want a boring sandwich."

She arched an eyebrow. "How do you know what I want?"

"I don't. Not really. But I'm pretty sure you're

146

running a calculator in your head that's adding every-thing up and wondering how you're going to pay anyone back."

She dropped her gaze. "Is that so wrong?"

"No. But it's also unnecessary. Nobody here is keeping tabs on what you eat—or what you wear. That was your aunt and uncle. Not us."

She bowed her head. "All right. I want the pasta with the lobster. How did you know?"

"Because of the way you ate the pasta Alfredo I made."

She grinned. "You're a very good cook."

"I pay attention to what I'm doing. That's all it is really."

"Well, I don't know how to cook. So I appreciate it very much."

"I guess this means you won't have dinner waiting when I get home from work?" he joked.

She shook her head. "I'm afraid not. Am I already a failure as a wife?"

He liked that she could banter with him. That meant she wasn't taking this too seriously after all. He went over and picked up the hotel phone. "It's okay, Ella. I don't think either one of us knows how to do this whole married thing."

"I know one thing we're supposed to be doing," she said. "But apparently that is not something you are willing to teach me."

He pretended not to hear her.

———

It didn't take long for the food to arrive. Ella dove in, uncaring that she was once more eating fattening pasta.

The sauce was creamy, buttery, and the lobster chunks were fat and juicy. It was heaven on a plate.

They were sitting at the table in the suite, a waiter having laid out all the food before retreating. Cash had ordered a steak. Ella closed her eyes and moaned.

"Jesus, Ella. You have to stop that shit."

Her eyes popped open to find Cash regarding her intensely. "What?"

"Making those noises."

"Oh. Sorry." She twirled the fork in the pasta, her cheeks heating as she considered his words.

"Hey."

She looked up, hot embarrassment swirling in her belly.

"Forget I said that, okay?"

"No, you are right. It's rude to make noises while eating. Aunt Flavia would be horrified."

"Fuck Aunt Flavia."

Ella gaped for a moment—and then she burst out laughing. Oh, how many times had she wanted to say that but never had?

"Yes, fuck Aunt Flavia. Fuck her good."

It felt so awesome to get that out. To say such rude words. To mean them.

"Uh, Ella... Princess, you shouldn't talk like that."

Ella blinked. "Talk like what? Fuck? You said it."

"Yeah, I did. But you shouldn't." He closed his eyes and put a hand over them for a second. "Fucking hell," he muttered.

Or at least that's what she thought he said.

"It's not proper for a lady in your, uh, position," he continued.

"In my position? You mean exiled, broke, and running from an arranged marriage with a sheikh? That position?"

"No, honey," he said, and her heart kind of squeezed at the way he said honey. As if he really meant that she was his honey. "I mean that you're royal. And while I don't care what the hell you say, you might need to be careful for the next time you're in public. You know?"

"I would never say such things in public," she said, scandalized. "I'm not a fool."

"No, I don't think you are."

"Then don't tell me what to say. You said it. I can too. Fuck Aunt Flavia. And Fuck Uncle Gaetano too."

"You're killing me, Princess."

"Why?"

"Because you're so wholesome and unworldly. And then you say shit like that. So matter-of-factly. As if you talk like a sailor all the time."

"They are just words, Cash. It's not a big deal."

He sliced off a piece of steak. "Not supposed to be."

"Then why do you get so worked up?"

His eyes glittered hot for a second. "I'm trying to figure that out."

Ella took another bite of her pasta. She didn't moan this time, but she wanted to. So good. So rich and forbidden. Aunt Flavia had told her that men wanted their women thin. That a plump woman was unattractive. Ella had watched enough television to know that was probably true. She took one more bite and carefully set the plate away. She hadn't had the discipline when he'd cooked for her the other night, but she did now.

Cash frowned. "Is there a problem with the food?"

"Of course not. I'm finished."

"But there's three-quarters of it left. You've barely eaten any."

"It's okay. I need to be careful anyway."

"What does that mean?"

"It means I don't want to get fat."

His expression was thunderous. "Is that you talking or your aunt?"

"It's me."

"Bullshit. It's your aunt and her notions about how thin you need to be."

"Do you like fat women, Cash?"

"Sometimes. It depends."

Well, that wasn't the answer she'd expected. "Sometimes?"

"If she's comfortable in her own skin and loves who she is, yeah, sexy as fuck." He shrugged. "I pretty much love women in general. And while I won't lie and say it doesn't matter to me what a woman looks like, I've found that what I consider sexy isn't limited to a specific set of physical qualities."

She thought about that. And then, because she was still hungry, she reached for the pasta.

Cash's expression softened. "Don't let those people control what you do anymore, okay? It's your life, not theirs."

"Old habits are hard to break," she replied, twirling the fork in the noodles. "But I'm trying."

"That's good."

She took a bite. "What about you, Cash? Have you considered that maybe some of your rules need to be rewritten?"

He lifted one eyebrow. Then he laughed. "Touché, Princess. And no, some rules are good ones."

"Even when they are silly and outdated?"

"To you, maybe. They aren't silly to me."

Ella sighed. She'd never really thought she'd so desperately want a man to initiate her into sex, but here she was.

Wanting. Aching. Desiring him to hurt her so she could get that part over with and get to the good stuff.

"If I promise not to get emotionally attached to you, will you consider it?"

He blinked. "You can't promise that."

"Can't I? It's about as realistic as your certainty that I'm going to fall for you if we have sex. I imagine there's a fifty-fifty chance one of us is right."

He dropped his fork and shook his head. "I've never met anyone like you."

"Nor I you. Here I thought virginity was a prize for men. You've certainly proven that I've been misinformed."

Before he could answer, a loud thud sounded from the corridor outside the suite. Ella jerked her head in that direction. Cash was on his feet in a second, weapon drawn from somewhere on his body and pointed in the direction of the sound.

He glanced back at her, his expression so deadly serious that her heart plummeted into her stomach. "Get in the bathroom and lock the door. If I don't come for you in five minutes, don't open the door." He tossed her his cell phone. "Call Hawk and tell him what's going on."

"I don't know how to use it. I've never had a phone—"

"You can use a computer, right?"

"Yes."

"Then you can use a phone. Find Hawk's name in the address book. Follow the prompts to call him. Now go."

Chapter Nineteen

CASH STRAINED his ears toward the sound as he rushed to the door. A quick check of the peephole revealed a man in a hotel uniform shoved against the opposite wall. The man holding him was one of Hawk's.

Cash didn't holster his Glock as he yanked the door open. "What the hell is going on out here?"

"This is a reporter," Hawk's man said. "Caught him trying to slide a microphone under the door."

Cash glanced down at the snakelike apparatus lying across the carpet. It was small, thin. He yanked it off the ground and studied it. Sure enough, on the end of the snake was a small receiver.

The man against the wall didn't look apologetic at all. Though he did look measurably concerned that he was being held against his will by a man with a weapon.

"What the hell do you want?" Cash demanded.

"A story," the reporter said.

"So you'd listen in on private conversations between a man and his wife?"

"It's nothing personal. It's news."

"What outlet are you with?"

"Star TV."

Star-fucking-TV. Nothing but a gossip rag in television form. The kind of network that gossiped about everything from which star was being dumped to who'd gained weight and who was paying off God and everyone not to give away a secret. Vile shit, mostly, and little of it true.

If Star TV had found their room, well, it was probably time to move on.

Hawk came striding down the hall, looking pissed as hell. Gina wasn't with him, which was a good thing considering who this scummy bastard represented. Guess Ella had figured out the phone after all. Smart girl, his princess.

His princess?

Cash shook that thought away. Nope, not his princess. Just a smart, sexy, bookish princess. *Don't forget the porn*, a little voice whispered.

God, he was trying really, really hard—*jeez, don't say hard*—to forget the porn. The fact that she'd watched it and she was both worldly and virginal at the same time. How the hell did that happen in this society?

Hawk grilled the man while Cash dragged his mind back to the problem at hand.

"Get him out of here," Hawk growled when he was satisfied.

"Yes, boss."

"Hey, what about my equipment?" the man wailed as the security guard frog-marched him down the hall.

"Trespassing, buddy. We're keeping it."

"I'll sue!"

The guard didn't even slow down. "Do you really want to get into a pissing contest over this shit? I'm not thinking the casino will take this kind of thing lightly, you know? Spying on guests, invading their privacy…"

The grumbling and arguing continued as the two men disappeared down the hall. Hawk turned to Cash.

"Is Ella okay?"

"She's probably a little scared, but otherwise she's fine. I made her lock herself in the bathroom and call you." He drew in a breath. "I think I need to get her out of here. Back to DC and a somewhat normal existence."

"I don't disagree. You won't be as visible there. HOT will make sure she's protected until the attention dies down. And if you need me, I'll be there too."

"I appreciate that. You and Gina have done so much already. I don't know how to thank you."

Hawk shrugged. "We're family. Once HOT, always HOT. I'll have your back and you'll have mine. It's what we do."

Yeah, it's what they did. It was always true of a SEAL team and even truer of the brothers and sisters he'd found in HOT.

"You ever need me, I'm there," Cash said.

"Thanks, man." Hawk nodded his head toward the closed door. "Better go tell your wife the trouble has passed. I'll let you know what time I can get you out of here. We're staying for now. Gina has a show in the next couple of days."

"Yeah, sorry we'll miss that." He meant it too, because Ella had been more than a little starstruck over Gina at first. She was a fan and she would have enjoyed the concert. But there'd be more concerts.

Would there?

Not with him, there wouldn't. Once they got back to DC, Cash didn't think they'd spend too much time together before they went their separate ways. Even if she was still a virgin, the damage had been done in the eyes of the world. Antonella Rossi was no longer as pure as new snow. Her value as a commodity her relatives could sell had been eroded overnight.

"Next time," Hawk said.

"Sounds good."

They parted ways, and Cash went back inside, locking the door behind him. He was thinking about how he and Ella would live in his apartment for the next week or so— thank God there was a spare bedroom now his roommate had gotten married—when something came flying at his head. He barely saw it in time to duck, but he managed to drop to the floor as the object sailed over and smacked the wall.

A second object—a human object—barreled into him as he pushed upright, knocking him flat again. She was small and fierce, and he rolled her until she was beneath him. He caught both her wrists in one hand and locked them tight to prevent her from breaking away.

"What the fuck, Ella?" he demanded.

She was twisting like a tiger, but she stilled when he spoke. "Cash?"

Her hair covered her face, blinding her as she lay on the floor beneath him. Her chest heaved, her breasts rising and falling with her exertions. The buttons of her shirt strained from the wrestling they'd done, gaping in a couple of places. His dick began to harden.

He pushed her hair aside, revealing a flushed face and flashing eyes. Before he could get a word out, she attacked.

"You didn't announce yourself," she accused. "You could have been anyone!"

Cash frowned. Yeah, he'd walked inside and locked the door behind him—but he hadn't announced himself. Hadn't told her to come out, that it was safe.

Which meant, dammit, that she'd opened the bathroom door anyway. That she'd thought she could stop whomever broke in and tried to attack her. With a fucking *book*.

"What the hell were you doing anyway?" he demanded. "You weren't supposed to come out until Hawk or I told you to."

Anger seethed in his veins, boiling furiously, scouring his insides. She'd risked her safety. She'd disobeyed.

"I called Hawk. I knew he was coming. What if someone got you, Cash? I was trying to help. I was here to distract him until Hawk arrived."

He didn't know what to say. Just didn't. Fury, frustration—and a healthy dose of lust—rolled through him.

Take her. She's yours. She wants you.

The voice didn't stop, and his dick swelled. Any second and she'd know it too.

He dragged his thoughts back to the anger. Propped it in front of his mind's eye and focused on it. *Anger. Danger. Fury. Yes, that's it. Be pissed. Don't think about fucking. Don't think about being balls deep in her tight wetness—*

Oh, hell.

He was losing this battle. Losing it so spectacularly that at any minute he was going to start peeling off her clothes and drowning in her gorgeous body.

Fight it, Cash. You're a damn SEAL!

Yes, he was a SEAL. He could face hardship, deprivation, danger. He could conquer anything he set his mind to. Including the temptation to devirginize a princess. He could most certainly conquer that impulse. He'd been tempted a couple of times to ring the bell during SEAL training, to give up and let the instructors know he was done. That he'd never be good enough.

Only the memory of what waited for him at home if he failed had kept him going. But he *had* kept going, and he'd conquered his impulses. Surely he could do that now.

He could annihilate this one small impulse to thoroughly corrupt Ella body and soul.

She shifted beneath him then, moving her hips, pressing her center against his aching cock.

"Ella, don't."

"Don't what?"

"Move. Don't move."

But she didn't obey. Of course she didn't. She arched upward, the contact between them setting off sparks behind his eyelids.

"I can't help it," she whispered. "It feels—it feels amazing, Cash."

He rocked against her, hard as stone. Pressing his cock against that sensitive spot she was trying to gratify. She whimpered and grasped his biceps. Squeezed her fingertips into his muscles so hard he was pretty sure she would leave a mark. If not a physical mark, then a psychological mark he would feel for a long time to come.

"You shouldn't ask me for this, Princess. It's getting too hard to keep control. I'm going to snap and do everything you ask—and some things you haven't thought of—if you aren't careful."

Her dark eyes searched his. "That's what I keep hoping, Cash. I want it to be you. Not because I love you, but because I know you'll do it right."

No virgins, his brain said. *Why not?* his heart asked.

Ella wasn't like other women. She was logical and levelheaded. She wasn't going to get tangled up over him. And he wasn't going to get tangled up over her. They were married, but it was an arrangement. They both knew it. And if she left the arrangement with a little knowledge about how to please a man, how bad would that be?

Besides, what if he *didn't* touch her and she chose a guy later who thought she was more experienced than she was simply because she'd watched porn? What if she didn't tell the truth and that guy hurt her when he took her virginity? Ella didn't deserve an awful experience. She deserved to be initiated with skill and patience, brought to orgasm again and again before she took that ultimate step.

He had the control for it. The patience. He could make it good for her. When she moved on to someone else, she'd know what to expect. What to demand.

Maybe he'd been thinking about this all wrong. Maybe he *owed* it to her to make sure she had a good experience.

Yes, that's right. He was a fucking philanthropist. Santa Claus, but with sex instead of presents.

He dropped his lips to her neck, ghosted along her skin until he reached her ear. She shuddered beneath him, her fingers curling into him again. Her breath hitched and a growl of possession rolled through him.

"I give up, Ella. You win."

———

She won?

Ella blinked, confused for a moment—but then his mouth took hers in a hungry kiss and her body melted into the tile beneath her. She wrapped her arms around his neck, lifted her head, and opened her mouth so that his tongue could plunge inside and dance with hers.

It was the kind of kiss that changed a person. A shattering kiss. A soul-grabbing kiss that stole her breath and her sense and turned her into a creature of sensation rather than reason.

"Bed," he muttered as he dragged his mouth away. "Not on the floor like animals."

"I don't care," she gasped, hugging him tight when he tried to rise. And she didn't. She simply didn't want this to end, which she feared it would when he got a little distance between them.

She didn't know what had happened to make Cash change his mind, but whatever it was, she didn't want him to change it back again. Or maybe she did, because suddenly she was scared. Just a little bit.

She knew there would be pain when he took her, but she hadn't thought it would happen. He'd been so adamant, and she'd gotten accustomed to the idea that she couldn't persuade him. It had perhaps made her bolder than she would have been otherwise.

"Bed," he said again, untangling her arms from around his neck and climbing to his feet. He pulled her up with him, tugging her against his body. His hands on her hips dragged her in close, let her feel what was waiting for her beneath his clothes.

"I'm not going to hurt you, Princess," he murmured, cupping her face, his thumbs stroking her cheeks. "I can stop whenever you ask me to."

She put her hands on his wrists, held them lightly. "Why did you change your mind?"

"Because I'm selfish, Ella. Because I'm aroused and aching and if I don't do something about it, my balls are going to turn blue. But more than that, I *know* I can make this good for you. I'm not sure the next guy can, and I don't want that to happen. You believe I'll do it right, and I will. You still want me to?"

Ella sucked in a breath. There was only one answer, no matter how hard her heart beat or how hot her skin got. "I'd be lying if I said I wasn't scared. But yes, I want you to be the one. I trust you."

He bent and hooked an arm behind her knees. She squeaked as he swept her up and against him. Then he carried her toward the bed and laid her down on it. He unholstered his weapon and set it on the night table before he followed her down, one knee beside her hip, his body dominating hers as he pressed her down into the mattress.

"Cash," she breathed as he stretched out on top of her. His palms were beside her head, holding his body up, keeping him from crushing her. His mouth lowered to hers by slow degrees. Too slow, because she lifted her head to close the distance, sighing when their mouths met.

His tongue stroked into her mouth, tangled with hers, left her feeling weak and hot and achy. Her body responded to his kisses with a surge of wetness and an ache deep inside that she'd never quite felt before.

His fingers went to the knot at her waist where she'd tied the shirt, and her heart skipped. He undid the knot quickly, tugging it open, and then he unbuttoned her shirt with one hand, his mouth never leaving hers. He'd shifted to the side, his weight pressing into the mattress beside her, his body still partially on top of her but not suffocating her.

When her shirt was unbuttoned, he pushed it wide open, revealing her skin to the cool air circulating in the room. His mouth left hers then, trailed down her neck to her collarbone and then farther down to the swells of her breasts. She threaded a hand through his hair and rubbed it between her fingers. She liked that she could touch him freely now.

He made a noise of approval—at least she thought it was approval, as his tongue continued to explore the swell of her breasts. When he dragged one cup down to expose her nipple, her heart throbbed with anticipation.

His eyes met hers over the dusty pink of her nipple. "Beautiful."

She didn't think her nipple could get any tighter, but she was wrong. It thrust up toward his mouth, demanding attention.

"No one has ever licked this pretty nipple, have they?"

"No."

"Touched it?"

"Only me."

"Show me, Princess."

"Cash, I don't think—"

"Show me, honey. I want to do it right for you."

The heat of shame flared over her skin, but she did as he asked. She closed her thumb and forefinger around her nipple and pinched it softly. Sensation streaked from her nipple to her core. Ella bit her lip and tried not to moan. She wasn't successful.

Cash's eyes were heated as he watched. Instead of taking over, he dragged the cup from her other nipple.

"Keep touching yourself, Princess," he said. And then he stuck out his tongue and licked the tip of her aching flesh.

Ella gasped. Liquid heat flowed between her thighs. Her pussy tightened as if he were touching that instead of her breast. Every lick of his tongue over her nipple made a corresponding ache happen down below.

She thought she might die of pleasure simply from his hot tongue licking around her tight flesh—but then he sucked the little bud into his mouth. Sweet pleasure spiked through her body at every tug and pull. And when he lightly nibbled her tight peak?

Heaven.

Chapter Twenty

IT WAS TOO MUCH. Too much pleasure, too much sensation. Ella cried out, her fingers curling in his hair. Both hands, because she'd stopped tweaking her own nipple a while ago now. She tugged harder than she should probably. But he didn't stop. He licked and sucked until she squirmed beneath him, until she thought she would die from the pleasure.

When he lifted his head to look at her, he grinned, arching an eyebrow. "You like that, sweet Ella?"

Her heart hammered. Tiny beads of sweat popped up everywhere on her skin.

"Yes." She was hoarse. Why?

"Are you scared?"

She shook her head.

"I think you are. But I promise you don't have to be. We won't do anything you don't want to do."

"I want to do everything."

His eyes darkened. "Jesus, some of the things that come out of your mouth. What do you want, Ella? Tell me."

"I want…" She swallowed. "I want you to lick me. There. And I want to lick you."

"That's going to happen. Maybe not the licking me part, at least not this first time. But baby, I'm going to lick you until you scream."

She thought of the video, of the man with his head between the woman's legs—of the way she'd panted and cried out as he licked the very heart of her—and a shiver skated over her skin. She'd wanted that for so long. Desired it every time she read a new romance novel. Imagined it as she brought herself to orgasm with her fingers.

"I want that," she said. "So much."

Cash sat up and grinned. "Today is your lucky day, Princess."

He undressed her with quick, efficient movements, though he left the bra with her breasts pushed up high and firm over the cups. He stripped off the shirt, skimmed the capri pants down her thighs, dragged her panties off and tossed them on the floor.

"You too," she said as he started to lower himself onto her again.

"You want to do it?" he asked.

She nodded. He stayed on his knees, spread his arms wide, and she climbed upright and dragged his T-shirt up and over his head, taking care to run her palms up his abdomen and chest on the way.

His eyes were hot when his head emerged from the fabric. She lifted herself up and kissed him on impulse. It wasn't a bad impulse, because he caught her to him and tangled his tongue with hers. His hot palm splayed over her back, pulled her bare skin against his bare skin.

It was heavenly. Her body felt like hot wax, pliable and formless.

But it didn't last because he gently pushed her away.

"Finish the job, Princess," he said, dipping his chin toward his abdomen.

She followed his gaze; her belly flipped at the sight of all that muscle. The tattoo over his pectoral, the ridges and bumps of hard muscle. The trail of dark hair that went from his belly button to beneath his waistband.

Ella unbuckled his belt, then unbuttoned him with shaking fingers before sliding his zipper down. On impulse, she pressed her lips to his chest, licked his nipple the way he'd licked hers. He growled and tugged her down to the bed, kicking out of his pants before pressing his naked body to hers.

She opened her legs instinctively, cradling his big body between them. His hot, hard cock slid against the groove of her sex.

"Holy shit, you're wet," he groaned. "So damned wet."

"Isn't that good?" she asked, confused for a second.

"Yeah, it's good. Damned good."

He dipped his head to her other nipple, tugged hard, and Ella cried out. It was almost too much—except it wasn't. It was just right. Cash teased her nipple into an aching peak before he started his slide down her body, tasting her with his hot mouth as he went.

When he reached her mound, he licked a trail along the top where the waistband of her panties usually lay. She grew light-headed, but he didn't stop. Instead, he slid down and settled between her thighs.

"Such a pretty pussy," he said, staring at her. She knew what it looked like down there. She'd studied herself with a mirror. Pretty was not the word she'd use, but the fact he did made her feel beautiful and confident.

"You want me to lick it?" he asked, and her belly flipped again. She had some world-class gymnastics going on inside there.

"Yes. Please."

Cash slid his thumbs into her seam, pushed her open, and dropped his tongue into her heat and wetness.

Ella bowed up off the bed. "Cash! Oh—"

She couldn't speak because he licked a trail from the bottom of her slit to the top where he curled his tongue around her clit and sent sparks exploding behind her eyes.

She couldn't breathe. Couldn't believe what was happening to her or how amazing it felt. The videos had taught her a lot, but they hadn't taught her how it felt. Novels did a pretty good job of making it sound wonderful —but this was so much better than she'd imagined.

Cash was relentless, spreading her open, licking and sucking her clit into his mouth and then dipping down to plunge his tongue into her body before climbing back up to her clit again. When he slipped a finger inside her, she whimpered.

"Does it hurt?"

"No." It didn't, but her hymen blocked the way before he'd gotten too far.

He got about half his finger into her, but the rest couldn't get past the barrier. Still, he began to work his finger back and forth, stretching her a little bit as he did so.

The feeling was foreign and intrusive, but it was also overwhelmed by everything going on a little higher up. Cash pulled her sensitive flesh into his mouth, sucked hard enough to make her see stars.

It was good. So good. She grabbed fistfuls of the covers as he attacked relentlessly. Everything within her tightened unbearably. It was almost painful how much she needed release, how desperate she was to reach the apex. His finger still worked to stretch her, but the distraction of it paled as her orgasm slammed into her and stole her breath.

Ella's body shook, her legs stiffened, and Cash's name burst from her lips as she came. So many sensations flooded her at once. It wasn't the same as when she came by herself. Not at all.

This was more intense, hotter, the plunge to the bottom sharper and sweeter by far.

She thought that would be the end of it, that he'd crawl up her body and press his dick inside her. That now was when she would feel the ripping and tearing of delicate tissues.

But that's not what happened at all. Cash brought her to another orgasm with his mouth, made her hover on the edge longer, and then watched her plunge farther and faster than before.

Ella was spent, and yet somehow she remained restless and achy. In spite of two bone-melting climaxes, she needed more.

This time, Cash did move up her body, licking and kissing her naked skin along the way. When his mouth met hers, she was shocked at first. He tasted salty and a little sweet. It was her taste, and that somehow embarrassed and aroused her at the same time.

"You are fucking amazing, Princess," he growled against her lips. "So beautiful and responsive."

She didn't know how to answer that. He kissed her again and then rolled away and stood. It took her a moment to find her voice.

"Where are you going?"

"Need a condom, Ella."

He disappeared into the bathroom. A moment later he was back, ripping open a package and taking out a pale rubber disk. She watched him roll it on, thinking she'd never seen anything so beautiful in her life as Cash McQuaid—her husband—rolling a condom on with one hand while his eyes burned intently into her.

"You still want this?" he asked before putting a knee on the bed.

If she'd been in love with him, she would have loved him even more in that moment than she ever had before. "Yes, I want this. I want you."

———

Hell, he'd given her every opportunity to put a stop to what was happening, but she hadn't. Cash didn't want her to either. Every time he asked, his heart stopped while he waited for her answer. Because, hot damn, he *really* wanted to get inside her. Now that he'd allowed himself to let it happen, he *needed* it to happen.

He let his gaze slide over her sweet body. His balls tightened in anticipation. Ella was lovely, though she had more angles than he liked. If she were naturally skinny, then fine. But she wasn't. He was sure of it because of the way she said her aunt restricted her food intake.

He'd like to see her with a few more pounds, see how lush and beautiful she would be then.

Cash considered how best to make this first time happen. How to get past the initial pain of breaching her hymen and on to the good stuff. But he didn't really know. She was his first virgin. All he knew was that he had to make her feel good. Make her wet.

He glided a finger along the seam of her body as he lowered himself beside her. She gasped and arched her back as he skimmed her clit. She was so wet. So hot.

"I'm not going to lie to you, Princess. It'll probably hurt at first. I don't know how to change that. All I know is once you get through it, it does get better."

Her throat moved as she swallowed. "I know. I've read about it."

"You scared?"

Her eyes went a little wide. "Yes," she admitted in a soft voice.

"Me too."

She blinked. "You? What are you scared of?"

He pinched her clit softly, gently. A soft breath escaped her.

"Hurting you, Ella. I don't want to do that, but that's how it works."

"It's okay, Cash. I'd rather it was you than…"

Her throat moved as she swallowed and a spike of anger pierced him. The thought of her lying beneath Sheikh Fahd, scared and alone, while he took her virginity against her will, made Cash's chest ache. No woman deserved to be violated like that.

Cash slipped a finger inside her, as far as it would go. It wasn't far, but he had immense patience. He wasn't going to push her any faster than she wanted to go.

"I know, Princess. Still doesn't make it any easier for me to do it."

He dipped his mouth to hers and kissed her again. The tension in her body melted away, leaving her pliant and warm in his arms. He didn't stop circling her clit, teasing it, until he felt the shudders of a fresh orgasm shake her. She dragged her mouth from his and cried out. While she was still shaking from the tremors, he rolled onto her body and positioned himself between her legs.

He didn't have to ask her to spread them. She did it automatically. He pressed the head of his cock against her entrance. Her fingers curled into his biceps and he stilled.

"You can tell me to stop, Ella. I will."

"I know. Please, Cash. Kiss me."

He dropped his mouth to hers. And then he began the process of inching forward. Ella trembled beneath him, and it nearly killed him that she did. He wasn't sure why he felt so protective toward her.

"Just do it, Cash," she said as she gripped his arms hard. "Get it over with."

"You sure?"

"Yes." Her eyes were dark pools. He saw fear in those eyes, and trust. It was the trust that undid him.

He glided a hand down her hip and dragged her leg up to wrap around him. She wrapped the other one around him as he gripped her hips and lifted her. Then he pushed forward harder than before. When she squirmed, he didn't stop. Not unless she asked him to, and she didn't.

She closed her eyes, her forehead knitting tight as she endured the pain. Cash almost stopped anyway, but then the barrier gave way and he suddenly slid fully inside her. Her eyes popped open.

Their gazes tangled. Something swelled in his chest. Some feeling he didn't quite understand. This was a first for them both, so maybe it was just an acknowledgment of that.

"Wow," she said, and Cash laughed. It wasn't what he'd expected to happen at this point, but that's also what made it so Ella.

"What's wow?"

"You. Inside me. I didn't think it would happen."

"And how is it? Okay?"

"It hurt at first, but now it's more of a dull pain. I feel full of you and it aches. But I think I like it."

He was having trouble thinking as her tight walls gripped him hard. All he wanted to do was thrust until he exploded. But he had to make it good for her. He'd promised.

"Then hang on, baby doll. It's about to get a whole lot better."

Chapter Twenty-One

ELLA WANTED to remember everything about this night, but it was moving so fast she couldn't keep up with all the details. She tried to commit every word he said to memory, but she knew she would never remember it all. And if she kept trying, she wouldn't experience this moment as fully as she should.

They were naked—well, except for the bra she still wore—they were entwined, and Cash was buried deep inside her. She was no longer a virgin. He shifted his hips, withdrawing from her body and then thrusting forward again. She ached, but it wasn't a bad ache. It was, as she'd told him, a full-of-him ache. She would know for days, once this was over, that it had happened, because she would have a reminder with the soreness.

He took his time with her, moving slowly and deliberately, though each thrust was a little harder than the last. Their mouths tangled again, tongues stroking, breaths mingling. She suddenly thought that she would never have a more perfect night than this one.

And then, between the bittersweet ache of his possession and the little sparks that zipped through her from time to time, it happened. Her body caught fire. Something within her came to life as he moved, some new spark kindled, and she suddenly wanted *more.*

He must have sensed it because his movements grew harder and faster. All the pieces of her that had been floating aimlessly came together and focused on the blazing light at the end of the tunnel.

This. This was what she'd wanted, what she'd watched in those videos—that moment when pure pleasure took over and built toward a shattering climax. It was really happening. She was going to come this way, and she couldn't wait for it.

But she couldn't quite find her way.

"Cash," she gasped when he dropped his head to her breasts and sucked a nipple into his mouth. He tugged harder than he had before, and a spike of hard pleasure shot down into her core. It was as if there were a conduit between her nipple and her clitoris because the more he sucked on one, the more the other ached.

He knew she needed more. Somehow, he knew.

"Come for me, Ella," he commanded her.

Just like that, she obeyed. How could she not? She shouted. She knew she did, even though she wasn't conscious of it happening. She heard the echo of it in her ears as her body came unglued. As heat and pleasure spiraled through her, sent lightning bolts of sensation into the outposts of her toes and fingers.

It was like her previous orgasms, yet unlike them too. She'd never climaxed with anything inside her before. Not a man, not fingers, not a dildo. Nothing. It was... sensational.

"That's it, baby," Cash said to her, his mouth at her ear,

his tongue wreaking havoc on her senses as he sucked the skin of her neck and her earlobe. "Keep coming."

She did. He didn't stop moving inside her, and she didn't stop trembling as her orgasm rippled through her in waves.

She was still coming when he joined her, his body stiffening as he groaned. She didn't know that's what it was at first, but then she felt his cock pulsing inside her and knew that must be what was happening. She wanted to watch it happen, but it was too late for that.

All she could do was stare at his face and watch it there. His eyes closed tight and his neck corded with muscle as he stiffened. His mouth fell open as he groaned. She'd never seen anything more beautiful than Cash McQuaid while he climaxed.

When he finished, when her own orgasm subsided, he kissed her on the forehead and got up to go take care of the condom. She felt empty without him inside her. As if he'd taken a part of her away when he'd withdrawn.

He returned with a washcloth in his hand. "There might be blood," he said before she could ask.

She pushed up on her elbows and spread her legs. The blood shocked her, even though she knew she would have it. It was the evidence of her virginity, the proof that her value had plummeted. She felt relieved and strangely sad at the same time.

Cash sat beside her and tended to the blood even though she hadn't asked him to. She'd expected he would hand her the cloth, but he didn't. It was warm because he'd thought of that, and he wiped away all traces of her virginity—except where it had stained the sheets—while she looked at the back of his head and thought she might cry.

Not for her virginity. Never for that.

No, it was for herself. Because he'd been right about her even though she'd insisted he was wrong. He'd said she would make this mean more than it should, and he was right. Her heart throbbed with feelings. Her eyes blurred with the strength of the emotion storming inside her.

Was it love? Or gratitude? She didn't quite know, but whatever it was, it hurt. Not because it felt bad, but because she knew he didn't feel the same. He talked about going their separate ways, about this marriage ending as soon as possible—and all she wanted right now was to lie in his arms and think about the future. A future *with* him. A future in which they stayed married and made love as often as possible.

"How are you feeling?" he asked her as the cloth moved between her legs.

"A little sore. But also—wow. I had no idea, Cash. Thank you for giving me this gift."

He frowned. "You make it sound like my motives were pure. They weren't. A hard-on is a difficult thing to ignore, especially when you've been getting them without relief for days."

"I think you're stronger than that."

"You've never had a hard dick, apparently."

"I think I just did."

His eyes dropped closed. He shook his head. "Jesus, Ella. You slay me with some of the shit you say."

"I like to keep you guessing."

"You do a good job of it."

He finished wiping away the blood and took the cloth back to the bathroom. When he returned this time, he reached for his pants. Disappointment flared in her belly.

"Where are you going?"

His expression was a little bit hard, a little bit cool. Or

maybe it was simply aloof. But it was such a change from a few moments ago that she was having trouble reconciling it. What had happened to change his mood?

"I'm not going anywhere. But I need to make some calls. You can stay in bed if you like. Have a nap. I'll wake you when I hear something from Hawk."

"About what?"

"Our departure. We're going home."

———

Okay, so he was an ass. Cash shoved a hand through his hair and grumbled to himself as he walked into the living area of the suite and picked up his phone.

Go back there, get in bed with her, and hold her.

No. He shook his head. No, he wasn't going to do that. He wasn't going to make this cuddly and sweet for her. It was bad enough he'd given in to the urge to fuck her. He stared at his phone for a second, then lifted his head to gaze out at the lights of Las Vegas. What had he done?

He'd just taken the virginity of a woman who would be a queen if her family hadn't been deposed. Him, Cash McQuaid from Iowa, a kid whose mother had left him and whose father hadn't cared enough about him to realize his new wife was abusive toward his son. All the times his step-mother was nice in front of his dad and then pushed him away when his dad's back was turned. All the times he'd believed her, because he was a fucking kid, and then had his heart ripped out anew when she rejected him.

All he'd wanted was some affection. A hug. Someone who cared about his day at school and who was excited when he brought home a lame art project.

"Fuck," he said beneath his breath. Why was he

thinking about this shit? Ella's childhood hadn't been any better. Besides, he'd escaped long ago. Ella had only been free of her family's shit for a handful of days.

His phone buzzed and he put it to his ear. "Yeah?"

"Hey, man. I can get you both on a charter at eight p.m. It'll put you back in DC early, but it might be best to arrive at an odd time anyway."

Cash looked at his watch. "Two hours. Thanks."

"I'll send an escort when it's time to head for the airport."

He and Hawk talked a little bit more about logistics, and then they ended the call. Cash turned and stared at the bedroom door. He didn't want to go back in there. Because he didn't want to see her tearstained face, her sad eyes, her confusion. She would be confused. He was certain of it. Because he was.

Dammit, he *was.*

That was the problem. For a man who always knew precisely what he was doing and why, he was suddenly wound up about his purpose and whether or not he'd done the right thing. He didn't want to see regret in her gaze. Or, yeah, sadness.

Still, there was shit to do and he wasn't the sort of man to avoid the difficult things. No, he charged in and took care of what had to be taken care of. He walked into the bedroom and stopped. The bed was empty.

He followed the sound of water and found her in the bathroom, standing naked with her hair piled on her head while steam built in the shower enclosure. Her back was to him, but she must have sensed his presence because she turned and he was faced with a jaw-dropping view of her beautiful tits, tiny waist, and the neat triangle of hair at the apex of her thighs.

Her skin was smooth, creamy—and abraded in places

where he'd dragged his stubbled jaw over it. They were his marks of ownership. And then he saw it—another mark he'd put on her, the one on her neck when she'd been coming, a love bite that left little doubt what she'd been up to. It wasn't anywhere that was going to be covered by her hair either.

Great.

"We're leaving soon," he told her, though his dick was starting to throb to life and his veins were beginning to flood with arousal and the urge to drive into her again.

"I won't be long."

She didn't put her arms over her body to hide herself. But she was blushing. He could see it in the pink flush spreading over her cheeks and down her neck and collarbones. He knew the kind of strength it took not to do the instinctive thing. Not to react.

God, he admired her. More than he wanted to. But Ella was amazing. She really was a queen, even if her family hadn't let her know it. He'd never met any of them, but he knew she was worth more than all of them put together. And maybe that's why they'd kept her down— they knew it too, and they couldn't stand it.

Because he couldn't help it, he shot her what he knew to be his most winning grin. "Need help in the shower?"

Her tongue darted over her lips. And then she shook her head. "I think it will be better for me if I say no."

Disappointment stomped his burgeoning arousal into the ground. But it wasn't anything he didn't deserve.

"Whatever you say, Princess," he drawled, even though her rejection stung. "Holler if you change your mind."

"I won't."

He tipped his head to her and started to back out of the room. "As Your Majesty wishes."

She frowned, but she didn't say anything. Instead, she

opened the shower door and stepped inside. He knew that move.

Dismissed.

Chapter Twenty-Two

HAWK'S SECURITY team came for them half an hour before departure. The airport was close and they were flying on a charter, so they didn't need to be there too early. They were still acting with an abundance of caution even though the news of Cash and Ella's marriage had filtered out to all the news outlets by now. Her family knew, Fahd knew— what could they do now?

Cash didn't put anything past them, which was why he appreciated the security. Desperate people did desperate things. He didn't know if they *were* desperate, but he didn't want to take that chance.

"Mendez wants to see you when you arrive," Hawk said as he walked with them to the elevator. "He'll send an escort to meet the plane."

Cash resolutely didn't allow his gut to tighten at the mention of his commanding officer's name. Mendez was one badass motherfucker. He'd taken on a vice president, a Russian oligarch, and probably saved the world from certain destruction on more than one occasion. The man was a legend—and he wasn't someone you wanted to piss off.

Not that Cash had done anything wrong. He'd saved the girl. Nothing wrong with that. Except now he'd gone beyond the parameters of the mission and made it personal.

Like getting married wasn't personal?

Yeah, but that was cover. Actually taking the principal to bed on a mission? Not quite by the book.

"Any word on Fahd or her relatives?" Cash asked in a low voice.

Ella was ahead of him, one guard flanking her and one leading. He and Hawk had dropped back to talk, but he still pitched his voice low just in case.

"Fahd has left the country according to the report I got about an hour ago. Her family is still in Virginia. They haven't stirred since the press conference they gave when news of the marriage broke."

He didn't expect they would deviate from the official story. How could they without admitting they'd been forcing Ella to wed against her will? If they insisted she'd run away and been kidnapped, they had a long road ahead of them to convince anyone she'd married him because she'd been coerced. The photos of the wedding, the pictures and video from their night out with Gina and Hawk—it was all much too convincing to fight.

Though why did he have a pit in his belly anyway whenever he thought of them doing just that?

Hawk's gaze slid to Ella and then back again. "Be careful, Money. With her."

The pit in his belly widened. "I will. Her safety is my priority."

"That's not what I meant."

Hawk gave Cash a significant look that let him know

the man had noted the mark on her neck and the apparent tension between the two of them. Before Cash could reply to the charge, they reached the service elevator and everyone stopped.

Hawk held out his hand and Cash took it. "Good luck."

"Thanks."

He gave Ella a brief hug, and then they were in the elevator and plunging down to the lobby level. The doors slid open onto a hallway where staff rushed between the public areas. No one batted an eye at their appearance. Hawk's men ushered them out the back door and into an armored car. Only a few moments went by before they were pulling away from the curb and rolling toward traffic.

It took a good fifteen minutes to reach the airport. The jet waiting for them wasn't as big as Gina's, but it was still nice and lushly appointed. Cash could get used to this life of private jets and high-roller suites. Who couldn't?

Most of his flying took place on military transports with minimal comforts. He wasn't complaining, but when you got to see how the other half lived, it was kind of shocking to think this was the way some people traveled all the time.

Hell, maybe she should have married Fahd. She'd have had every luxury in the world if she had.

He had a visceral reaction to the idea of her standing beside another man and pledging herself to him. Of her virginal body being stripped of her wedding attire while another man got to enjoy the unveiling of flesh no man had ever touched before.

Except me.

Holy shit, he'd never thought that was a turn-on. The idea that he'd been her first. Her only. But it was.

And it only made him want her again. He wanted

to show her everything, give her all the pleasure she could handle, teach her everything they could do together.

She lifted her gaze from the contemplation of the menu a flight attendant had handed her. She hadn't spoken much to him since he'd left the bed earlier. She hadn't been impolite, but she hadn't been her usual self either.

"I'm sorry," he said, and her eyes widened.

"For what?"

"Earlier. Walking away when you needed me to stay."

Her gaze dropped. "I didn't. I was fine."

"But you would have liked it. If I'd stayed with you, both of us naked, talking. Maybe touching. Maybe doing it again."

Her dark eyes boiled with hot emotion. As if he'd cracked into the heart of her. But then she slammed the window shut, and he was left wondering if he'd imagined the simmering cauldron behind those eyes.

"Yes, it might have been nice. But you had things to do. I understand."

Impulsively, he reached for her hand. She started to pull away, but he tightened his grip. Just enough to stop her. And then he loosened his hold so she still could if she wanted.

She did not.

"I did have things to do. But I could have handled that better. I could have spent a few minutes giving you what you needed."

She blinked. Her pink lips were shiny with lipgloss. He wanted to mess them up. "And what about you, Cash? What do you need?"

He felt as if she'd stabbed a dagger into his heart and twisted it. Why? It was an ordinary enough question—

And then it hit him. No one ever asked him that. No sexual partner, no friend, nobody. *What do you need?*

So many things. So many damned things.

He squeezed her hand before letting go and put on his easygoing face as he slouched in the seat. The one that said he didn't care what happened so long as it was good. "Nothing, babe. I'm good."

"Are you?"

His heart hitched for a second. Hurt and anger flared. He stuffed them deep. Gave her a wink and a smile. "Yeah. Just fine." He tipped his chin at the menu still in her other hand. "You figure out what you want to drink yet?"

The flight attendant arrived as if on cue and took their drink orders. When she left, Ella gave him a serious look.

"What happens when we arrive?"

Cash shrugged. "Not much. We'll be met by my team, and we'll go talk to the boss. Or I'll go talk to him. Not sure about you."

And he wasn't.

Her skin paled. "I don't want to be without you. Not yet. You're the only person I know outside of my family. Please don't let them take me somewhere away from you."

In any other circumstance, he'd have been alarmed by a woman he'd slept with saying those things to him. Begging him not to leave. But not this time. He understood where she was coming from.

"I don't think that's the plan, Ella. We put too much into this story to turn around and call it into doubt. We aren't being separated. Not yet."

She seemed to relax then. The drinks arrived and she sipped the sparkling water she'd ordered. Her fingers were long, elegant. The wedding band on her ring finger seemed naked without a diamond residing beside it. He wasn't going to put one there, of course. Didn't mean he couldn't notice it would look better if she had one. As if he could afford to put one there anyway. At least not the kind royalty deserved.

"It's been a long day," she said after a few moments. "So many things have happened."

"I'd say it's been a long few days."

"Well, yes. But today I learned I would be a queen if circumstances were different. And I finally lost my virginity."

Cash dropped his gaze to her neck and the mark there. He wanted to give her another one. Hell, he wanted to be inside her again. As soon as possible.

"Any regrets?"

She lifted her lashes, her dark eyes boring into his. "Many. But none of them involve you."

———

It was still dark when the plane landed at a private airstrip in Maryland. Ella blinked awake as a hand gently shook her. She shifted in the seat and winced at the soreness of her interior muscles. She'd expected it would hurt a bit, but it was surprising how much it did. Then again, it was like working out. When you worked a body part that hadn't been worked in a long time—or ever in the case of her vagina—then you had to deal with a bit of soreness at first. It would get better with time—and more workouts.

Which she really hoped she got, though she couldn't be sure she would. Cash had grown so serious since they'd left the hotel, so businesslike. Once they'd gotten airborne, he'd stopped talking altogether—and she'd finally given up and fallen asleep.

"What's wrong?" he asked now.

She turned her head, their gazes colliding. The cool mint color of his eyes struck her as one of the prettiest things she'd ever seen. The dark rim around his irises intensified their prettiness. Not that she thought he'd appreciate that word. *Pretty*. Cash was a lot more than pretty.

"Nothing's wrong. I'm fine."

"You didn't look fine."

She sighed as she sat up and stretched. "I'm sore, Cash. Bits of me are still recovering."

"Oh. Sorry."

"You did your best. I think it's to be expected. Non-use and all that."

He looked so chagrined that she didn't expect him to snort. "Jesus, Ella. You always make me laugh, even when I don't want to."

"It's a gift," she said, though she wasn't sure it was any such thing. Still, the fact he laughed—the sound of his laugh—did things to her insides. Made them fluttery and happy. He was a dangerous man in more ways than one, only the danger was to her heart. Her poor, unloved, starving-for-affection heart.

He took her hand and wrapped his fingers around it. The aforementioned heart fluttered and trembled.

"Yeah, it is. You ready?"

"What happens now?"

The cabin depressurized as the exterior door opened.

"We get in the waiting SUV out there and go where it takes us."

"You don't know where that is?"

"I suspect I know. But it's nowhere you've heard of or will hear of. So we go. Or not. Depends."

She turned to look out the window. There was indeed an SUV there. A black one with a man standing near the door. Two other men stood nearby. They looked dangerous too. Intense and determined.

Cash helped her up, and they walked down the aisle to the stairs that had been rolled up to the plane. He stepped out first, then turned and waited for her to join him. They walked down hand in hand while he slowed his steps for her.

At the bottom, the two men strode up. They were both grinning. It made her feel a little better. A little less apprehensive.

"Congratulations, Money," one of them said. "Never thought to see the day."

"Shut up, Camel," Cash growled. "You too, Cowboy. Not a word."

The one named Cowboy snorted. But he turned his attention to her. "Your Highness, welcome. Don't pay any attention to this jerk," he added, nodding toward Camel.

Camel? She thought it an odd name. A homely desert animal with a humped back? This man was not homely. At all. He was tall, dark-haired, and strikingly handsome. So was the one named Cowboy—except he was the bigger of the two. Wider, more muscular. Not that Camel wasn't muscular, but he was leaner.

"Thank you," she said when she remembered to stop staring and open her mouth.

"Boys, this lady is my wife," Cash said, tucking her arm into his and stepping closer to her. "Princess Antonella Maria Rossi McQuaid—or however that works. Not quite sure of it yet."

"Call me Ella," she said. "Please."

"Ella, these two idiots are my teammates. Alex Kamarov and Cody McCormick. You can call them whatever you like, including asshole—they'll answer to it."

"Jesus, Money," Camel said. "Do you really talk like that in front of your lovely bride?"

"He does," Ella replied. "But it's okay because I tend to shock him too."

Camel's eyebrows went up. So did Cowboy's.

"You don't say," Cowboy replied. "I'd love to hear all about it."

"No you wouldn't," Cash interjected. "Mind your own business. You taking us somewhere in that land yacht or are we gonna camp out on the tarmac at this ungodly hour and shoot the breeze?"

"Nope, we're going," Camel said. "After you."

They went over to the SUV where the man waiting for them opened the doors. "Welcome back, Money," he said. "And congrats."

"Thanks, man. Ella, this one is Adam Garrison. You can call him Blade—or asshole. Same thing applies."

Blade laughed. "Ma'am, you can call me whatever you like."

"Watch it," Cash growled as Blade took her offered hand and kissed the back of it. "She's married."

"For now," the man said with a wink.

Ella laughed. Okay, so she liked Cash's friends. Cash helped her into the SUV and climbed in beside her. The others piled in as well. Their luggage—which wasn't much —was loaded into the rear of the vehicle, and then they were speeding away from the plane and out onto a dark access road.

Ella yawned and tried not to nod off as they sped through the night. She wanted to hear everything these men said, but she was disappointed because they didn't say much. There was some teasing about her and Cash's marriage, but they kept it light. Ella sat up straight and tall in the back seat and tried not to lean against Cash, but after the second time she jerked herself upright, he tugged her into the circle of his arm, draping his fingers over her shoulder where he could twirl her hair.

She felt the quiet stillness of the vehicle then. The way the conversation sort of died off for a moment, the silence seeming heavy, before one of the men said something about someone named Viking.

Lord, she would never keep up with these people and their names. Real names, nicknames—they all blurred together for the time being. Too many people. Too many names. Though she thought maybe she'd met Viking before, back at the fishing cabin.

After a short trip, they turned into what appeared to be a military facility. A guard stood by a building in the center of the road, checking the identification of everyone who entered. Before Ella could stir, Cash lowered the window and held up her passport along with his own identification. The guard looked at everything and then waved them through.

"Where are we?" she asked softly.

"It's where I work. We need to find out what the plan is for keeping you safe, where we'll be staying, that kind of thing."

"You promised," she said, trying to keep her voice low. She got the impression the other men heard her anyway.

"I know, Princess. Don't worry."

She couldn't do anything else.

Chapter Twenty-Three

"Wow, Money," Cowboy said after they'd gone through the security checks to get into the secure areas of HOT HQ.

They'd left Ella in the area of the building that housed the temporary quarters. Victoria Brandon, a contracted sniper to Alpha Squad, was with her. She was safe, but Cash had hated to leave her side. He could still see the fear in her eyes that she'd kept hidden from everyone else. But he knew it was there because he knew her.

An odd thought when he'd only known her a few days, but there it was.

"That woman," Cowboy continued. "Holy shit, what a body."

Cash tried not to be annoyed. Before Cowboy had gotten tangled up with Miranda, he and Cash had spent a lot of nights prowling the bars and clubs together. They assessed women frankly and appreciatively. Discussed tits, asses, and pussies—and what they intended to do with them—without a second thought.

But if Cowboy went there right now…

Cash stopped. Cowboy stopped. They stood in the middle of a darkened hallway with cameras bearing down on them, capturing every move they made. And every word too.

Cash turned and faced his teammate. His friend.

"Not another word, buddy. Not about her. Ella's not one of the women you pick up in a bar. She's a lady. A *princess*. And she's my wife, so please don't make me mop the floor with you for everyone in the control room to see."

Cowboy's jaw dropped open. And then he burst out laughing. Cash stiffened.

Until his friend backed up, both hands in the air, and shook his head. "Holy shit, Camel was right. You've fallen for her."

Cash's gut tightened. "What are you talking about? She's a lady, that's all. Don't talk about her like she's a slut. You wouldn't talk about Miranda like that. Don't do it about Ella either."

Not that he had anything against sluts. God knew he was a man slut. Or had been. Until recently anyway. Would be again.

Maybe.

"Camel dared me. Sorry, man. No disrespect. None at all."

Camel entered the corridor from behind them. He'd been talking to one of the guards back there and hadn't gone through when they did.

"Motherfucker," Cash said, spinning as Camel walked up. "You told him to say that?"

Camel's grin spread ear to ear. "As much grief as you've given him over Miranda—I couldn't resist. Sorry."

"Not to mention," Cowboy added, "that crap you pulled when you took on the job of playing her husband on the mission to smoke out Victor Conti—yeah, you fucking deserve it."

Cash growled. "Jesus, asshole. *That* was a job. And you acted like you couldn't stand Miranda. Someone had to be her husband for the op. We all gave you the chance—you refused."

"Yeah, but then you rubbed my damned nose in it every chance you got. I wanted to kill you for making her laugh. For pretending she was yours." He shrugged. "Doesn't feel so great when you're on the receiving end, does it?"

It was probably too late to play it cool now that he'd blown like a pressure valve. He went for offended protector instead. "No matter what you think, I'm not in love with Ella. I barely know her. But she's a sweet girl. She doesn't deserve you assholes talking about her like she's fresh meat."

"Barely know her? What's that mark on her neck?"

Shit.

"It's called verisimilitude. Look it up."

Cowboy snorted. "I know what that word means, dickhead."

"I don't," Camel mumbled.

Cowboy kept going. "You're trying to tell me you put that mark on her to make this marriage thing look real? Sure thing, bro. I believe you."

His tone said he clearly did not.

"As fun as this is, you two want to keep the colonel waiting or what?" Camel asked as he started to walk backward. "'Cause I'm gonna have to get on into that briefing room without you if so. I am not making that man wait another second."

Shit. Mendez.

"C'mon," Cash grumbled. "If you're done having fun at my expense?"

"For now," Cowboy said.

They strode down the corridor and through another two security doors before they reached the one they were looking for. A thumb and retina scan later, the door slid open and they entered a room where their commanding officer lounged at a long table with one hand propped against his cheek and the other tapping on a computer keyboard. The rest of the SEALs were there too, as well as Ghost, the deputy commander.

"Glad you boys could finally make it," Colonel John "Viper" Mendez said, looking up, one eyebrow arched mockingly. He motioned to the empty chairs. "Have a seat."

Blade was already there. He'd gone ahead of them once they'd arrived at HQ. He shot the three of them a grin that Mendez couldn't see and mouthed the words *You're fucked.*

"How's the princess, Money?"

"Fine, sir." He tried not to think about the love bite on her neck. How prominent it was. How he shouldn't have done it. *Dumb ass.* "A bit weary, but holding up."

Someone snorted and then coughed to cover it. Cash had to work at not glaring at the entire pack of dickheads. They were so fucking amused by this. All he'd wanted to do was go fishing, dammit.

Mendez's gaze swept the group. He knew they were having fun, but his patience only went so far.

"That's enough, boys," he said mildly. "Money was in the right place at the right time and he did what any of you would do. Now, maybe he deserves some shit for teasing the hell out of the rest of you when it comes to women, and maybe those of you who've gotten married take particular pleasure in ribbing him since he once declared that dating was a buffet and you guys were stuck with the same entrée every night—"

Holy shit, Mendez knew about that?

"But we're going to take this shit serious and make sure that girl stays safe. Got it?"

"Yes, sir," everyone said in unison.

Mendez nodded. "Good." He tapped a key and a slide came up on the overhead. It was a picture of Sheikh Fahd. "Intel says he's returned to Qu'rim. We think he wanted to marry the princess because a royal wife—especially a queen in exile—would bolster his claim to the Qu'rimi throne if the rebels succeed in overthrowing King Tariq bin Abdullah."

He let his gaze slide over them. "It's possible he's given up on the idea now that the princess is married and presumably no longer a virgin."

Cash's neck grew hot. Pray to God none of these assholes saw any color flaring on his face. He'd drop the first one who made a disparaging remark about the state of Ella's virginity—and he'd do it in front of the colonel with the full knowledge that it was going to cost him.

"It's also possible that he has not," Mendez continued. "Which means we're going to have to keep an eye on things surrounding her, at least until we get some kind of confirmation he's moved on. And then there's her family."

A new slide popped up. This one featured her aunt and uncle, two people with petulant expressions and an air of entitlement that oozed from their photos. Cash wanted to punch them both in the mouth.

"They've been hounding the State Department since they've learned where she went. They insist she has no legal right to marry without the approval of her guardians.

They want the marriage dissolved and the princess returned to them."

"No."

Cash hadn't realized he'd gotten to his feet until the colonel looked up. Everyone else had tilted their heads up as well. He spread his hands on the table and slowly sank down again.

Don't overreact.

But somebody had to speak for Ella. Somebody had to tell them what had happened to her.

"They kept her a virtual prisoner," he said, his heart hot as the words tumbled out. "They denied her money, friends—hell, they even denied her food. She hasn't been allowed any freedom to be her own person. They can rot in hell for all I care."

Cash thought that Ghost covered a smile as he absently ran his pen back and forth on the paper in front of him. Mendez didn't crack a smile, but his expression softened for the barest of moments. As if he understood.

"We aren't letting them have her, son. Believe me, we aren't. *I* won't let it happen, I guarantee you that. But I need you all to know what's going on. This is a briefing, like any other mission briefing you've attended. You need the whole picture. Understand?"

"Yes, sir. Sorry, sir."

"All right. So let's discuss protection plans. Who, what, where, why. We're looking at a week or two, maybe longer if something happens. Princess Antonella appears to be a hotly contested prize in a dangerous game of tug-of-war. Her relatives want her back, Sheikh Fahd has plans for her that we can't be certain have changed, and there's a fringe movement in Capriolo that wants to use her as a lightning rod in their plans to gather support for a return to the monarchy."

Cash's belly tightened. All those people who wanted Ella for their own reasons. Not one of them cared what she wanted. What she needed. She wasn't a person to them. She was an object, a prize to be won. To be used.

He frowned. Had he treated her like an object? He hoped not. Thoughts of her beneath him rolled through his head. Yeah, he'd used her—but he'd given her something in exchange.

But was it enough? Or was he just as guilty as the rest of them?

———

The woman named Victoria was stunning. Absolutely stunning. She was wearing a wedding ring, which Ella was oddly thankful for, but she still managed to draw the eye no matter how hard Ella tried not to stare. Ella attempted to keep her attention on the magazine she was reading, but she did a poor job of it.

Victoria smiled when their gazes met. "It's okay. You can stare."

Busted. "I'm sorry. I'm being rude. But you're so pretty, and yet here you are with a gun strapped to your side. Do you work with Cash?"

Victoria laughed. "A woman can't be pretty *and* lethal in your world? Yes, I work with Cash. Sort of. Mostly I work with another team, but I was here when you arrived, and the colonel asked if I'd stay with you."

"I think I would be fine here alone. Would I not?"

The security they'd gone through to get inside this place had been fairly extensive. She didn't think her aunt and uncle would jump out of any hallways. Nor would Sheikh Fahd, assuming he cared to do so.

"It's not your safety that was in question. It was more that he thought you might not want to be alone."

"Oh." Ella closed the magazine on her lap. "I am accustomed to being alone. It's truly not a problem. If you have things to do, I mean."

"I'm fine. My husband isn't home, and my sister and her husband are busy tonight. I was on the range. Practicing." She pressed her palm to the gun on her hip. It was a big gun.

"I've never shot a gun before."

"No? You should learn how. It's a good skill to have. Especially for a princess, I'd imagine."

"I should. If I'd had a gun the day Cash rescued me, perhaps it never would have come to that. He could have gone on his fishing trip and never met me."

Except the thought of never meeting Cash made a cavern open in her belly.

Victoria unsnapped the strap holding the weapon in place. Then she pulled it out, ejected something from the long handle and dropped it on the table, did something else that made the top of the gun slide back with an audible click—something small and golden fell out of it, but Victoria snatched it up and pocketed it. Then she pulled the top of the gun a couple of more times before walking over and holding it out.

"Here, take it. It's empty. Feel what it's like in your hand."

Ella got to her feet and eyed the weapon. Gingerly, she reached for it.

"It's okay. Don't be afraid of it. You can't hurt anyone. But don't ever point it at a living thing you don't mean to kill, even when it's empty. Got it?"

"Yes." Ella took the gun. It was light in her hand. The

body was black, and the handle was black and sort of rubbery with little nubs on it.

Victoria stood beside her and turned her toward the back wall. "Hold it straight up, one hand wrapped around the grip."

"Grip?"

"The bottom part there."

Ella did as she was instructed. There was a white dot on the front of the weapon and a white U-shaped notch on the back.

"Bring your other hand up, wrap it around this one…" Victoria helped her get the right hand position, wrapping her left hand around her right, positioning both thumbs on the left side of the gun. "Never wrap your thumb around the other side. When the slide comes back as you're firing, it'll hurt something fierce. Keep both thumbs on this side. Now line up the front dot with the tops of the posts on the rear sight. Try to keep both eyes open."

Ella followed the directions. She squinted at first, but then it got easier.

"When you're ready, squeeze the trigger. Slowly."

"But I don't want to shoot."

"It's empty. You aren't going to shoot anything. You're practicing, feeling the give of the trigger."

Ella squeezed and the trigger popped like there was a spring somewhere inside. "Oh."

"Now don't let it out. Hold it for a second. Very slowly, let it out until you feel a little click."

Ella did. The trigger clicked and she stopped.

"Excellent. Now pull the trigger in again."

It popped same as before.

"That's the reset point. You don't have to let it fully out before firing again. That knowledge could save critical seconds—and accuracy—when you need it."

"Wow."

"You've just had your first lesson," Victoria said, taking the weapon away. "It'll be different when you have live ammo, of course, but this is a start."

She picked up the thing she'd tossed on the table. "This is the magazine. It's loaded with bullets."

She handed it to Ella, and Ella turned it around in her hands, studying it. It was heavier than she'd expected. When she handed it back, Victoria took the bullet from her pocket and inserted it into the top of the magazine. Then she jammed the whole thing into the grip of the gun, dragged the slide back quickly, and holstered it again. The entire operation took about a second.

"Why do you pull the top back?"

"Because I'm chambering a round. It's called racking the slide. The gun is ready to fire now. I don't recommend doing that usually, but I'm a professional and this is my job."

Ella was more than a little awestruck at the idea of this woman taking down bad guys. She wanted to know how to do that too. How safe would she feel then? If she had a skill like Victoria's?

The door opened and Ella whirled as Cash came striding in with the same guys as before—and Viking, one of the other guys she'd met back in the cabin a few days ago. She knew him now that she saw him again. Hard to forget with that blond warrior-god thing he had going on.

They were *all* big and imposing men, faces set in grim lines as they filled the room.

Ella's heart skipped a beat. "Is everything okay?"

Cash spoke first. "It's fine, Ella."

"They always look that way," Victoria said, giving Ella a quick grin. "It's in their DNA to be serious."

"Don't let her kid you," Viking said, jerking a thumb at

Victoria. "That's one of the most serious—one of the *scariest*—women I've ever met."

Victoria laughed. "All right, I'm out of here, guys. Unless you still need me?"

"We're good," Cash said. "Thanks for staying."

"No problem. It was great to meet you, Ella. Remember what I said—and get one of these guys to show you more, okay?"

"Okay. Thank you."

"Show you more what?" Cash asked when she was gone.

"How to shoot a gun," Ella said. "I held hers and pulled the trigger."

His eyebrows rose. The other guys didn't seem surprised at all.

"Oh, but there were no bullets," she added.

"Yeah, I kinda figured."

"What happens now, Cash?"

He glanced at his teammates. "We're taking you somewhere safe. Your aunt and uncle are claiming you had no legal right to marry, and they're asking for you to be returned to them."

She must have made a noise or given a look because he reached for her hand and squeezed it.

"You're their queen. Don't forget that part. They can't make you do anything you don't want to do."

No, they couldn't. But that didn't mean they wouldn't try. And if they had her under their control again? It didn't matter if she was a queen if she had no money or power to fight them.

"I have not forgotten."

"Good." He squeezed her hand again. "I won't let them take you, Ella. I promise."

"I know that."

She smiled, though inside she felt nothing but dread. Aunt Flavia and Uncle Gaetano were ruthless people. They'd lied to her for years simply so they could control her. The fact she'd married Cash wouldn't stop them from trying to regain that control—and whatever benefit they stood to gain by selling her in marriage to anyone willing to pay them enough for her.

She'd run away, married Cash, and she still wasn't her own person. Would she ever be free? Or would she always be running?

Chapter Twenty-Four

FORTY-EIGHT HOURS. That's how long he'd been married. He glanced at Ella. His wife.

She was reading again. A romance novel this time. He could tell because of the shirtless guy on the cover and the provocative title. Ella read whatever she could get her hands on. Fortunately, this house they'd ended up at had books. If it hadn't, he wondered what she would do then.

They'd left HOT HQ and driven south to a small house located on five acres. One of Hawk's safe houses. Camel and Blade were with them for now, though the composition of the team would change over the next few days. If nothing happened in the outside world that was deemed a threat to Ella, then the guys would pull out and Cash would take her back to his place and start to help her figure out what she was going to do with her life.

There was no set date for a divorce, but the colonel had said probably a month or so if nothing happened to change it.

One month. Cash turned that over in his mind, expecting relief to flood him at finally having an end date to this ruse.

Instead, he felt nothing but a strange kind of disquiet. Like hearing the low hum of something you couldn't quite identify and therefore couldn't make go away.

The bad part about having his guys here was that Ella had her own room. She might technically be his wife, but this mission was designed with her as the object being guarded. Pretending to a be a couple wasn't necessary in front of the team.

And yet Cash wanted to touch her. Wanted to take her in his arms and explore her passion the way he had last night. There was so much she didn't know yet. So much he wanted to show her.

But maybe it was better this way. He'd worried she would grow attached to him, hadn't he? She couldn't do that if they didn't get personal anymore. If he was one bodyguard among many.

They'd been here for hours now. When they'd first arrived, Ella had gone to bed and taken a nap for a few hours before rising and dressing in a pair of jeans and a tank top with a light sweater to keep from getting a chill. Cash had napped too, but in a different room and not for long before rising again to help the other guys.

He stood and strode over to the window, gazing out at the cloudy sky that threatened rain. Camel was out there, checking the perimeter again, and Blade was on the mission computer. It was a normal, boring day on guard duty. The job they had was challenging and explosive, but much of it was also mundane. The exciting parts were tremendously exciting, but most of it was preparation and waiting for shit to go down.

Blade sat back and ran his hands through his hair.

"What?"

"Nothing," Blade said. "Nothing at all."

Cash took his meaning. There was *nothing* going on,

and no apparent reason for three operators to be stuck out here with a princess. But they all knew it was necessary, at least for now.

Blade stood and stretched, then went over to turn on the television. He sank down on the couch. "Anybody care if I watch *Overhaulin'*?"

"Nope," Cash said.

Ella looked up, blinking like a startled rabbit. "I don't mind."

Cash was pretty sure she didn't even know what *Overhaulin'* was. She met his gaze for a long moment as Blade flipped to the station he wanted. Cash felt a hard sizzle begin in his groin and work its way up the length of his penis until he was as hard as a rock.

What the hell was happening to him? Since when had he just looked at a woman and ached for her?

Ella closed the book and set it on the side table. Then she rose, her eyes on his—her eyes hot—before she walked into the hall and disappeared.

Cash watched her for a long moment. When he looked back at Blade, the man hadn't moved. So he followed Ella. When he reached her bedroom door, it was slightly ajar. He hesitated only a moment before pushing it inward.

She was standing by the bed, hands clasped in front of her body as she faced the door. As if she'd been waiting for him.

"What's going on, Ella?"

"Nothing." She shrugged. "Everything."

"I don't know what that means," he said, shaking his head.

"I don't either. I'm scared, Cash."

It pierced him to the bone. "You don't have to be. I won't let anything happen to you."

"I know you will try. That's all I can hope for."

It killed him that she was worried. That she didn't believe he was going to protect her. "I'll do more than try," he growled.

She dropped her gaze. "I know."

Frustration hammered him. "What more do you want from me?" His voice was only slightly rough.

"I-I don't know," she whispered.

"Ella——" He raked a hand through his hair and forced himself to stay where he was. Not to go over and take her in his arms or lose himself in her.

Her head lifted, her eyes shining. "I want you inside me again," she said on a rush, as if she had to say it fast or not at all. "I want to come with my body wrapped around yours. That is what I want."

Cash closed his eyes. It wasn't just his penis that was hard now. It was all of him. Hard as fucking stone. That wasn't what he'd expected her to say. And yet it was exactly what he wanted to hear if he was honest with himself.

"You've been reading a romance novel."

"Yes. And the hero did wonderful things to the heroine. Things I want too. But I know you aren't a romance hero, Cash. I know this is temporary."

"Do you? Because you don't act like a woman who knows she needs to be careful."

"Careful of what? Of you? I think that horse has left the barn, don't you?"

Cash wanted to laugh. And snarl with rage at the same time. "You aren't a virgin anymore, Princess. We don't have to do anything a second time. The damage is done."

"Damage?" Her eyebrows climbed her forehead. "I don't think of it as damage. I think of it as..." She seemed to be thinking about something.

He prompted her. "As?"

Her dark eyes met his. "A revelation," she said simply.

His gut—his heart—melted with heat and need in a way it never had before. He clicked the door shut behind him and closed the distance between them, taking her in his arms. She didn't hesitate as she wrapped her arms around him.

"You play with fire, Princess," he growled before taking her mouth in a hot kiss.

There was something about kissing Ella. Something about her sweetness and fire that inflamed him beyond measure. He wanted her. *Needed* her. He didn't understand it—didn't much care to at the moment.

He just wanted to bury himself inside her. He was operating on autopilot and unable to disengage the mechanism.

The kiss was scorching hot, tongues tangling, lips pressing tightly together, teeth scraping. Cash filled his hands with Ella's breasts, kneading them before ripping her tank top off and unsnapping her bra.

When his lips closed over one tight little nipple, she cried out, her fingers curling into his shoulders. He licked and sucked both nipples, making them hard and wet and tight beneath his tongue.

Ella wasn't passive though. She tugged his shirt up and off and then ran her hands over his chest, squeezing the muscle, exploring. Cash went for the fly of her jeans, peeling them down her legs and dropping them before he picked her up and pushed her back on the bed.

It didn't take much for him to push her legs open, and then he was falling to his knees between them.

"Cash," she said brokenly. "You don't have to—"

"I want to," he told her. And then he opened her with his fingers and slipped his tongue into her sweetness. Her back bowed off the bed and her breath sucked in, her legs shaking as he licked her again and again.

He showed her no mercy, licking and sucking her sweet flesh until she uttered a sharp cry, her entire body shaking as her orgasm exploded. The whole time, all he could think about was the fact he was the first. The *only*. She was his. His alone.

It was an insane thought for a man who didn't believe in lasting relationships. Who didn't believe in soul mates or finding that one person who completed you. It was all bullshit, perpetuated by those silly books she read and by greeting card companies who wanted to frighten men to death on Valentine's Day. *Buy this shit for your sweetheart or else!*

And yet there was something supremely special about knowing this woman trusted him enough to share her body with him. That he'd been the first one to show her what sex could be like.

She went limp beneath him and he stood to unbuckle his belt and drop his jeans. But he hesitated as he gazed down at her, her skin flushed a pale pink, her eyes heavy, her lips begging for his kiss.

His dick jutted out from his body, hard and ready. Ella pushed up on her elbows, her eyes widening with some effort. Then she sat up until her face was at a level with his dick, and his heart squeezed tight.

"I want to do to you what you did to me," she said, and his every dream came true.

"Ella," he breathed. And then, "No, you don't have to."

She scooted up and wrapped a hand around him as his entire body stiffened. "I want to. Teach me, Cash. Teach me how to make it good for you."

He stood above her, his muscles tight and quivering. Ella squeezed him, her heart hammering. His cock was soft and hot and hard all at once. She didn't wait for him to answer her before she stuck her tongue out and licked around the tip of him.

He groaned, and triumph shot through her. She licked again. He tasted salty at first, but that quickly went away. His hand came up to the back of her head as she opened her mouth and took the tip of him inside.

She'd never done this, but she'd watched the video. She knew what was supposed to happen. She just didn't know how it felt to do it.

Except that now she did, because she opened her mouth wider and took Cash in. He groaned again, his other hand coming up to grasp her hair. He had both hands on either side of her head as he began to slowly move, pushing his way into her mouth and then pulling out again.

It was the most natural thing to put her hands on his hips, to circle them around to his ass and grip him as he pumped in and out of her mouth.

"Ella," he said on a low moan at one point. "Jesus fuck, what the hell are you doing to me?"

She couldn't answer. How could she? Her mouth was full of him.

And her pussy ached with need for him. She dropped a hand to her center, circled her clit with quick fingers as Cash fucked her mouth. His movements grew a little faster, a little harder. Her jaw ached, but she didn't want him to stop. She cupped his balls, kneaded them.

Suddenly he jerked away from her, cussing. A jet of hot semen shot onto her breasts. Cash kept pumping his cock with his fist, spending himself on her skin. She reached up to touch the thick, warm liquid, dragged a finger through it, traced it around her nipple.

Cash was staring at her, his chest rising and falling as if he'd run a couple of miles before engaging in sex. His hot gaze followed her finger as it rounded first one nipple and then the other.

"How in the hell—?" He swallowed. "I don't know whether to hate your aunt or thank her for showing you porn."

Ella leaned back on the bed and grinned. "You should thank her. It's probably the one thing she did right."

Because she wasn't afraid of sex. Not really. She'd been worried about how much it would hurt the first time, but really that hadn't been so bad. And now? Now she wanted to try everything with this man. She craved him like a drug. She didn't fear him.

She wanted everything he could give her—and more. Ella pushed that last thought aside. She didn't want to think of the more, or what it meant. She couldn't. Because that way lay heartbreak. Cash didn't feel the same and never would. He'd told her so more than once.

"I wanted to be inside you," he growled. "But you fucking ruined that."

Ella blinked. "Did I? Is it ruined? I thought you enjoyed it."

"I enjoyed it, Princess. I wanted to enjoy it longer." He scraped a hand through his hair. "The last time I came that fast, I was probably sixteen."

She looked down at his cock. It was still erect. "Can't you go again?"

"Soon, baby." He went into the adjoining bathroom and came back with a towel that he used to wipe the semen off her chest. Then he dropped it and sank down on top of her, thrusting his tongue into her mouth and taking her that way for long moments.

Ella sighed into his mouth. She loved the feel of his body on hers, the simple act of kissing him. How much her life had changed over the past few days. How much she wanted it to continue with him as a part of it.

"Damn, you are hot," he said after they'd been kissing for a while. "So fucking hot."

"You're kinda hot too, Cash."

"You sure you're up to this?"

She still ached from the first time, but there was no way she was saying no to this man. Not when her body burned so hot it hurt. She nodded.

He rolled over and took her with him until she was on top. "You control it this time," he told her. "Do what feels good."

He reached for the bedside table. He'd laid a condom there when he'd returned from the bathroom. He handed it to her, and she tore it open as she lifted herself to sit upright, straddling him. It wasn't hard to roll on, and when she was finished she climbed up and sank slowly down. Her body stretched, sore tissues burning with the intrusion.

As if he sensed her discomfort, he slipped his fingers between them and began to stroke her clit in slow, teasing circles. Her body relaxed as sparks zipped along her nerve endings, sharpening the pleasurable sensations and dulling the painful ones.

Cash slid his other hand around and teased her back entrance, and the sparks zipping through her turned into comets. She moved faster, rising and falling, her heart beating harder, her breath catching in her throat as the pleasure grew nearly unbearable.

"Cash," she cried out as the world exploded into a million stars.

"Yeah, Ella. Like that. Honey, you are so beautiful when you come. You make me ache with need."

"I love—" Ella swallowed, her belly clenching with the weight of what she'd nearly said to him. The words that would have changed everything. Her, him, the way they were together. "I love the way you make me feel," she choked out. "The things we do together."

"I love it too," he said, his voice husky. And then he rolled her beneath him and began to move, seeking his own climax. When it hit him, when his body stiffened and his hips jerked, Ella buried her face against his neck and bit his salty skin as first one tear and then another slid down her cheeks.

She'd been trying to avoid disaster when she'd escaped her wedding to Sheikh Fahd. Instead, she'd run headlong into it. Her heart was never going to be the same.

Chapter Twenty-Five

THE DAYS PASSED much quicker than Cash thought they would. He'd expected the time spent away from work and civilization would probably be boring, but it turned out to be anything but. He taught Ella to shoot a pistol, and she took to it like a fish to water, handling the Glock with skill and confidence. After a few days' practice, she could make a nice cluster in the center of a target.

But it was the other thing that happened between them that made the days fun. Namely, he and Ella couldn't keep their hands off each other. Oh, they did a good job of it while his teammates were around, but the second they had opportunity, they disappeared into her bedroom to fuck like rabbits.

He took her up against the wall, in the shower, on her hands and knees, in front of the mirrored dresser where he could watch every shudder of pleasure rippling over her creamy, smooth skin. He made her come innumerable times, biting her fist, biting the pillow, biting him while she muffled her cries.

He fucked her hard and soft, fast and slow, over and

over. There wasn't anything about Ella's pleasure he didn't know by now. He'd tasted her, savored her, teased her into oblivion. He'd come hard and often inside her body, always cloaked since she wasn't on any birth control, but he longed to fuck her with nothing between them. To really feel her silken heat gloving him as he stroked into her tight, wet pussy.

That was a fantasy that would have to wait. If it ever happened. Because this thing between them had to end. It had been over a week since he'd taken her virginity, and though he wasn't exactly tired of fucking her, he would be before this was over. He knew he would because it was coded into his DNA. Cash McQuaid did not stick with the same woman for more than a few rounds. He was like his dad in that respect. A serial womanizer who engaged in shallow relationships at best while looking for the next hot body to give him a new fix—though his dad had succumbed to marriage twice for some reason.

Maybe that's why Cash's stepmother had hated him. He'd been his father's mini-me, the same good looks, the same swagger. Maybe looking at him reminded her too much of what his father got up to when he was by himself. The nights he came home late, stinking of beer and whiskey and, no doubt, a hint of feminine perfume.

Then again, his father had met her in a bar, so she'd known exactly what she was getting when she married Dan McQuaid. Her problem, not Cash's. Even if he hadn't known why she hated him when he was a kid.

The first light of dawn crept across the floor of Ella's bedroom. Cash spent all his nights in here with her. His teammates knew. Of course they did. Nobody said anything, but they weren't stupid. The first time someone had given him a sly look and a wink, he'd returned it with a stony face that said *don't go there or I'll clean your clock.*

He didn't want them thinking those thoughts about Ella. She was sweet in her sexuality, pure. She didn't have any inhibitions, but she'd also never encountered anyone who tried to make her feel dirty for liking or engaging in sex.

Holy hell, he loved that she loved sex. He loved bending her over and sliding into her from behind, watching his cock sink into her and knowing that he was the only one who'd ever done that to her. All the begging and pleading she did with him to make her come was for him alone. She'd never asked anyone else to do those things to her. It was a huge turn-on.

Yeah, it surely was, because he was growing hard again. She lay beside him, naked, on her belly with one leg bent and the other straight. So pretty. It wouldn't take much to wake her. He could slip inside her, stroke her into an orgasm, and give them both a hell of wake-up call.

Except his phone buzzed on the dresser, ruining the fantasy. He fumbled for it, finally grabbing it, and read the text. It was from Camel.

Wakey wakey, sleepyhead. Blade says orders from HQ.

Shit. Cash sat up and slipped from the bed. He grabbed his jeans and dragged them on, then shuffled to the door and opened it quietly. He closed it behind him and walked down the hall, jaw cracking in a yawn as he entered the kitchen.

His teammate looked at him. There was no smirk, but there was a frown.

"You know, if you'd actually do some sleeping instead of—"

"Watch it," Cash interrupted, knowing what word was likely coming next. "That's my wife you're talking about."

Camel rolled his eyes. "Pretend wife, *amigo*. Even if you're really married to her, it's not real and you aren't in love. You are in lust though. That much is obvious."

A peal of anger rolled through him like thunder. "It's not like that."

"Really? You planning to stay married then? Start a family? Because you sure are spending enough time practicing on your wedded bliss."

"Camel, for fuck's sake," Cash growled.

Blade walked in from the opposite direction and poured a cup of coffee. "You two fighting again? Maybe y'all should get married instead of Money and Ella. They allow that kind of thing in the military now."

Camel frowned.

Cash growled some more. "Yeah, that'd be great if I liked sucking dick," Cash said. "Not my thing. Though maybe it's Camel's."

"Don't know," Camel said coolly. "Never tried it."

"Jesus, can you two stop? You're giving me a fucking headache."

Cash didn't know why, but he suddenly found that funny. "Just when Camel was about to offer to suck your dick."

"Nope," Camel said. "Not happening. Though I'd let either one of you suck mine under the right circumstances. Namely, the end of civilization as we know it and the death of every last woman alive."

"So what are the orders?" Cash asked.

Blade sipped his coffee. "Colonel says we're to return to HQ. Beyond that, I don't know."

"Maybe you're off the hook," Camel said. "Maybe

there'll be divorce papers waiting for you. Sign 'em and you're free."

Cash frowned. Divorce papers. He should want those pretty badly, but all he could think about was Ella lying in bed in the next room, her body naked beneath the sheets. If he went to her now, she'd be warm and wet and perfect. And he'd be lost.

"Yeah, maybe so," he said, his mind half on Ella and half here.

Blade snorted. "Yeah, I don't think you want a divorce."

Cash frowned. Of course he wanted a divorce. Because what would it mean if he didn't? "Can't happen soon enough. I don't want or need a wife."

Camel cleared his throat. Cash frowned harder.

"What? You think just because I spend a lot of time alone with Ella, it means something? It doesn't, asshole. It's nothing more than what it looks like, okay? Soon as this is over, we're going our separate ways—and you and I can double-date with those babes you were talking about last week."

Camel was making faces at him. Significant faces. Cash closed his eyes as the truth began to dawn on him. *Shit.*

He knew who he'd see when he turned around. He didn't know what she would look like. Devastated? Angry? Embarrassed?

He pulled in a breath and turned. A rock sat in his belly at the sight of her. Beautiful, sensual Ella. She didn't look pissed or embarrassed. She looked haughty. Regal.

Of course she did.

"What's for breakfast?" she asked coolly.

Camel nearly tripped over himself heading for the pantry and swinging it open. "Cereal? Bagels? Or would you like some eggs and bacon?"

Ella glided over to the island, her face showing no emotion whatsoever. Except for the tightness at the corners of her mouth, he wouldn't have known she was affected by anything he'd said.

"Ella," he began.

She held up an elegant hand, silencing him. Such a princess, his girl. *His girl?*

"No explanations, Cash. We both know what this is. And we'll both be happy when it's over and our lives begin again." To Camel she said, "Cereal is fine. Thank you."

Camel brought out every box they had, as if they hadn't all been here a week and didn't know what was in the pantry. Ella selected one. Blade got a bowl, milk, and a spoon and set it in front of her.

She didn't move, and they rushed to pour everything for her. Cash watched in amazement. His heart throbbed. He wanted to grip her chin and press his mouth to hers. Then he wanted to take her back to the bedroom and claim her in the most primitive way he knew how.

That wasn't going to be possible anytime soon. Hell, it might never be possible again if there were divorce papers waiting at HQ. He'd have to sign them. She'd sign them. They'd go their separate ways.

Everything inside him rebelled against the idea. She was *his*.

His teammates were watching him. His emotions were in turmoil. If he stood there much longer, he'd do something desperate. Like get down on his knees and beg her forgiveness—and to hell with his teammates and the incessant ribbing he'd endure for it.

Cash grabbed a cup, poured some coffee, and walked outside where the early morning air could clear his head.

"I'm sorry," Cash said.

Ella didn't look at him. Her heart pounded but she didn't look. She wanted to, but if she did she'd melt. Because her heart had fallen for this man, and she didn't know how to make it stop.

She loved him—desperate, lonely fool that she was—and he couldn't wait to be rid of her. To eject her from his life.

You've always known he didn't want to be married.

Yes, she'd known. But she'd begun to hope. The way he touched her, the way they were together—yes, it had made her hope. But what did she know about sex other than what he'd taught her? For all she knew, it was this way with everyone when you were attracted to them. Still, deep down, she'd felt as if what they had was something special.

Clearly she'd been wrong.

Ella closed her eyes as the hopes she'd cherished struggled frantically against the chains she'd bound them in. Because she couldn't set them free again. It would only hurt more than it already did. He'd told her what the score was when they'd embarked on this journey. He'd tried to keep her at a distance so she wouldn't get hurt, but she'd insisted on getting closer.

Her fault. All her fault.

"It doesn't matter," she replied. "You only told them the truth."

They were standing in the bedroom where she'd gone to get her things. He'd followed her. Just like that first day when they'd arrived here. She'd wanted him so badly. She'd been reading a romance novel. A sexy one that made her ache inside, especially when she thought of Cash doing all the things to her that the hero did to the heroine.

Cash had followed her into this bedroom and made every fantasy she had come true. She was definitely not a virgin anymore—nor was she naïve or inexperienced. Cash had showed her everything, given her everything.

Ella shook herself. Today was different. Today they were leaving. Returning to the building where she'd met Victoria and held a gun for the first time. She had no idea what was going to happen today, but she had to be prepared for anything.

Even divorce papers and a goodbye. Because Cash wouldn't mind those things at all. He'd said so just half an hour ago.

He blew out a breath. "It's none of their business, okay? I reacted because they wouldn't leave me alone about being married to you."

Ella managed to lift her head and meet his gaze. His green eyes were troubled. She could almost feel sorry for him if she weren't so angry and hurt by what he'd said.

"You did what you had to do."

He gripped her arms. "I like you, Ella. A lot. I don't want to hurt you."

"I know that. You've been nothing but helpful. You saved me, Cash. I'll never forget that."

"You're talking like this is goodbye."

"Isn't that what you want?"

He exploded. "No. It's not what I want."

"But you want a divorce."

He let her go and stepped away. "It's not a real marriage. It's not like we dated for months and decided to get hitched. We don't even know each other. Not really."

"You know everything about me there is to know. I've left nothing out."

"It's not enough. Right now this thing between us is about sex. It's new and exciting. But that's not enough to base a marriage on. We aren't *married* for real. We're pretending to be married because it's what had to be done."

She was trying to understand him. "So it's fine to keep having sex? But not to be married?"

He frowned. "You're twisting this."

"You're fine with a divorce, but you don't want the sex to be over. That's what you said. You specifically do not want to say goodbye yet. Surely that's not for my sparkling conversation alone."

He blinked. "I never said I didn't like talking to you."

"We don't talk, Cash. Not much anyway."

His brows drew down. "We talk about the things that matter."

"Do we?"

There was a knock on the door before he could reply.

"Time to hit the road," Camel called out.

"Yeah, yeah," Cash said.

Ella started for the door, but he caught her by the arm and swung her around. Then he took a step into her and kissed her hard. Ella's anger started to melt whether she wanted it to or not. She tried to resist, but her body had other ideas. Ideas that would have seen them naked and entwined if there were time.

Cash broke the kiss and stared down at her with flashing eyes. "We aren't finished, Ella. I promise you that."

Chapter Twenty-Six

HE WAS LOSING his fucking mind. Cash had never felt this way before. Hell, he didn't know what *this way* even was, but he wanted to destroy anyone who got between him and Ella. Not because she was his wife or anything. It was just that she was so innocent and sweet and he didn't want her hurt.

He wanted to protect her. Help her transition to her new life. And he damned sure didn't want to be the one who hurt her.

He had though. He knew he had, and it bothered him. He'd tried to apologize, but in true Ella fashion, she'd gotten all stoic and unemotional on him. Accepting of her fate even when she was scared inside. He knew she was scared because he knew her. Because, damn her, they *had* talked over the past week. About a lot of things.

He hated how she shut down and pretended not to care, but that too was Ella.

Ella, the girl who'd lived for fourteen years with no emotional support besides books and movies. The girl who'd learned to have sex from pornography but wanted the kind of love she read about in romance novels.

Jesus.

He couldn't give her that love, but he could be more careful with her. He could avoid talking about double dates with Camel and how he couldn't wait for a divorce.

His gut twisted at the thought of the word. *Divorce.*

Yeah, he wanted it. Of course he did. But he didn't need to keep repeating it in front of Ella for God's sake. She had enough to deal with.

He went out and got into the SUV, joining his teammates and Ella. They rode the hour back to HOT HQ without much conversation. Mostly they listened to satellite radio. Ella grooved to Taylor Swift, Ariana Grande, Gina Domenico, Demi Lovato, and Bruno Mars. She knew all the words.

They made it back to headquarters just as the workday was getting started. Colonel Mendez met them in a conference room that was not in the secure area of the facility. Ghost walked in behind him, his expression unreadable.

Ella was sitting in a chair, hands folded over her belly, her expression serene. Cash would bet she was anything but serene. She'd learned to hide her emotions over the years so she didn't rouse the ire of her aunt and uncle. She was using that skill now, he was certain.

Mendez introduced himself to her. She stood and put her hand in his.

Holy shit, was she stammering? Fuck. Mendez had that effect on women even though he was probably old enough to be Ella's dad. Bastard was good-looking and confident as hell though. Not to mention he was a certifiable badass. After that shit in Russia not too long ago, the man was practically a celebrity in Special Ops circles.

Ghost was quieter but no less interesting. Cash didn't know his story yet. Nobody really did, come to think of it.

"I imagine you're ready to get on with your life," Mendez said to Ella after the introductions were made.

"I would like that, yes. I'm grateful for all you've done to make it possible," she said. "For all Cash has done."

"It's what we do, Ella." She had, predictably, told everyone to call her Ella rather than by her royal title. "But we aren't quite done yet. We've been doing our research—and it seems you're the owner of the Virginia estate that your aunt and uncle live on. Not only that, but the entire Rossi fortune belongs to you as well. They've been living off allowances from your funds, not the other way around."

Ella looked stunned. She put a hand to her throat. Cash wanted to go to her, but she didn't once look at him. "I… Wow."

"I've been talking to Jack Hunter this morning. Gina's attorneys are ready to help you sort everything out if you wish to use their firm. You can sell the estate or live on it. It's up to you. But there's no doubt it all belongs to you. Your aunt and uncle no longer have access to any of the accounts as of late yesterday."

"I'm not sure…"

"It's a lot to decide. You don't have to figure it out yet." Mendez glanced at Cash. "There's also the matter of your marriage to my operator. You can divorce, though I'd recommend staying married a while longer. At least until the media attention dies down in a month or two."

Cash's gut roiled. He had no say in this—but he wanted one. Still, he kept his mouth shut and waited to see what she would say.

"I… am I free to go?" Ella asked.

"If that's what you want. Jack can send a private security detail for you. If you and Cash want to work something out where you stay with him for a few days, that's an option too."

She didn't even look at him. "No, that's all right. I'll hire Jack's people. And I'll get a hotel room." She looked confused for a moment. "I can do that, right?"

"You can. It's your money, Ella. It's always been yours."

She frowned. "I wish I'd known that a long time ago."

"It's not your fault you didn't. My guys will stay with you until you have your security in place. I'll have my secretary book a hotel room for you. You can meet with attorneys and security personnel there. When you're satisfied, you can dismiss my operators. You and Cash can arrange for the divorce paperwork at your convenience."

"Thank you. I'm so grateful for your help." She turned her gaze on Cash finally, but it skittered away and danced over to Blade and Camel. "All of you. I owe you so much."

"You don't owe us anything," Camel said before Cash could find any words. "This is what we do."

Her gaze slid to him again for the briefest of moments. He got the distinct impression she was dismissing him from her life when her gaze moved away.

"I will never forget you," she said softly. "Never."

Something boiled up inside him. "Colonel," he interjected, his voice sounding strained. "How can we be sure Ella is safe? What about Fahd?"

Mendez fixed him with that dark, piercing stare. "This isn't a military operation, son. We've done everything we can, and Ella now has the ability to hire her own security. She won't be unprotected. As for Fahd, he's still in Qu'rim —and he's arranged to marry another princess."

There was nothing Cash could say to that. Fahd was an opportunist, and he'd clearly pounced on another opportunity when this one hadn't worked out. He'd never been interested in Ella so much as he'd been interested in what he perceived he could gain from her status as a queen in exile. If he'd found someone else to exploit, then all the better for Ella.

Mendez turned back to Ella and took her hand again. "It's been a pleasure, Ella. Should you need anything from us in the future, you can contact us through Jack. He can always get in touch with us."

"Thank you. I hope I won't need anything, but it's nice to know."

Mendez and Ghost left the room. Cash frowned hard at Camel and Blade. Finally Camel rolled his eyes.

"Hey man, let's go get some coffee. I didn't have nearly enough this morning."

"You drank four cups," Blade said, clearly not taking the hint.

"Yeah, well, I need more. My eyes aren't twitching yet."

"Get out," Cash said. "Now."

Blade's eyebrows rose. Then he snorted. Cash didn't much care.

"Yeah, fine, I get it. So, coffee then. Let's roll."

They both walked out, and Cash was left alone with Ella. He didn't move. She didn't either. She'd sat back down and she lifted her head to meet his gaze head-on. But she made no movements toward him.

Damn her.

"I don't want to end like this," he finally said when the silence stretched too long.

Ella laughed and shook her head. "Cash, you've wanted nothing but an end since you first picked me up. What's changed besides the obvious?"

He blinked. "The obvious? What are you talking about?"

She folded her arms over her chest. Glared. "Money."

"That's my name. So what?" He wasn't used to her calling him by his team name, but whatever.

"No," she said, shaking her head. "I'm talking about *my* money. It seems I have some now."

He frowned at her. Hard. Anger flared. "You think I'm interested in your *money?*" He was indignant. "Princess, I went to bat for you when you had nothing but the clothes on your back. I've jumped through hoops for you, married you when you were poor, protected you—until five minutes ago, you had absolutely nothing." He held up both hands, the anger spiraling hard within him. "You know what? Fuck it. I don't give a shit. You want nothing to do with me now, fine. But money has nothing to do with what's happened between us. Nothing at all."

Ella shot to her feet, her face red with the sudden emotion she couldn't contain. "Then what *does*, Cash? What's it about? Do you care about me? Want to be with me? Because I care about you, you dumb ass. You told me I wouldn't be able to keep my feelings separate from the sex, and you were right! I care. I'm head over heels in caring about you. I don't want to lose you or this thing we have, but I don't want to go on either." She pressed a balled-up fist to her chest. "I don't want to keep going knowing I'm the only one whose heart is on the line. The only one who feels more than desire. I want more from you, Cash."

He was stunned into silence. Simply stunned. What she was saying… God, it terrified him. Because it wasn't real. It was just hormones and emotions and some really, really hot sex talking.

She closed the distance between them. Put her hand on

his chest. Her eyes glittered with unshed tears as she gazed up at him. She was the most beautiful woman he'd ever laid eyes on.

"I want *this*, Cash," she whispered. "I want your heart. If you can't give that to me, then maybe it's best if we do say goodbye."

———

She hadn't intended to say any of those things to him. But he'd gotten so mad when she'd mentioned the money—and yes, she'd known she shouldn't do that; she'd known it wasn't about money at all—that she'd lost whatever control she'd been holding on to.

She hadn't wanted him to know she cared. Hadn't wanted him to know he'd been right and she'd been a silly virgin all along, falling for the first man to have sex with her.

But he did know because she'd lost control of her tongue.

She stood with her hand pressed to his heart for what seemed forever but was in reality only moments. That organ beat strong and hard—maybe a little more quickly than usual—beneath her palm.

Something flickered in his gaze and hope flared for the briefest of moments. But then it died when his gaze shuttered and all emotion went dormant. Cash was good at shutting down. Good at keeping his distance.

Except for the moments when he'd been buried inside her, whispering hot words in her ear while he came. Then he'd been open and raw. But he always put distance between them after.

"I don't know if I can," he said, his voice on edge.

She dropped her palm away, balled it into a fist at her

side as if to keep his warmth and the essence of his heart-beat with her always.

"Then I can't go on this way," she said sadly. "I'm like an infant in some ways, you know. I have to learn how to live on my own, to forge relationships with others, to pay bills and build the life I was never allowed to have. I would do that beside you, with you—but you don't seem to want that. You want me in your bed, but not in your heart. It's not enough for me, Cash."

He shoved his hands in his pockets. So cool. So unaf-fected. "I don't know how to do that, Ella. I—" He swore. "I had a shit childhood. I don't know what love is. I've never had it, so I don't know how to give it."

Ella arched an eyebrow. "I had a shit childhood too—at least after my parents died. Love is what makes you so happy inside that you could burst. Love is wanting the best for someone else, even if the best for them isn't necessarily the best for you. Just because it makes them happy."

"I want you to be happy."

"I would be happy with you."

He blew out a breath and moved away from her. Her heart crumbled as he did so. Because she'd lost him in that moment.

"You only think you would, Ella. You have no idea what my life is like. You're a princess, and now you can have the lifestyle to go with it. I'm a SEAL. I live my life on the edge. I leave for weeks at a time, often with little notice, and there's always a chance I won't come back again. That's not a life you want."

Ella frowned. "I think I get to be the judge of what kind of life I want."

"Yeah, you do. But you need to try this other life before you make that kind of call. You're still young. Sheltered.

You have to experience more than just a forced marriage with me."

Her heart throbbed. "So you want me to date other men? Sleep with other men?"

He stiffened. Growled. Subsided. "That's up to you."

Ella wanted to scream. Just moments ago he'd said he didn't want it to end like this, and now he was shoving her away like she'd just revealed she had the most deadly, contagious virus ever discovered.

She started to tremble. It was anger, not fear.

"You have no guts, Cash McQuaid. You're a coward—oh, not in the big stuff," she said as he spun on her, eyes flashing. "You'll face down a hundred armed men with your bare hands, but you won't once risk letting down the guard around your heart. Even if it means you get hurt, even if nothing turns out the way you expect it to and you have to pick up the pieces later, you have to take risks—otherwise, what the hell are you doing with your life?"

Chapter Twenty-Seven

WHAT THE HELL was he doing with his life?

Cash had been asking himself that question for the past five days. After that explosive confrontation with Ella, things had happened fast. Blade and Camel had returned to the room. The colonel's secretary had arrived with information about the hotel she'd booked—the Ritz, of course. Nothing but the finest for a princess.

He and his teammates had taken Ella to the hotel and gotten her settled. That was the point at which things spiraled out of his control. He'd been angry, but he'd thought they would still have a chance to talk once they'd both cooled down. Maybe he'd banked on her fondness for him to make it happen. Or maybe he thought they'd be left alone at some point and he'd have his chance.

He'd been sadly mistaken. As soon as they arrived at the hotel, the calls and parade of people started. Lawyers, hairstylists, personal shoppers, real estate agents, bankers, and finally, a new security team.

Cash hadn't wanted to leave her there with Hawk's people, especially since these were different people than the ones who'd been with them in Vegas, but he'd had no choice. Once Hawk's team signed on, the SEALs were done. They had jobs to do and missions to prepare for back at HQ.

So he'd been coming in early for the past five days, spending time on the gun range blowing up targets—and blowing off aggression—while watching the news for glimpses of Ella.

He'd been rewarded a few times. There was footage of him and Ella in Las Vegas, but no mention of the state of their marriage. When Ella was asked where he was, she said he was busy working. Mendez had said they should stay married for another month or two, but for all Cash knew, a set of divorce papers could arrive any day.

Ella's aunt and uncle were out on bond after being charged with fraud. They'd been forced to vacate the Virginia mansion where they'd been living for the past twenty years, along with Ella's cousins. Apparently her father had owned the estate as well as the Rossi fortune, and it had only ever been in trust to her aunt and uncle while they raised her. She'd been due to inherit everything on her twenty-first birthday, which had come and gone while her aunt and uncle kept racking up the debt and forging documents in Ella's name.

Sheikh Fahd stayed in the Middle East, doing deals for oil and secretly—or not so secretly—supporting the Freedom Force in their bid to overthrow the king.

Cash was happy for Ella. He was also somewhat jealous of the man who always appeared with her. He was a security guard, but a handsome one who always seemed to have a hand on her elbow or against her back, guiding her. Former military, because Cash recognized the posture and mannerisms. Maybe he'd already insinuated himself into Ella's bed.

That was a thought that sent Cash back to the range with more ammunition. When he started pretending the targets wore that guy's face, he knew it was time to quit for the day.

"Hey, going to Buddy's?" Camel asked when they bumped into each other in the locker room.

Buddy's Bar & Grill was a spot where they hung out during their off time, playing pool, eating fried food, and watching sports on the various televisions hung around the place. It wasn't fancy, but it was good food and cheap entertainment.

He didn't want to go. He'd have to be social, have to pretend nothing was eating him up inside while he laughed and flirted with the waitresses.

And then, because it pissed him off that he'd even considered saying no when he never would have before, he said, "Yeah, I'm going."

Cash did his workout, cleaned up, and headed out for Buddy's. Everyone was there when he walked in. The noise practically knocked him back through the door when he opened it. Laughter and voices swarmed over him in an aural wave that froze him on the spot. He started to turn and go, but Viking waved at him.

Cash walked inside, let the door shut behind him, and headed over to their group, which was gathered around a couple of tables. Alpha Squad was there and Echo as well. The tables were packed with operators and their significant others. Cash surveyed the scene as he strode over.

Viking and Ivy. Cage and Christina. Cowboy and Miranda. Richie Rich and Evie. Knight Rider and Georgie. Billy the Kid and Olivia. Kev and Lucky. Hawk and Gina, as incognito as she could possibly be in a bar with a hat hiding all that famous blond hair. Brandy and Victoria. Iceman and Grace. Flash and Emily. Fiddler and

Sophie. Double Dee and Annabelle. The only ones missing were Mendez and Kat, but nobody really expected the commander and his lady to hang out with the operators.

Ghost was there too, but over in a corner with a leggy brunette with long, daggerlike nails. The deputy commander liked to drop in from time to time, check things out. At least Ian Black wasn't there, though Cash wouldn't put it past him to show up. Not that anybody really liked Black.

Especially not Cash, since one of the times he'd been on an operation with Black, he'd taken a shot in the arm when a group of tribal nomads tried to kill them all in the desert. That was when they'd rescued Christina and a group of civilians who'd gotten caught in Qu'rim when the rebels took the capital city of Baq.

"Hey, Cash Money," Camel said, ambling over from the pool table, cue stick still in his hand. Blade was still playing pool with their other teammates, Ryan "Dirty Harry" Callahan and Zack "Neo" Anderson.

"Hey, man."

Camel had a beer in his other hand. "Remember those girls I told you about?"

Cash frowned. "Not really, no."

Camel tipped his head to the bar where two busty blondes with short skirts sat drinking fruity drinks.

"Not interested, Camel. Get one of the other guys to join you. Or, hell, take them both home and have a great time."

Camel shook his head. "Dude, you still pining after your princess?"

Cash's gut boiled. "Nope, not pining at all. Just not interested."

Camel closed the distance between them until they were inches apart. Cash didn't move.

"Know what I think?" Camel asked.

"Nope. Don't care either."

"Man, you're an idiot, you know that? Ella is amazing, and you're the lucky jackass who got to pluck her off that road and marry her. You spent a whole week using every excuse in the book to be alone with her—I know you weren't playing checkers in that bedroom—and now you aren't interested in hot, easy, no-strings sex when it's staring you in the face? Yeah, you're hung up over your princess. Wishing you could take her to bed and do every dirty thing you can think of with her instead of one of those ladies at the bar."

"Camel," he growled, considering punching the dude in the nose and to hell with it. "Get out of my face with that shit. And *don't* talk about Ella like that."

"Like what, jerk-off? I got nothing but mad respect for that gorgeous babe. You're the one with the dirty mind where she's concerned."

"She's still my wife. I'm allowed."

Camel snorted. "You're in over your head, Money. I don't know what the hell you did, but you need to pull your head out of your ass and get to her hotel room before one of Hawk's dudes romances her out from under you."

Cash blinked. And blinked. His heart twisted in his chest. His belly churned. He thought of Ella beneath him, her eyes closed in blissful enjoyment, her lower lip caught between her teeth before she stiffened and let out a short, sharp cry of pleasure. Her breasts jiggled, her pussy gripped him hard as her orgasm rolled over her, and he couldn't get enough of her reaction.

He'd made it last on purpose. Teased and tormented her into just one more second of bliss. He'd thought, when his dick was inside her body and his tongue in her mouth, that there was nowhere else he'd rather be in this world.

He missed that feeling. Wanted it back again. Hell, he didn't know if it was love—didn't think it was, actually—but he was willing to find out. Or maybe he didn't know shit and this *was* love. He still didn't trust that the rug wouldn't be yanked out from under him. He didn't trust because he'd learned not to as a kid. His mother leaving. His stepmother ignoring him unless she wanted to prove to his dad that she cared before ignoring him again. People who were supposed to care couldn't be trusted. They had agendas, and not one of those agendas was in his best interest.

But Ella. Jesus, sweet Ella. She had no reason whatso-ever to need him now. To want him. She was a princess with money of her own. She didn't need a Navy SEAL. She needed some dude who could treat her right.

You can treat her right, Cash. Wealth or lack of it has nothing to do with this.

He glanced at Hawk and Gina. They were happy. Their hands were always entwined, or their arms were around each other. They touched and kissed. And Gina had more money than God. Didn't seem to bother Hawk.

"Hey, man—you okay?" Camel asked.

Cash shook his head and focused on his teammate. Clarity was a blinding thing when it finally struck—and it had thanks to this dumb jerk. Cash grinned. "Don't take this the wrong way, but I could totally kiss you right now."

Camel backed up a couple of steps. "Dude, you've lost your mind."

"No, I think I've found it." He settled for wrapping a shocked Camel in a quick bear hug. And then, because Cash loved a good joke as well as anyone, he planted a kiss on Camel's cheek.

"Aw, fucking hell," Camel said. "You just cost me a hot night with those two ladies."

"Nah, I doubt it. They might even think you're hotter now."

Cash strode over to where Alpha Squad sat. Hawk looked up at him with interest. Gina stood and gave him a hug.

"Honey," she said softly. "How are you?"

"Fine, thanks."

"But not with Ella." She sighed. "I had such hopes."

Cash shook his head. "You always have hopes. You'd pair off everyone in this bar if you could."

Gina flashed her megawatt smile. "I'd like to try."

"How's it going, Money?" Hawk asked.

"I need to see Ella. Can you get your guys to let me in? But don't tell her I'm on my way," he added.

Hawk took out his phone. "Sure. I'll let them know you're coming."

"Thanks."

Cash took his keys from his pocket and flipped them around his finger while waiting for Hawk to give him the all clear. A few seconds later, it came.

"Good luck," Hawk said. Gina smiled a knowing smile and Cash gave her a salute.

"You're diabolical," he told her. "But smart."

Gina laughed. "Go get your girl, Cash. You can thank me later."

Cash headed out to the parking lot and climbed into his Mustang with the bullet hole he hadn't gotten fixed yet. He needed to, but it was like erasing Ella somehow. He took a deep breath. He had no idea what he was going to say to her when he got there, or if she'd even listen.

Still, it was a twenty-minute ride. He'd think of something. He had to.

It had been a long day. Ella kicked her shoes off and walked into the exquisite master bath of her hotel suite. When she got there, she frowned at her reflection. Her eyes were sad, her expression dark and unhappy.

Why?

She'd gotten more than she'd hoped for when she'd run from her wedding day. She'd just wanted her freedom. She'd gotten so much more—and with it came restrictions of a different kind.

She was sought after by reporters, bankers, lawyers, companies wanting sponsorship deals. She had to deal with the tangled mess of the Rossi estate while also trying to discern if the people advising her were giving the best advice. Since they'd come with a recommendation from Gina, she thought they were.

Yet after so many years of being uninvolved, it was her responsibility to make sure she understood everything her lawyers wanted.

First there was the Virginia estate to deal with. She thought of keeping it but ultimately decided it had to go. She'd never been happy there. Why prolong her memories by tossing out her aunt and uncle and cousins and moving back in? She hated the place and all it represented, so it was going on the market.

Then there was the purchase of a new home. She didn't want a mansion. She wanted something much smaller, more easily managed. She'd been to Gina and Hawk's home on the Eastern Shore. She liked it. It was a big house, but not a huge house. Built in the style of a historic home—or renovated, she wasn't sure which—it was classic and elegant. A real home instead of a showy place meant to impress guests.

That's what she wanted, so she set her lawyers and her real estate agent to the task of finding such a place—or finding property where she could build. A view was imperative. Security was imperative.

There was the money to deal with as well. Her aunt and uncle had run down the family fortunes quite a bit, but only so far as they could get their hands on it. There were vast sums they'd been unable to touch. She didn't know how they'd intended to obtain them, though she thought it might have had something to do with her marriage. Perhaps they'd agreed to split the money with Sheikh Fahd.

She'd come into her fortune at the age of twenty-one, but there were other sums in trust that she could not reach until she was twenty-five. Perhaps her parents had known what kind of people her aunt and uncle were after all.

Whatever the case, Ella now had more money than she could ever spend. She was rich—and she was still alone. Her parents were never coming back. Her aunt and uncle and cousins despised her.

And Cash… Oh God, Cash. The man she loved with all her being, even though she'd been telling herself for a week now that it wasn't real. That she'd been silly and virginal and that he was right after all. She needed more experience. More time. She should totally be fucking the hot bodyguard that Hawk had provided her—

But she couldn't. She wanted Cash, not Ben. Ben was indeed hot—but he wasn't Cash. Wasn't the man who'd been so sweet and tender with her, who'd taken her virginity and still made the experience pleasurable.

Oh God, she missed him.

Ella pinched her cheeks to stop the tears and dragged in a few deep breaths. She would get over this. *She would.*

She changed into a pair of silk pajama pants and a silky tank, then tied a robe over her sleepwear. She slipped on a pair of fuzzy mule slippers, feeling decadent in the small heel with the furry pom-pom on top.

Tonight she was reading a book and going to bed early. Tomorrow she'd start again with the estate management.

Ella settled onto the couch. There was a knock on the door of the suite. Her bodyguard was in the living area and would answer it. It was probably room service. She'd ordered a salad and steak—she'd wanted the pasta, but it made her think of Cash so she'd impulsively picked steak. She waited for Ben to let her know her food was here.

There was a pop and a crash and Ella shot to her feet, her heart pounding. A moment later, the door burst open.

It wasn't Ben at all. A man dressed in hotel livery stalked toward her. Except he held a gun instead of a steak. And it was pointed at her.

Chapter Twenty-Eight

Cash took the elevator up to Ella's floor. His heart had started to pound when he walked into the lobby. This place was for rich people, not people like him. Ella was not only rich, she was also royal. What the hell would she want him in her life for?

Still, he was determined to see this through. If she told him to get out when he stood in front of her again, well, he'd know, wouldn't he? He'd know he'd been right all along and that her love for him had been a scam.

He more than half expected her to kick him out. Ella was young, inexperienced, and there was no way she'd be satisfied with a man like him for the rest of her life. She only thought she was in love. Probably, in the past five days, she'd realized she'd only been infatuated. She had a new bodyguard now, a guy with all the same basic equipment Cash had—maybe he was warming Ella's bed and making her body sing every night now.

The thought was an acid bath to Cash's stomach. He didn't want anyone else touching Ella. The idea of it made him want to smash something.

He reached her floor and headed down the hallway. Before he got to her door, however, some instinct he'd honed over years as a SEAL ghosted through him. He drew his weapon. A moment later, her hotel door loomed ahead, a slice of light coming through the cracked opening. Cash charged, sweeping the gun around him as he went.

He flattened himself against the wall and waited. What he really wanted was to kick the door open, but he told himself to be calm. To assess the space first. He spent a few seconds peering inside, shifting his angle until he made out a hand. A male hand.

Fuck.

He kicked the door open and burst into the room, sweeping it with the weapon as he moved quickly through the suite.

There was no Ella. Her bodyguard lay on the floor, a room service cart upended beside him. Blood spilled in a puddle around his body.

Cash returned and stooped to check the guy's pulse. It was there, but thready. He dialed 911 as he ripped the tablecloth from the cart wreckage and went to work trying to stabilize the man on the floor. Once he'd stanched the blood flow, he dialed Hawk.

"Hunter," the former HOT sniper said.

"Got a situation here," Cash replied. Then he reported in rapid succession what he'd found and what the status of Hawk's man was.

"Be right there. Don't move."

Cash let his gaze slide over the room, looking for anything he might have missed. Panic clamored on the other side of the walls he'd erected, trying to get through and rattle his calm.

Where was Ella?

Who had her?

Was she still alive?

The paramedics arrived, along with hotel security, and went to work. Security peppered Cash with annoying questions that weren't going to help find Ella. By the time Hawk arrived, his man was being wheeled out. Hawk burst inside, looking like a thundercloud.

"Where's Robert?" he asked.

Cash blinked. "Robert?" Hawk couldn't mean the man on the gurney because he'd seen his face and would have known who it was. "That guy was the only one I found. Are you telling me there was another?"

Hawk nodded. "I had a two-man team on her. *Fuck!*"

Cash was trying to stay numb. Trying to stay cool. "Think he did this?"

Hawk looked furious. "Maybe. I hope to hell not." Hawk swore again. "All my guys undergo rigorous background checks."

About that time, a man rushed through the door, looking a bit wild-eyed as he surveyed the scene. He wore dark jeans and a button-down shirt. There was a holster on his belt with a Glock tucked inside.

"What happened?" he asked.

"You tell me, man," Hawk said, his jaw clenched. "Where the fuck did you go? Two-man team at all times," he finished, his voice hard and unforgiving.

"I—" The guy, whom Cash could only assume was Robert, swallowed. "My wife's cheating on me," he said. "I got a text that she was headed for a hotel with her lover. I went to get evidence."

Hawk exploded. "You *never* fucking leave a mission until it's over. Jesus Christ, Robert, you *know* that. You were a Ranger."

"She threatened to take my kids," Robert yelled back. "I can't let that happen."

"You'll have plenty of time to follow her around now. You're fired," Hawk ground out.

Cash wanted to go medieval on the guy's ass, but there were more important things to worry about.

"Fuck him," Cash said to Hawk. "We have to find Ella."

Hawk nodded, his eyes still flashing with anger. "We'll start with the security footage. I'll get my team on it."

Cash started for the door.

"Where are you going?" Hawk asked.

Cash turned back to him. "HQ. I need to get my team —and prepare for a mission."

———

Ella managed to stay cool—in spite of the man with the gun, in spite of the hood over her head, in spite of the fact she'd seen Ben sprawled on the floor and clutching a gunshot wound.

But the minute she realized she was inside a plane was the minute her cool evaporated. The plane sped down the runway and then lifted into the air. A few minutes later, the hood was yanked from her face. Her hair covered her eyes, but she blew it away until she could see.

Aunt Flavia stood there with a sour look on her haughty face, her arms crossed, anger evident in every tense muscle of her body.

"You little bitch," she hissed. "How dare you think you can steal from us! After everything we did for you. After we raised you as our own and tried to give you a good life."

Hot outrage bubbled inside her. "I did *not* steal *anything* from you—you stole from *me!*"

Ella didn't see her aunt's hand dart out until it was too late. The slap across her face knocked her head to the side. Her bones rattled and a throbbing began in her left temple. Her hair was in her face again, but this time she didn't get a chance to blow it away.

Her aunt slapped her from the other side and then grabbed a fistful of her hair and yanked hard until Ella saw stars.

"Ungrateful, evil little bitch," her aunt spat out. "You don't deserve the Rossi name. You never have. That horrendous mother of yours—" Aunt Flavia gave up trying to speak and made angry noises instead.

"Leave her alone, Flavia," Uncle Gaetano said. "If you damage the goods, Fahd will be angry."

Flavia let go and gave Ella's shoulder a shove. Since she was strapped into her seat, she didn't fall. If she'd been standing, she probably would have. But that was nothing compared to the horror that filled her at what her uncle had said. At *whose* name he'd said.

"Sheikh Fahd? He still wants to marry me?"

Aunt Flavia snarled. "No thanks to you, you little slut. Yes, he'll still take you—though he won't pay as much as he would have before that stunt you pulled."

"I don't understand."

"It's not up to you to understand. It's up to you to *do your duty!*"

Anger and outrage still had Ella in their grip. And since her uncle had told her aunt not to hit her again, she didn't guard her tongue.

"You know you can't touch the vast majority of the Rossi money. It's not yours at all. It's mine."

Uncle Gaetano threw her a bored look while Aunt Flavia turned redder by the minute.

"You will sign it over," Uncle Gaetano said. "And you will do so happily."

"I won't."

"Oh, I think you will. If you wish to remain alive, that is. Because upon your death, dear niece, the money passes to the next heir. That would be *me*."

Ella blinked as fear tightened her throat. "Then why not kill me and be done with it?"

"We thought of it," her uncle said. "But the money stays in trust for the next five years if you die. It will *eventually* come to me. If you sign the money over, it will come much sooner."

"And if I'd rather die?" she threw at him.

He uncrossed his legs and recrossed them the other way. So casual. So unconcerned. "Don't be melodramatic, Antonella. Alive is always better than dead. And you will be a queen, which you will never be in Capriolo. The monarchy is dead there, even with that silly band of monarchists who want to bring it back. The people have spoken, and they will not return to those days. So die if you wish and make this inconvenient for us—or marry Fahd and be his queen. You will be wealthy and pampered and live out your days as a royal. Much better than tawdry sex in a tiny apartment with a soldier, don't you think?"

"And what if I agree to sign it over if you let me go? Just let me be free and you can have everything." She meant it too. Because freedom was far more important than a fortune. Freedom to be herself, to choose her life. To choose whom she loved. "I'll get a job, renounce my title and fortune. I don't care. Whatever you like—only don't do this to me. Don't sell me to a man I don't love."

"I am afraid that won't do, Antonella," her uncle said. "You will always be Princess Antonella of Capriolo. You will always be the queen in exile if you stay in the US. And how would it look if your aunt and I are rich and you are poor and living with a soldier? Or, worse, getting a job?" He shook his head. "No, it's better this way. You will thank us one day for looking out for your best interests."

Ella very much doubted that. Her uncle accepted a drink from a flight attendant who carefully avoided looking at Ella. Her aunt joined him and took her own drink from the tray.

Ella glanced around. The jet was opulent, with gleaming gold surfaces and leather couches and chairs. There was a pattern in the carpet that she tilted her head to study.

Qu'rimi Oil Exploration was written around the medallion that featured a hawk and crossed palm trees. There was also a curved sword and words written in what she assumed was Arabic across the bottom.

Sheikh Fahd. Of course they were in his jet. Of course he was still involved.

She thought of the man who insisted his hooded raptor accompany him everywhere he went and knew that a man like that would not take any insults to his person lightly. And he had certainly taken her flight as an insult.

Which meant, even if he was planning to marry her, he intended to punish her as well.

Ella shivered. She had no idea what a desert sheikh might do in order to assuage his wounded pride, but she didn't look forward to finding out.

Chapter Twenty-Nine

"HER AUNT and uncle have her. They're on the way to Qu'rim," Colonel Mendez said, brows drawn low, expression one of quiet fury.

"Fucking Fahd," Cage said. He had no love for Fahd, not since his wife—before she was his wife—had been in Qu'rim to meet with the sheikh and he'd flown away from the capital without offering her a ride when the rebels took the city.

Cash stood beside the table, unable to sit. Unable to reconcile the situation in his head. The colonel and Ghost were the only other men standing. Everyone else was at their seats around the conference table.

When he'd arrived, they'd already been here, wargaming the situation. He'd called Viking on the way and told him everything. Hawk had called too. Flavia and Gaetano Rossi had been watching Ella for days, it seemed. They'd hired a mercenary to kidnap her, and he'd taken his shot when one of Hawk's men left his post.

"What does Fahd want with her?" Cash asked. "She's still married to me."

Or at least as far as he knew. He'd gotten no papers to sign. Didn't mean she hadn't initiated the process.

"You think a little thing like that will stop Fahd?" Mendez asked. He shook his head. "It won't. He intends to marry her. He apparently never gave up on the idea after all."

"We have to stop him," Cash said, his voice tight. Ella would be afraid. He hated the idea of her being afraid. She'd been free of her family for almost two weeks, but now she was right back where she'd started. Except it was worse, because now she knew what freedom tasted like.

Mendez looked thoughtful. Cash's belly tightened. If the colonel said this wasn't a military op, they were sunk. He was sunk.

Cash's resolve hardened. He would call Ian Black if so. That rogue could get anything done. For a price.

"We're going to stop him, Money," Mendez finally said. "You boys get your gear and get ready. I'm calling Andrews for transport."

Cash's legs wobbled for a second. Andrews was Andrews Air Force Base, home of Air Force One—and one of the primary sources of their rides to various theaters. This time their theater was the Middle East.

The SEALs hurried to their lockers and grabbed their gear, checking weapons and packs. They'd have to make battle plans on the way. Study maps, figure out where best to intercept Ella and her relatives.

They boarded a plane within the hour and took off. They were a couple of hours behind Ella, but they could make that time up in the air. It was a long trip, and when they landed at a base north of Baq, it was midmorning.

There was a surprise waiting on the tarmac when they disembarked.

Ian Black stood there with arms crossed, chewing a piece of gum and looking supremely bored.

"Hey there, boys," he called when they trudged off the aircraft with equipment duffels on shoulders and weapons strapped to their bodies. "Long night?"

Viking, as their commanding officer, was the one who had to deal with Black.

"Long enough," he replied. "How about you? Spend the night in a cushy hotel room eating bonbons?"

"You know it, man," Black said. "Don't forget being fed those bonbons by a nubile young lady who misplaced her clothes."

"Can we cut the crap?" Cash interjected. "Where's Ella?"

Black let out a long-suffering sigh. "You fucking marine animals are too serious sometimes. Lighten up, fish face. They landed half an hour ago. She's being taken to Fahd's palace in the city."

"Palace? The fucker has a palace?"

Black shrugged. "It's a compound. He calls it a palace. I guess he's big into visualizing what he wants. If you visualize it, it will come," he intoned.

"What about the wedding? Is he actually planning to marry her?" Viking asked.

"So far as I can gather, yes. It'll be a sunset ceremony in his gardens, according to my information." He glanced at his watch. All operators wore a watch instead of using cell phones for time, because phones could jeopardize mission security. Black was Special Ops, all right. "That gives you a few hours to figure how you're gonna bust in there and rescue the girl. Best keep nap time to a minimum, boys."

"You got a schematic for this place?" Cash growled. "Or you just want to bust our balls?"

Black smiled a lazy smile. "I've got it."

"All right," Viking said before Cash could pounce, "let's get into the war room and figure out the plan. Ella is counting on us."

————

After a forced nap—in which she did not nap at all—Ella was taken to a bathhouse within the palace. Made of artfully crumbling stone and mosaic tile, it was lovely, with a soaring domed roof and hot water pouring from a spigot into a clear pool. Another spigot poured cool water.

She was disrobed by servant girls who ignored her protests, and then immersed into the pool. They joined her, soaping her body and then rinsing her skin with ewers of water poured over her head. Ella sputtered and spat, but they didn't stop.

Her hair was washed, dried, and woven with flowers. They painted henna designs on her feet and hands while her limbs trembled and they ringed her eyes with kohl. All the while, she kept imagining the dark sheikh with his hooded hawk and the hard look in his eyes. What would he do to her when he finally had her in his bedroom?

Would he strip her naked and take his pleasure, or would he turn away in disgust because he knew she'd been with another man? If all he wanted her for was her title, what incentive did he have to actually copulate with her?

Ella hoped he had none, though she very much feared she was going to be proven wrong on that score. Men, she knew, didn't need much of an excuse.

She was wrapped in silk robes, each one more elaborate than the last, and draped in jewels that hung between her breasts and lay against her skin. Skin that was visible through the narrow slits in the robes.

"Come," one of the maidens who'd been tending her said when the preparation was done, smiling as if Ella were being bestowed a great honor.

Ella hesitated.

The maiden took her hand. "Come."

"No," Ella whispered, hanging back. "No."

Her heart pounded and she felt suddenly light-headed. She didn't want this. She was married to Cash—whether he liked it or not—and she didn't want Sheikh Fahd. How could she lie beneath him after what she'd experienced with Cash? How could she pretend it was okay?

At least it won't hurt.

No, it wouldn't hurt because she'd had enough sex to make sure it didn't. Unless the sheikh took her in a place that Cash had not.

Fear froze Ella's heart, her throat, her feet. She couldn't move.

"You will come, Princess," the maiden said again. Firmer this time. Less smiling. "The sheikh awaits."

"No," she whispered. "I cannot."

"You have no choice, Princess. The sheikh is your lord and master. You will come."

"Who are you?" Ella asked, horrified at how unfeeling this girl was. How certain that Ella should go willingly and that it would be a great honor for her.

"I am nobody, Princess. You will come."

Ella wanted to scream. To cry. Fear glued her feet to the ground. But then she got mad at herself. Why was she cowering? Hiding? She would go to Sheikh Fahd with her head held high. She would be defiant and completely unsuitable. Perhaps he would be so disgusted with her that he would let her go. Tell her aunt and uncle the deal was off.

She marched out of the room behind the maiden. The

others followed. This one led Ella through cool corridors upon which the shadows grew long. When she reached a doorway, she stopped and knocked.

"Enter," a dark voice said.

Ella's heart throbbed as the maiden swung the door open. The sheikh stood there, imposing and cool in his white desert robes and dark headdress with the golden cords holding it in place. There was a sword at his waist and a winking jewel on his hand. He was resplendent— and a little frightening.

Ella followed the maiden into the room. Her aunt and uncle stood off to the side, looking smug. There was another man. A secretary, perhaps.

"I have papers for you to sign, Princess," Sheikh Fahd said. "You will sign them and then we will be married."

Her heart pounded. Her chin lifted. Defiant. "And if I do not?"

Because would the sheikh threaten her with death? What good would it do him?

"You will sign, or you will be punished."

Ella searched for something to say. Finally it hit her. "You would have me sign over my fortune to them? What if it could be yours?"

Sheikh Fahd's eyes gleamed. "I have enough money. I don't need more."

She lowered her lashes. "Can a man ever have enough?" she asked softly.

He didn't speak for a long moment. Her aunt sputtered. Her uncle stiffened. Ella wanted to laugh. Fahd did laugh, but it wasn't an angry sound. It sounded like genuine amusement. She was encouraged.

"Perhaps not," he murmured.

"Sheikh Fahd, I have a lot of money that my parents left me. I don't know what these people told you"—she cast her relatives a withering glance—"but they have no right to that money. It can be yours. I would rather it was yours than theirs."

Aunt Flavia was close to exploding. Uncle Gaetano looked furious.

Ella pressed on before her aunt could speak. "They have no right to it. You, as my husband, do. Surely it will help you in your quest."

"My quest?"

Ella lowered her gaze. Had she gone too far? She only knew that he wanted to be king of Qu'rim because Cash had told her. "Your quest to do what is right and best for your country," she said softly. "Let the money help Qu'rim as it cannot help Capriolo."

Fahd shot her relatives a glance. They looked positively outraged. It must be killing them not to speak, but she knew they were working hard to show deference to Fahd.

"Sheikh Fahd," her uncle began. One of Fahd's eyebrows lifted. "The girl is mistaken. The Rossi fortune cannot be transferred to someone who is not a Rossi. It is law."

Ella wanted to laugh at that blatant lie. Her attorneys had spent a great deal of time over the past five days telling her exactly what she could do with her fortune. The answer was *whatever she wanted*.

Fahd ignored her uncle. He snapped his fingers and the man who'd been standing off to the side hurried over.

"Come," he said to Ella, holding out his hand with the hint of a smile. "We will be wed first. Then we shall decide what is to become of your money."

Chapter Thirty

CASH SAT in the van with his teammates, M4 slung over his chest, Glock at his side, extra magazines stashed in his belt. The SEALs were dressed for combat in tactical suits and armed to the teeth.

"This is Delta Whiskey. What's our ETA?" Viking asked Black via radio back to his HQ. "Over."

They'd been crawling through a traffic jam for the past half an hour. Black was tracking their progress via satellite and trying to give them alternate routes. Waze wasn't a thing in Qu'rim yet, and Google Maps hadn't caught up with all the changes now that the city was a war zone much of the time.

Cash was about to lose his frigging mind. Ella had been in Qu'rim for about six hours now. She hadn't moved from Fahd's palace, but what was going on in there? What had they done to her by now? The possibilities killed him, but his team hadn't been able to move until they had a plan and good intel. Rushing the op was bad juju, and they weren't about to do that.

The mood in the van was somber, and the guys didn't

say much. Ella was fifteen minutes away from Black's HQ on a good day. Fahd's palace in Baq was a recent acquisition that he hadn't managed to completely modernize yet. That was good for the SEALs when it came to Fahd's security measures—meaning they were still rudimentary, which Black's schematic of the buildings had confirmed.

There were cameras and alarms, but nothing state of the art. More like what you'd get for typical home security in the suburbs back home. Adequate against thieves but a joke for experienced operators.

Black's voice came over the line. "India Bravo copies. ETA twenty-eighteen. Unless you get a miracle and someone parts the traffic for you. I'm still looking for a route. Over."

"Shit," Viking said before lifting the receiver again. "Copy that, India Bravo. Let us know. Over and out."

"We could run faster than this," Camel grumbled.

Cash started for the sliding door. Someone grabbed him and slammed him down again. "No, not happening." It was Cage who'd growled in his ear. "This is fucking Qu'rim, and you'd stand out like a sore thumb. We all would."

They would. They were a badass Special Ops team on a mission. They weren't in civvies, they were in full-on spec ops gear. Yeah, they'd stand out. They'd be a target too. There were Freedom Fighters in the streets these days, and they didn't give a shit about civilians. If a SEAL team appeared in full gear on the streets of Baq, people would panic that they'd be in the line of fire.

The van crawled along for another fifteen minutes— and then, just when Cash was ready to blow his top, they shot forward and started to move. Dirty Harry, or DH for short, was behind the wheel, and he mashed the accelerator to the floor. Ten more minutes and they were swinging into position on a side street near Fahd's compound. It was full dark now, which was good. They'd originally planned to go at sunset, but the traffic had changed that plan.

Now they piled out of the van and headed for their insertion point, a part of the razor-wired wall that butted up against a nearby house. They scaled the wall, cut the wire, and dropped into the compound. Voices came from the courtyard. Glasses clinked together as if there was a celebration happening.

Viking stood at the head of the group and frowned. "Fan out. Find Ella. Let's avoid the gathering if we can. If not, no shooting unless someone shoots first. Sounds like a party."

He called back to Ian Black at HQ and reported what they'd found.

"Let me dial in the coordinates."

They exchanged surprised gazes. Black had access to an infrared satellite camera apparently, because he was back in a few moments with the news. Dude was dialed into the intelligence community at levels they could only guess at.

"Twenty people in the courtyard. More inside, probably servants. Fahd appears to be having a party."

"You could have warned us about this earlier," Cage grumbled.

"Didn't know. It wasn't on his schedule. Unless it's a celebratory gathering. He might have married the princess already."

"It's not legitimate," Cash said coldly. "She's married to me."

"Wouldn't stop him. This is Qu'rim. And he'll never take her back to the US, so there's that. It's a minor diplomatic issue to him, nothing more. He will also, very likely, file an official annulment of your marriage with the Qu'rimi government just to cover his bases."

"Not if I can help it," Cash growled.

Black chuckled. "Go get your princess bride, tiger."

The rest of his team was staring at him. Not that he could see their eyes in the helmets and NVGs, but he could feel it.

"Pussy whipped," Cowboy said with a more than a hint of amusement.

Cash's skin flooded with heat. He'd teased these guys relentlessly about their wives and girlfriends. Swore up and down that there wasn't one single woman in this world that could make him want only her.

Well, he'd been wrong. Seriously wrong. Right now, he wanted Ella back in his arms. Back in his bed. Back in his *life*.

Was that love? Maybe it was. And if it was, he was in it. Because he couldn't imagine his life without her now. For the past few days, he'd missed her charm and wit, the way she got lost in her books, the faraway look in her eyes when she closed something she'd been reading. He missed how she lost herself in their lovemaking, how she shocked him and teased him and made him so hard it physically hurt. Mostly he missed her sweetness and the way she smiled at him when she looked up and caught him staring at her.

He missed Ella—and he was going to get her back. She'd said he had no guts because he couldn't admit he cared. She'd been right. He hoped like hell she hadn't changed her mind about him because he'd fight to change it back again.

"Yeah," he said to Cowboy. "I guess I am." He pulled the Glock from its holster. "Let's go get my woman, fellas. You can laugh at me all you want after she's safe."

Cage clapped him on the back. "Welcome to the club, sailor."

"What club?"

"The club where men like us have figured out that we're nothing without the special women in our lives."

"Lock and load, boys," Viking said. "We've got a princess to rescue."

————

Ella politely refused the glass of juice someone offered her and stood quietly by Sheikh Fahd's side. They had married in a brief civil ceremony overseen by the man she'd assumed was a secretary at first.

And she had not signed any paperwork. Fahd had seemed to conveniently forget he'd intended for her to sign a thing. Her aunt and uncle were utterly furious. They'd hissed at her when Fahd left her side to attend to some things, but she only smiled at them. That angered them further.

Her aunt might have hit her if not for Fahd's body-guards standing nearby. They had watched and listened, and Ella's relatives had controlled their tempers.

Now she looked out on a crowd of business associates and friends. Fahd had planned a party to show her off, it seemed. People had come to congratulate them. One couple turned out to be Capriolan. She'd found that out when they dropped to their knees in front of her.

"Your Majesty," they'd said.

Ella had been horrified. "Please, don't kneel. I don't want you to do that."

They'd stood, looking at her in awe. After a few moments, they'd moved on.

Ella could see her aunt's stiff form out of the corner of

her eye and knew that the woman was livid. She clearly hated the idea of Ella being queen of Capriolo—and anyone acknowledging her as such—when her husband was second in line. Not for the first time, Ella considered it truly a miracle that she'd not been smothered in her sleep years ago.

She was standing and staring off in the distance when someone screamed. Instantly, her attention was jerked back to the moment. A group of black-clad men rushed into the gathering, rifles slung low and aimed menacingly at the crowd. Fahd's bodyguards were swiftly disarmed and made to lie on the ground, hands behind their heads.

"The rest of you do the same," one of the men said in a rough voice. "Except you, Princess," he added when Ella started to drop to her knees.

Her heart slammed her rib cage, but she obeyed. As the rest of the guests dropped to the ground and lay down, she stood and watched. Fahd's face twisted in fury as he lay in his white robes on the tile of the courtyard patio.

"Who are you? What right do you have to enter my home and treat my guests this way?"

The man who'd spoken stalked toward them. He was tall, big, but she couldn't see his face behind the balaclava he wore beneath a helmet. There was a microphone that curved from his ear to his lips and a visor was over his eyes. He lifted the visor slowly, and Ella's heart began to race so fast it skipped over a couple of beats.

"I'm Ella's husband, asshole," Cash snarled. "And I'm here to take her back."

He reached for her fingers with a black-gloved hand, tugged her against his side. She went willingly, her body melting in that way it did only for Cash.

He was here. He'd come for her.

She couldn't seem to form any words as she stared at

his profile. He was big and menacing and so gorgeous to her eyes that she could cry for joy. Once more, Cash McQuaid was standing up for her. Rescuing her.

God, she loved him.

The sound of a helicopter in the distance began to grow louder. She ignored it at first, but the helicopter was soon directly overhead, the wind gentle at the beginning and then beating the palm trees like a hurricane as the craft lowered itself onto the helipad Fahd had built for his personal use.

"That's our ride, honey," Cash said. "You ready to go?"

She nodded.

"Run as fast as you can, okay?"

"Okay, Cash."

He gave her a quick kiss on the mouth and pushed her toward the helipad. Something flashed off to her side, drawing her attention. Her aunt had something shiny in her hand, something she'd dragged from her purse. It only took Ella a split second to realize it was a gun.

Everything seemed to happen in slow motion then. "Look out," she cried, though the weapon was pointed at her.

Cash's head turned—and then he leaped in front of her as a flash erupted from the gun. A second later, Cash grunted and dropped with a groan. Ella screamed. She reached for the gun strapped at his side as he rolled toward her—

And then she lifted and fired at the woman standing on her feet now, gun pointed, another flash exploding from the barrel as she fired at them again.

Ella's hands shook as adrenaline flooded her system. She emptied the magazine—and her aunt dropped like a stone. A moment later, someone dragged Ella into his arms

259

and lifted her over his shoulder while she screamed at him to let her go.

But he didn't. Instead, he ran toward the helicopter. She bounced on his back, trying to see behind her. Trying to see Cash.

She was flung into the helicopter and her rescuer climbed up beside her. The helicopter was a blur of bodies as men jumped into the craft.

And then they were lifting off and Ella was trying to be heard above the impossible din of the rotors. Tears rolled down her cheeks as she frantically tried to communicate that she wanted Cash.

The men were removing visors so that she could get a look at them. Viking, Cage, Camel, Blade. She knew these men.

It was Camel who took her by the shoulders. His mouth moved, but she couldn't make out the words. The guns had been so loud, and the helicopter drowned out everything. Her ears rang and everything was dull.

Finally Camel turned her forcefully toward where a man lay against the rear bulkhead. Cash's eyes were closed and his face was pale. Ella's heart stopped.

And then she flung herself at him.

Chapter Thirty-One

SOFT LIPS PRESSED against his face. Liquid dripped onto his skin, and he opened his eyes to see Ella hovering over him, tears sliding down her cheeks. He couldn't hear what she said because it was too fucking loud.

But he got the gist of it. She'd thought he was dead. Thought her bitch of an aunt had killed him when he'd leaped in front of her to stop the bullet.

He took her face between his hands and dragged her down to him. Then he kissed her hard, his tongue sliding between her lips to duel with hers. She melted instantly, her body going limp against him. He kissed her until he was pretty certain she must realize he wasn't dying.

Hell, he wasn't even bleeding. But stopping a rain of bullets with a bulletproof vest wasn't exactly a picnic. That shit hurt. He'd be bruised in the next couple of days. He'd taken three hits from that gun. The other three had gone wide. Thank God the damned woman had only had a pocket .380 instead of a double-stack 9mm. He did *not* like to think about how that would have gone.

So he was sore and the breath had been knocked out

of him. He'd made it back to the helicopter because Blade had dragged his ass. He hadn't wanted to leave Ella's side, but he'd known Camel was getting her.

Holy shit, she'd grabbed his Glock and fired back. He still couldn't believe she'd had the presence of mind to do it. Or the bravery.

Damn, his girl was awesome. Cash kissed her again and pulled her close. She looked worried, but he gave her a grin. She was fucking hot with all that black stuff around her eyes. He let his gaze drop to the skin showing through the silk of the robes she wore. He didn't like that others could see her bare skin, but he had to admit she looked amazing.

The helicopter took them to the airport where a transport waited for them. Black had helped arrange it all, including the pickup of the van they'd left around the corner from Fahd's place. They'd discussed returning to Black's HQ, but he'd assured them he'd have a ride waiting. The dude hadn't let them down.

Cash thought maybe he wasn't such a bad guy after all, no matter what he pretended to be.

Cash disembarked from the helicopter and walked toward the plane on his own power. Ella had her arm around him as if he needed to be supported. Camel shot him a look and Cash merely grinned. No way was he pushing her away. Sweet, sweet Ella. His princess bride.

As soon as they were on the plane, Ella turned to him. "Did she hit you? Are you bleeding?"

She was a little bit loud, but it was understandable after the gunfire. When he'd been teaching her to shoot, she'd worn hearing protection. This was her first time experiencing gunfire without.

"I'm wearing a vest, Ella. She knocked the breath from me, that's all. It's like being hit by a baseball bat—and since she got three shots on target, I took a beating. But I'm fine."

"Oh no," she gasped, her eyes wide. "I'm so sorry."

"Honey, it's fine." He put his hands on her shoulders and gazed into her liquid brown eyes. "You okay?"

Her gaze dropped. "I'm fine. Nothing happened." She sucked in a breath and lifted her gaze again. "I think I killed her, Cash."

He squeezed her shoulders. "You might have. I think it's more likely one of these guys did it though."

He could see her thinking about it. "I emptied the magazine. How could I have missed?"

"Trigger control, baby. You're still new to firing a weapon." Even with a gun as accurate as a Glock, even with the practice she'd had, she'd never fired under pressure. Her shots had likely gone wild. One of his teammates had dropped Flavia Rossi because she'd been an active threat. Not that he blamed whomever had done it. He was just glad it hadn't been him. Not because he didn't dislike the bitch for all she'd done to Ella, but she had been part of Ella's family. He didn't want that hanging over them.

"She did seem to stay on her feet for a few seconds after I fired." Ella's brows drew together. "I thought I killed her—but maybe it wasn't me at all."

"Did you want it to be you?"

She thought about it. "No, I don't think so. I hated her, but she wasn't all bad. How could she be if my cousins and my uncle cared for her?"

As mean as she'd been to Ella? Starving her, stealing her money, forcing her to marry someone she didn't love, kidnapping her—and then deciding to kill her? No, there wasn't an ounce of kindness in that woman's body.

But Cash wouldn't say that to Ella.

"Right, honey," he said, pushing her hair from her face.

Stroking her skin and thinking how close he'd gotten to never touching her again. He dragged a thumb over her bottom lip, and then he pressed his mouth to hers again. It was a light, sweet kiss even though what he really wanted was to devour her.

"Jesus, get a room!" Cowboy shouted at them.

Ella giggled. Cash wound his fingers in hers and leaned back on the seat. The plane took off and climbed skyward.

"Thank you for rescuing me," she finally said. "Again."

Cash turned his head on the seat back and gazed at her. "I will always rescue you, Ella. Always."

She squeezed his hand. "I believe you will. But Cash…"

She hesitated, and he squeezed her hand in return so she would look at him. "What, Princess?"

"What does it mean?" she asked simply.

His belly tightened for a second. But then his heart swelled and overruled the fear in his gut. "It means I'm yours for as long as you want me. And even when you don't."

She looked very serious. "I will always want you, Cash McQuaid. I'm your wife and—" She bit her lip. "And I love you. You're the best man I know."

Emotion detonated in his heart, his brain. No one had ever thought so highly of him. Or loved him like she did. He knew it in his soul now. And he knew he wasn't ever letting her go.

"I love you too, Ella McQuaid. No way in hell am I divorcing you."

She sucked in a breath that emerged as half laughter, half sob. "I think I have two husbands now. I married Fahd today, you know. I had to."

Cash wished he'd killed the fucker when he had the

chance. "It's not legitimate. He'll back down when the pressure is on. Promise you that."

Ella sighed. "You know I believe anything you tell me, right? You could promise me the moon and I'd believe you."

"Not the moon, baby. But I promise to take care of you and make you as happy as possible."

"You do make me happy."

He frowned. "You sure you want to spend your life with someone like me? You're rich, beautiful, sexy. You could have anyone—"

She put a finger over his mouth. A hennaed finger. Designs swirled over her hands, up her arms. *Sexy*.

"I want *you*, Cash. All of you. You're the only man for me." She laughed. "You told me I'd fall for the first man I had sex with. You were right. I fell hard. I'm still falling, every time I look at you."

He was raw inside. "You're my first love, Ella. My *only* love. I promise you I've never said those words to another woman in my life."

She stretched up and pressed her mouth softly to his. "I know."

"How do you know?"

"Because I know you."

It hit him in the gut, those words. She knew him. *Knew*. Somehow, even though they'd only spent a short time together, she just did.

"Yeah, you do."

And it was the best feeling in the world. Finally, he'd found his home. With Ella, the woman who rocked his world and made him *feel* for the first time. Without fear, without reservation.

Ella, his virgin princess bride. His wife. His soul.

His.

———

Two weeks later…

Ella rolled over in bed and slowly opened her eyes. She often wondered if she was dreaming, so she took her time waking up in case she found herself back in her aunt and uncle's house because she'd been imagining the whole thing.

Her eyes opened and… Nope, not a dream. Relief and happiness rushed through her, making her giddy. Beside her lay her husband. *Her husband.* He was gloriously naked. The covers were thrown back off his magnificent body, and his penis was at about half-mast.

Ella crept from the bed and went to take care of morning necessaries. Then she returned, sidling over and pressing her naked body to his side. He stirred. And then he rolled over and dragged her beneath him. Ella giggled as her legs and arms parted for him.

"Morning," he said as he dropped a kiss on her shoulder.

"Morning, Cash."

"Mmm, just what I wanted this morning," he said, pulling a taut nipple into his mouth.

Ella sighed and moaned, but he didn't linger long. Within moments, he was between her legs, licking her into an orgasm that had her shuddering with pleasure and thrashing on the pillows as it crashed through her.

He laughed as he stood and headed for the bathroom. She heard water running and knew he was brushing his teeth and washing his face. When he returned, his cock jutted from his body.

He slipped on a condom, because they'd agreed they

weren't ready for kids just yet and she hadn't been on birth control long enough to be safe, and then he was inside her, stretching her wide and taking her places she'd only dreamed of before she'd met him.

"I love you," she cried out when she came again.

"You'd better," he growled before he found his own release.

His big body pressed hers down into the mattress, but he was gentle about it, shifting so he didn't crush her. He lifted his head and gazed down at her. "I've never been scared before, but I'm scared of losing you."

Ella ran her fingers up his biceps, into his hair. "You aren't losing me. I love you."

"I love you too, Ella. That's what scares me."

"Just let it happen, Cash. We'll get through it a day at a time."

His grin lit her world. "Yeah, I know. But I'm still getting used to it. Still wondering when you're leaving me for a better life."

She mock punched him in the arm. "You are my better life, you idiot."

He arched an eyebrow. "Well, yeah, that *is* true. I'm kinda awesome."

"You definitely are."

His expression softened into one that made her heart ache. "So are you. The most awesome woman I've ever known."

Her skin flamed hot at the praise. "I think you haven't known many women then."

"None like you, Princess."

They spent another hour in bed, cuddling, making love, and talking about anything and everything. When a ringing phone interrupted, Ella blinked at the unfamiliar sound.

Cash smiled softly. "It's yours, baby. Do you need me to change the ringtone to something more recognizable?"

Ella shook her head as she reached for her phone on the bedside table. She was still getting used to having her very own cell phone. Few people had the number, so if it was ringing, it was probably someone she wanted to talk to.

The real estate agent she'd employed was on the other end. "I have some houses for you to look at today," the woman said with the bubbly cheerfulness of a salesperson excited about making a sale. "Can you come in an hour?"

Ella put her hand over the phone and looked at Cash. "Houses in an hour?"

"Sounds good." He climbed from the bed and headed for the shower while she made arrangements with the agent.

In the two weeks since they'd flown out of Qu'rim, life had barely slowed down. Sheikh Fahd had renounced any claim to a union with her and complained bitterly that her relatives had tricked him into thinking she was marriageable when she wasn't. Ella had worried about being whisked away again in the middle of the night or something, but Cash—and Colonel Mendez—had assured her it wouldn't happen.

Apparently another man had gotten involved, someone named Ian, and whatever he'd promised Fahd had done the trick.

Aunt Flavia was dead. Ella would never know if she'd been the one to deliver the kill shot, but she believed Cash when he told her it was unlikely. And knowing how lethally accurate he and his teammates were, it was easier to believe it had been one of them. More likely as well.

Uncle Gaetano was currently being held in custody in Qu'rim, awaiting extradition—praying for extradition, in fact, since conditions in Qu'rimi prisons weren't exactly ideal—to the US on kidnapping and human trafficking charges.

Ella's cousins weren't responsible for their parents' cruelty, so Ella didn't cut them off entirely. But she did make them vacate the Virginia house. She'd also made them kneel in her presence when they'd come to see her at her lawyer's office. Cash had stood by with a stony expression, but he'd given her a nod of approval when she'd done it.

She hadn't been intending to do anything of the sort, but when Luciana had started whining to the lawyer about how unfair it was that Ella had inherited everything, she'd snapped.

"Kneel," she'd commanded.

Luciana had blinked at her like a deer in the headlights.

Ella had risen to her feet. "Kneel," she'd yelled, her entire body trembling inside as she stood there with clenched fists.

Luciana and her sister Julia had dropped to their knees in an instant, bowing their heads as they did so. "Yes, Majesty," they'd said.

Things went much smoother after that. Luciana and Julia had left the meeting white-faced, but they'd not left destitute. That was more than they deserved, but Ella felt it was right.

Now she and Cash climbed into his Mustang—he swore he was getting the bullet hole fixed but he hadn't done it yet—and headed out to meet the agent. The media hadn't yet found where she and Cash were living, but she wanted a more secure place for when they did.

They spent the day touring homes, each one more grand than the next. The agent was clearly impressed with Ella's status and thought she needed something commensurate with her station. Ella let the woman rattle on.

Cash didn't say anything, but Ella felt like he wasn't exactly comfortable in most of the houses. Truthfully, neither was she. Finally, Ella put a hand up when the agent had yet another grand location for them to tour. The woman stuttered to a halt.

"These are all too big," Ella said. "How about something around three thousand square feet. Maybe four. But no bigger. Something a family would live in and be able to grow in. Not a showplace to impress rich friends."

The woman blinked a few times. "Yes, of course, Your Highness. I know a few properties."

"Please," Ella said. "Call me Mrs. McQuaid."

Cash smiled at her, and her heart turned over at all the love she saw there. He reached for her hand and held it tight.

"Of course, Mrs. McQuaid. As you wish."

When they were in the car again and following the agent, she turned to Cash. "Why didn't you say something?"

He had both hands on the wheel. He glanced at her. "Because I want you to have whatever makes you happy, Ella. It's your money and your decision."

She touched his arm. "No, it's *our* decision. And it's our money, though I know you won't think so. But I lived my whole life without it, and I don't care if I have it now. All I care about is being with you."

"That's what I care about. And if being with you in an eight-thousand-square-foot house makes you happy, then that's what I'm doing."

"I want a home, Cash. With you."

He shot her one of those killer smiles of his. "Then

we'll find one we both like. And I'll strip you naked and make love to you in every single room."

Ella shivered. "I like that idea."

As if agreeing made it happen, the very next house proved to be the one. Set on ten acres near the Chesapeake Bay, the house was grand without being ostentatious. There were four bedrooms, three baths, a huge chef's kitchen for Cash, a small library for her, a pool, and lush grounds with blooming flowers and mature trees. The perfect place to raise a family whenever they got to that stage. And they would in time. Ella was certain of it.

They stood on the back porch that overlooked the yard. The terrain sloped gently downward. Because they were on a hill, they could see the bay sparkling in the distance. Ella's heart was full.

"This one," she said, gazing at the view in wonder. When she turned to Cash, he smiled. He wasn't looking at the view though. He was looking at her.

"Yes," he said. "This one. Always."

He gathered her in his arms and kissed her, and she thanked the universe for setting her on the path that had brought her here. Even if she'd technically stolen a car to do it.

Epilogue

ALEXEI KAMAROV—FOR though he was Alex, or Camel, to his friends, he would always think of himself by the Russian name his immigrant parents had given him—slept the sleep of the dead. He'd just returned from a mission with his team and it hadn't been a fun one. Twenty days in the desert, fighting through a thick tangle of terrorists in order to rescue a group of American students who'd been dumb enough to go on a backpacking trip through hostile territory.

But the SEALs had gotten them all and the students were home safe. Alexei had picked off the enemy one by one for a few days, weakening them until his SEAL team could move in and dispatch the remainder quickly and efficiently.

Now he slept, passed out on the king-sized bed in the house he'd rented in the suburbs, blissfully unaware of the world around him. Well, maybe not entirely unaware. A too-loud noise, a disturbance nearby, and he'd be on his feet in a second, holding the Glock he kept on the nightstand. Too many years in Special Forces had done that to him. He didn't process sounds and movement like a normal human being anymore.

Still, nothing disturbed him for a long time, and he slept. Until, eventually, there was a pounding on the door. Alexei blinked awake, his heart rate barely kicking up. Pounding on the door was nothing. Kicking the door in? Well, that would be quite a different matter.

But nobody kicked the door in. They just kept pounding. He sat up and grabbed the Glock, stuffed it in the waistband of the camo pants he'd fallen asleep in—at the rear, in the small of his back—and shoved a hand through his hair.

"Just a goddamn minute," he yelled. Lumbering to his feet, he shook his head to clear it, then shuffled into the bathroom and swished some mouthwash to kill the taste of three weeks of sand and deprivation.

After taking a piss, he washed his hands and started for the door. The pounding wasn't pounding anymore. But it was an annoyingly pervasive tap-tap-tap. A female voice punctuated the tapping with a few well-timed curses.

"I know you're in there, you rat bastard! Answer the goddamn door!"

Alexei jerked the door open in mid-tap and her fist arced through empty air. She stumbled forward, catching herself by pressing both hands to his chest. She caught herself quickly and flew backward as if he were an electric fence.

Alexei squinted at the brightness of the sunshine behind her. Damn, how long had he slept anyway? It had been around two in the morning when he'd gotten home.

Presently, he focused on the woman standing on his porch. She was about five-three, slender but not skinny, and she had pale purple hair. Seriously, purple hair. It fell in waves to her shoulders, skimming them as she turned to gaze at something off to her left.

He turned too, frowning when he saw the stroller. It was flat and covered, and he couldn't tell if anything was in it. Hell, it looked like one of those dog strollers he'd seen in the neighborhood once. But he didn't think there was a dog in this one. In fact, he kinda had a bad feeling about the whole thing.

The woman gazed at him, her expression hardening. "Are you Alex Kamarov?"

He hooked a hand over his head, on the doorframe, and let his gaze wander over her. She was cute. And sort of familiar, like maybe he'd seen her somewhere before. But he didn't know where. It would come to him soon enough.

"Yeah. Why?"

She jerked her head toward the stroller, then glared daggers at him. "Because you need to step up and stop shirking your responsibilities, that's why."

"Lady, I don't know who you are or what you're talking about."

She reached for the handle on the stroller, turned it so he could see the tiny baby sound asleep on her back. He could tell it was a girl based on the pink onesie. Her little face was angelic, and she had a head of black hair that was shocking in its abundance.

"I'm talking about your baby, Alex. Your baby."

Shock rooted him to the spot for a long minute. And then reality doused him with cold water. *Think.*

Yeah, he'd had his share of sexual encounters, but he was careful. Very, very careful. He never forgot the condom.

"You expect me to believe that's my kid? I don't even know you, lady. You could be anybody, making shit up for reasons of your own."

She looked scandalized. "How dare you? I am not making this up. Anastasia is yours."

Alexei glanced at the kid sleeping so peacefully. Then back at the woman who glared at him. She was angry and utterly determined. But why had she needed to ask who he was if she knew he was her kid's father?

It occurred to him this could be a joke. That Cowboy or Money could have put this girl up to it in order to scare him. Jesus, those two clowns. Both married now. Both out of their frigging minds.

Alexei grinned at the hot honey with the purple hair. He hated to disappoint her, but skepticism was practically his middle name.

"Sorry, babe, but you're going to have to prove it."

Her eyes hardened. The kid suddenly went from sleeping to crying. Panic crossed the woman's features as she pulled the baby from the stroller and cradled her. Blue eyes met his for a desperate moment. Then she bent her head and pressed a kiss to the baby's forehead.

"Hush, little angel. Hush. Auntie Bailey's got you. Shh."

Auntie? That certainly explained why she didn't recognize him even though she was insisting he was the father of her child. He was almost disappointed that he'd never spent the night with her.

The baby continued to cry and she continued to soothe, but she looked uncomfortable doing it. Like she wasn't accustomed to babies.

Shit.

He couldn't leave her standing on the porch. A beat-up old Volkswagen Beetle was parked by the curb. Did that thing even have seat belts?

He stepped back and held the door open. "Why don't you come inside until she stops crying?"

The girl looked at him with wide eyes. Desperate eyes. "I… I don't know…"

"Look, if I'm the father—and I'm not saying I am— you don't expect I won't ever want to see the kid, do you? Which means bringing her here to my house. So come inside and figure out what she wants."

"What she wants?"

"Diaper. Food." He cocked his head to the side. "You ever take care of a baby?"

She bit her lip. Then she shook her head. "I'm learning."

Alexei held out his hands, cursing himself six ways to Sunday as he did. "Give her to me."

"You? What do you know?"

"I'm the oldest of six. I know a thing or two. Now hand her over and come inside. Or stand out here and let her scream. Your choice, Bailey."

She blinked at his use of her name. And then she handed him the baby.

Also by Lynn Raye Harris

The HOT SEAL Team Books

The Hostile Operations Team Books

Book 5: HOT SHOT - Jack & Gina

Book 6: HOT REBEL - Nick & Victoria

Book 7: HOT ICE - Garrett & Grace

Book 8: HOT & BOTHERED - Ryan & Emily

Book 9: HOT PROTECTOR - Chase & Sophie

Book 10: HOT ADDICTION - Dex & Annabelle

Book 11: HOT VALOR - Mendez & Kat

Book 12: HOT ANGEL - Cade & Brooke

The HOT Novella in Liliana Hart's MacKenzie Family Series

HOT WITNESS - Jake & Eva

About the Author

Lynn Raye Harris is the *New York Times* and *USA Today* bestselling author of the HOSTILE OPERATIONS TEAM SERIES of military romances as well as twenty books for Harlequin Presents. A former finalist for the Romance Writers of America's Golden Heart Award and the National Readers Choice Award, Lynn lives in Alabama with her handsome former-military husband, two crazy cats, and one spoiled American Saddlebred horse. Lynn's books have been called "exceptional and emotional," "intense," and "sizzling." Lynn's books have sold over three million copies worldwide.

To connect with Lynn online:

www.LynnRayeHarris.com
Lynn@LynnRayeHarris.com

Made in the USA
Columbia, SC
14 January 2018